THEY KNOW WHEN THE *KILLER* WILL STRIKE

A FILM MILIEU THRILLER

MICHAEL J. BOWLER

They Know When The KillerWill Strike

First Edition: 2023

Paperback ISBN: 979-8-9886110-0-4
Hardback ISBN: 979-8-9886110-1-1
eBook ISBN: 979-8-9886110-2-8

Editor: Proof Positive Manuscript Services
Cover and Formatting: Streetlight Graphics

PROLOGUE

THEY SAT HUDDLED TOGETHER IN the darkest corner of a seedy smoke-filled lounge, finalizing their plans.

The loud voices all around ensured that no one overheard them.

"Just remember that you want to kill quite a few of the cast and crew. If even one or two 'accidents' happen, it will shut down the entire production, and you'll lose your chance."

"I know. What about your target? What's your plan?"

"That's my concern. You're the amateur here, remember? *I'm* advising you."

"I know. I was just wondering."

"Well don't. You have enough to worry about. After all, killing eight people during a film shoot is unprecedented. Everything must be perfect or some of them will slip through your fingers."

"They all deserve to die for what they did. And they will."

"That's the spirit. Now, let's go through the plan one more time and then get out of this hellhole. The smoke is killing me."

As the noisy patrons laughed and drank and surrounded them with foul-smelling smoke, the conspirators once more laid out their plot to commit mass murder.

CHAPTER ONE

I DON'T THINK IT WAS AN ACCIDENT

LEO SAT AT THE BOTTOM of the steps leading up to his expansive Victorian home, wondering if his mother's desire to fictionalize his brush with death at the hands of a serial killer might end up bringing real-world horrors back into his life. He knew his dread seemed crazy, and yet he couldn't shake the gut feeling that this movie was jinxed from the get-go. Still, he'd agreed—reluctantly—to be an advisor/consultant to appease his persistently pushy producer mother who, he knew, never would've stopped asking until he said yes. Fortunately, he wouldn't be alone on the set. His three—make that *only*—friends had also signed on in the same capacity, seeing as how they were fellow serial killer survivors and, like Leo, sought to ensure that their fictional alter egos were accurately portrayed on screen.

They all sat together on the steps awaiting the arrival of the actors who would portray them. That was another of his mom's "brilliant" (her own word) ideas: the actors portraying the four main protagonists would live with their real-world counterparts while the film was shot on location in La Costa, their small coastal town west of Los Angeles. Knowing his extreme shyness would pose a problem, Leo had objected, but his mother insisted, especially after she saw the actor portraying him.

"He's gorgeous, Leonardo," she'd gushed effusively. "Perfect for you."

Leo didn't even want to ask what she meant by that (though he was sure he knew), and he didn't have a chance anyway because she'd raved on about the pending production and how much fun it would be for them to work on something together for the first time in his seventeen years. She seemed to have forgotten that only a few months prior, he'd nearly died during the actual events she was now so eager to turn into the next hoped-for hit designed to generate box office gold.

Oh well, that was his mother.

"Aren't they supposed to be here by now?"

Leo glanced over at his best friend, J.C. Rivera, looking hot and uncomfortable in the designer shirt and pants he'd worn despite the eighty-plus degree July temperature surrounding him. Unlike J.C., who loved to show off his fancy clothes, Leo sported a plain tee shirt and old board shorts.

Blonde and petite Laura Benson, wearing a light summer shirt and shorts, glanced at her watch. "They still have five minutes, J.C."

J.C. grunted with disgust, causing Laura to toss Leo and Chet a grin. Leo had only met Laura that spring when she'd transferred to La Costa High, but she'd already proven to be a great and loyal friend, especially during those terrifying weeks when she, Leo, and J.C. sought the identity of the person who planned on murdering J.C.

Surfer blond Chet Hamilton, on the other hand, had been a bully most of Leo's life. Only his narrow escape from death at the hands of that same killer, and Leo's part in saving his life, had reformed Chet, folding him into their nonconformist group of oddballs who didn't fit the trendy, partying, self-absorbed mold of La Costa High School students.

Chet shrugged but said nothing as he relaxed beneath the warm sun in a tank top and board shorts. He used to arrogantly show off his ripped physique every chance he got, but that was before he'd nearly died. Leo knew he wasn't wearing the tank to impress the newcomers, but only because it was more comfortable in the hot summer weather.

"At least there won't be thirty-year-olds playing us teenagers like they usually do in movies," Laura commented, wiping perspiration from her lightly tanned forehead.

"I insisted on that," Leo commented dryly, "*and* those script changes I told you about."

"Thank God you got that garbage taken out of the script," J.C. spat, his lean face twisted with anger. "I already get enough crap from my mom on that front."

"Me too," Leo agreed, noting Chet frowning beside him.

"I guess my part in the story couldn't be changed much," he said, his deep voice tinged with regret. "I don't know if I can relive what happened, and how I used to be."

Laura took his hand in hers and squeezed gently. "You don't have to be there when they're filming something painful, Chet. None of us do." She glanced at Leo. "Especially you, Leo, when they film the part where you almost died."

Despite the heat, Leo shuddered at the memory. "I guess. I'll take it one day at a time."

Laura offered a reassuring smile just as a black SUV rounded the corner and approached Leo's house.

Laura released Chet's hand and sat up. "Looks like they're here."

J.C. grunted, "'Bout time."

The SUV eased to a stop in front of the house. Leo and the others rose to greet their onscreen counterparts. Since his mother was the producer, Leo felt obligated to approach the newcomers first, despite his social anxiety screaming at him to run and hide. As he rounded the rear of the large vehicle, the driver's side rear door popped open, and out stepped a tall guy with sleek side-parted brown hair followed by a shorter guy with a thick head of curly hair. Leo started forward, but then whirled at the sound of screeching tires approaching from behind.

A dark sedan with tinted windows careened toward the two young men standing beside the SUV. They turned at the tire noise, but Leo was faster. He darted forward and tackled both guys toward the sidewalk. Just as they tumbled to the grass separating the sidewalk from the street, a smashing of metal against metal filled the air. Sprawled on the grass with the two guys beneath him, Leo saw from the corner of his eye the dark sedan speeding off down the street.

"Leo!"

Laura rushed forward, J.C. and Chet on her heels. They reached out to pull Leo to his feet and then helped up the young actors, who looked stunned but unhurt. The driver of their SUV leaped from the car and joined them, visibly shaken by the event. He was a young man, probably just a driver who worked for the studio.

"Are you guys all right?" The driver looked terrified, as though he might get blamed for this incident.

The shorter boy with the curly hair broke into an amazing smile that caught Leo's eye. He looked directly at Leo and said, "Yeah, thanks to Leo. You move fast."

Leo was so captivated by that smile he almost made eye contact but quickly looked away, confused by what had happened, and how this guy knew his name. "How…how do you know me?"

The curly-haired guy dusted himself off, while the taller one did the same. Leo found a hand sticking out for him to shake.

"I'm Asher King," the curly haired one said, his voice firm but not especially deep. "I'm playing you in the movie."

Leo shook his hand, still avoiding eye contact but thinking how much his mother's description of Asher fit the young actor. Just then he found himself surrounded by another guy—tall and Latino, wearing a tank top—and a gorgeous girl with shoulder-length blonde hair, dressed in stylish summer attire. Both looked horrified.

"Are you all right?" The girl leaned in like a doctor to examine Asher and the other guy whom Leo had tackled.

"Yeah, Kristen, we're good," said the broad-shouldered, short-haired guy. He faced Leo and stuck out his hand. "Thanks, Leo. I'm Robert."

Leo shook his hand and Chet stepped closer. "Oh, you're playing me. I'm Chet." He shook hands with Robert, who grinned.

"You're obviously Kristen." Laura offered a warm smile.

The long-haired blonde, looking relieved that no one had been hurt, shook her head in amazement. "You always greet visitors like this?"

Laura shrugged. "Only actors."

Kristen chuckled. "I think we'll get along just fine."

The tall, well-built Latino noted J.C. staring at him as though in awe and stuck out his hand. "And you're J.C. I'm Diego. I've been looking forward to meeting you."

Caught off guard, J.C. composed himself and shook hands. "You have, huh?"

Diego smiled, another photogenic show of pearly white teeth. "Sure. I'm hoping you can show me some dance moves during the shoot. I saw some of your vids on social media."

J.C. offered up a smile equal to Diego's. "You got it, man." He eyed Leo. "Here's a guy who knows good dancing when he sees it."

Leo glanced quickly away from Asher, who'd been staring at him the entire time, and gave J.C. a shove to the shoulder. Then he led the group around the front of the SUV where the young driver stared in hopeless abandon at the missing rear door.

"The studio'll kill me for this."

He sounded so morose; Leo placed a hand on his shoulder. "We got your back on this one."

"Yeah," the others chimed in.

"It wasn't your fault, Ron," Asher assured him in a gentle but firm voice. "We'll tell 'em what happened."

Diego sprinted on long legs into the middle of the street and retrieved the mangled rear door. Trotting to the back of the SUV, he waited as Robert lifted the hatchback, and then he slid the busted door into the storage space.

"For a small town, you have some crazy drivers," Kristen commented to Laura.

"I've only lived here about six months, but I've never seen anything like that."

"Me either, and I been here my whole life," J.C. put in, directing his comment to Diego, rather than the girls.

Diego and J.C. made momentary eye contact before Diego glanced down as though uncomfortable.

Robert stepped forward and grabbed two suitcases, one in each hand, from the back of the vehicle and set them on the asphalt. That caught Diego's attention and he grabbed a third. Before either boy could reach for the remaining baggage, Kristen darted forward and reached past them to pull out her two bags, both of which were larger than any of the others. Laura stepped forward to help.

"The boys have been razzing me for bringing two bags for only one week," she told Laura with a heavy sigh. "They just don't realize what it takes for us girls to look gorgeous, right, Laura?"

Laura chuckled but didn't comment. Leo knew Laura wasn't into fashion or makeup, relying instead on her natural beauty, which in his opinion was considerable. He tossed her a smile when Kristen wasn't looking, and she returned it.

Looking like he was headed for his own funeral, Ron, the youthful driver, waved goodbye to his charges. "I'll see you next week. If I'm still employed."

They all assured him he would be and, looking slightly less disheartened, Ron drove off in the SUV, leaving the the group behind on the curb.

"Well, this is definitely a strange way to meet," Kristen announced to the group, "but I, for one, am excited about this shoot." She faced Laura. "I can't wait to get to know you, Laura, and pick your brain for details."

Laura shrugged. "I'm not sure there's much in there to pick."

J.C. stifled a laugh as Kristen eyed Laura quizzically.

"We can head over to my house," Laura told Kristen, pointing at a two-door coup parked across the street. "Later, guys," she added, casting a look back at Leo and the others as she strode across the street. Caught off guard by Laura's abruptness, Kristen grabbed her two large suitcases to follow.

"I can help, Kristen," J.C. blurted, stepping forward with a grin on his face.

She gave him a stony look and he stopped. "I can handle my own bags, thank you." She hefted the bags and waddled across the street after Laura.

J.C. shrugged and turned back to the others. "Well, I tried."

"Kristen's kind of the antisocial type unless she needs something from you," Diego said with a shrug of his own. "I know her pretty well. Where's your house, J.C.? I love the retro feel to this neighborhood, all these old-school homes."

"I'm around the corner. My car is the blue Beemer just over there." He pointed at a shiny new BMW coupe parked in front of the Queen Anne-style house next to Leo's. "You ready to go?"

"You know it. I can't wait to start picking *your* brain." Diego grinned, and it was an infectious grin that Leo found quite appealing. So, apparently, did J.C., because he laughed.

"I think you and me'll get along great, Diego." He reached for Diego's large suitcase. "Let me help you with this." He grabbed the leather handle and tried to lift the bag, but it barely rose a few inches off the pavement before J.C. grunted and let it drop. "What you got in there, rocks?"

Diego laughed. "Naw, just a few dumbbells so I can keep up my workout."

J.C. glanced at Leo. "Another fitness nut like you, Leo."

Leo couldn't help but smile. Other than dancing, J.C. had never been into fitness.

Diego grabbed his bag with one hand and lifted it with ease. The short sleeve shirt he wore stretched at the biceps and prominent veins bulged on his forearm. "I'm ready, J.C."

Looking sheepish, J.C. waved for Diego to follow and started toward his parked car. "I'll check in later, Leo."

"Okay." Leo watched them a moment before turning to Chet, Robert, and Asher.

Robert eyed Chet's physique and grinned. "I bet you got some weights at your place, Chet."

"Oh yeah. I don't surf anymore, but I still work out."

"Awesome," Robert said. "I'll be your workout partner while I'm here."

"That'll be cool." Chet glanced at Leo. "I guess we'll head to my house. See you tomorrow, Leo."

"Later," Leo replied as Chet led Robert toward his shiny black Z4 parked just up the street. Then he turned to Asher, who was gazing at him intently. "Well, Asher, let's go in and I'll show you around."

Caught off guard staring, Asher quickly smiled and reached for his old leather suitcase. "Awesome."

Perturbed by the other boy's ogling, Leo led the way up the stairs toward his front door.

Cassie Stewart sat at on a barstool in her kitchen, sipping coffee and reviewing the call sheets for the first day of shooting. As assistant director to Mr. K, her job was to make certain everyone was where they needed to be throughout the shoot. Donovan Quinn, the love of her life, sat beside her, reviewing costuming and other details for his script supervisor role on the film. In many ways, his job was harder than hers because films were shot out of order, and he needed to keep track of every detail to make certain scenes or partial scenes shot on different days looked identical.

She glanced over at him, relishing the soft features, mop of brown hair stuffed beneath one of his signature fedoras, and his mismatched retro clothing choices. Donovan was one of a kind, and she loved him with all her heart. Feeling her intense stare, he looked up and smiled. She blew him a kiss and he blew one back. Then they returned to the work at hand.

This film, as yet untitled, was their first foray into Hollywood, thanks to their former teacher, Mr. Ketchum, who, when hired as director, chose Cassie and many of her graduating class as cast and crew. They were all excited to be working together on a professional project. She and Donovan never had a chance to finish the feature film last spring that was to be their high school graduation project because of the copycat killings that had occurred, killings based on those in their script. With that case wending its way slowly through the courts, their unfinished film was considered evidence and had been confiscated by the police. The entire experience had been devastating, especially for Donovan, who was more sensitive and in touch with his feelings than herself.

Cassie shoved these thoughts aside to focus on the project before her. This film was a fictionalized version of a real serial killer incident that had happened earlier in the year down in the South Bay. She knew that four of the surviving teens, including the one dubbed "Hero Boy" by the press, were consultants on the film, and she wondered how they would feel reliving their worst nightmare. She could relate somewhat, but these kids had almost died, and that was worse than what she went through.

"Hey, D-Boy."

Donovan looked up from his paperwork, perfect eyebrows raised questioningly. "What's up?"

"How do you think the others are doing, you know, meeting their real-life counterparts?"

Donovan shrugged. "I know Asher was super excited to meet Leo. I think he's almost nervous about playing him."

"From what the media said about him, Leo sounds pretty amazing. I'm looking forward to meeting him too."

"Yeah."

She paused to collect her thoughts. "Does it seem kind of, I don't know, heartless, maybe, to make a movie so soon after something horrific happened?"

He nodded, his face clouding over. "I agree. Kids died and Leo and the others almost did too. I don't think I could be part of this film if I was one of the victims."

"Mr. K talked to the survivors and their parents and assured them he would not try to make the story anything other than a fictionalized version of what happened."

"I know. It still feels…wrong."

"Leo's mother is the producer. It was her idea."

He grimaced. "Like I said, wrong."

"Do you think we'll get a credit for those rewrites we helped Mr. K with?"

"Doubtful. Writing credits require a certain percent of the script to have been written, and we didn't do that. Plus, we're not in the guild."

"Well, we changed the two boys' relationship from boyfriends to just friends. That took a lot of tinkering."

"I don't think it's enough." He paused. "I wonder why the producer wanted that changed. It worked for me."

"You heard Mr. K. The real Leo and J.C. aren't boyfriends, so this makes it more accurate."

"That's true, but this isn't a docudrama."

She considered a moment. "Maybe the boys objected. Since everyone who knows them will realize the film is based on them, I'd probably want that part changed too."

Donovan nodded. "That's true. Kind of makes you wonder what sort of mother would want the world to think her son is gay if he's not."

"Even if he is, it's not her business." She fell silent. Neither her dad nor Donovan's mom would ever do such a thing to them. While she disagreed with the timing of the film (so close to the actual events), it was a chance for her and Donovan to make their mark in Hollywood, and she trusted Mr. K more than any other adult except her dad. So, she overlooked the unsavory aspects.

"Mr. K'll make sure the shoot is as painless as possible for those kids."

He tossed off a small smile, which practically melted her heart. "For sure."

They kissed, pressing their lips gently together for a few lingering moments, before reluctantly returning to their work.

Leo and Asher sat at the dining table, finishing up the scrumptious lasagna Sylvia made for them before she'd departed for home. Sylvia was their middle-aged housekeeper and had been with them so long, Leo thought of her as a surrogate mother, especially since he saw more of her than he did his real mom.

Leo had given Asher a tour of the house, and the other boy was impressed, especially with the gymnastics training room Leo's mother had installed when she thought Leo might become a great gymnastics star back in the day. He'd even asked Leo to show him a few moves on the rings and pommel horse, and Asher had attempted to replicate them as best he could, which bonded the boys in ways that surprised Leo. He normally was tongue-tied with anyone new, but Asher's open face and heart-on-his-sleeve personality made Leo feel like they'd known each other for years.

Asher pushed back his empty plate and stifled a burp.

Leo laughed. "It's just us, Asher. Burping's allowed."

Asher grinned. "I didn't want to sound like a tacky, tasteless pig."

Leo laughed again and swigged the remains of his milk in one gulp. He'd been so stressed about having a stranger in the house, and now he felt more relaxed than he did around his own mother. Crazy how things worked out.

As though reading his thoughts, in walked Leo's mom, setting her briefcase down on the far end of the table and approaching them with an enormous grin that showed off her perfectly white teeth. At forty-five, she looked thirtyish due to having some "work" done, with shoulder-length auburn hair the same color as Leo's, full lips, and striking brown eyes. In fact, Leo looked much like her, except his wavy hair only brushed his collar, but the soft features, full lips, and strong brown eyes easily identified him as her son.

She made a beeline for Asher and extended one well-manicured hand. "Asher, I'm so happy to have you in our home. I'm Cassandra Cantrell."

Asher politely shook her hand and offered up his amazing smile. "I'm happy to meet you, Ms. Cantrell. Thank you so much for letting me stay with you this week."

She pulled back her hand and took a moment to study both boys, her grin growing ever wider. "You boys complement each other so well. Both beautiful and photogenic. You'd make a lovely couple, especially paired up on screen. Of course, Leonardo wouldn't allow me to put him into modeling, Asher, but I clearly see why your mother got you into the business."

Leo was still reeling from the "you'd make a lovely couple line" and so was Asher, who looked like he was fighting to maintain a pleasant demeanor.

"Do you still model?"

Asher kept his composure, which impressed Leo. "No, not since I started high school. I'm actually kind of shy and it wasn't my thing."

"Yes, shyness was always Leonardo's excuse for not doing much of anything I wanted," she went on conversationally, as though Leo wasn't sitting right there, his face burning with embarrassment. "However, he did save those kids last spring and is helping me out now, so we mothers have to take what we can get."

Asher looked like he was going to say something in Leo's defense, but Leo caught his eye and shook his head. Instead, Asher just said, "Yes, ma'am."

"Well, I'm glad you're here. Help yourself to anything you need. I have tons of work to do before shooting begins tomorrow, so I'll retire to my office." She tossed off another smile and grabbed her briefcase from the table, sashaying from the dining room.

Mouth agape, Asher faced Leo, who just shrugged.

"That's my mother," Leo said, standing and grabbing both their plates. "You up for some gaming?"

Asher stood and picked up the empty lasagna dish. "Sure. I'll help you clear the table. It's the least I can do."

The boys enjoyed a couple of hours of gaming on Leo's X-Box, sitting on the floor up against his king-sized bed. Leo felt as comfortable with Asher as he ever had with J.C., who'd been his best friend since second grade. Asher, he could tell, was equally at home with him. The other boy finally put down his game controller and grinned at Leo.

"I admit defeat, oh great leader. You're clearly the master of Halo."

Leo laughed and set down his controller. "Naw. Just a lot of play time. Not much else to do in this town."

"Except stop serial killers," Asher said with an easy grin.

Leo knew Asher wasn't trying to offend, so he laughed. "Yeah, that too."

They fell silent, a rare awkward moment between them.

"So, you didn't like modeling, huh?"

Asher looked surprised by the question. "I didn't care so much when I was a kid. It was something my mom wanted me to do, so I went to the shoots. They told me I was cute, which I guess I liked, at first. I wore their clothes and posed how they told me. Then I'd go home and play with my toys because it was usually too late to play with other kids, not that I ever had time anyway."

He stopped, looking thoughtful. "I was lonely, Leo. Sure, there were other kids on the shoots sometimes, but we weren't allowed to play because of the clothes we wore. Kids at school who saw my picture at Target, or the mall would usually make fun of me, especially the boys. I had no real friends, and by the end of eighth grade I was tired of hearing everyone tell me how beautiful I was. I think most of that was just to stoke my ego, but it made me feel weird." He shifted position and looked right at Leo, who avoided direct eye contact, like always. "My mom created an IG account for my modeling pictures, and I never even looked at it till last year. Know what I noticed?"

Leo shook his head.

"I saw photos of me at like seven or eight posing with girls and my shirt was open, and the girl would be looking at me like, well, like she wanted me, and it was all supposed to look sexy. Can you believe it? Little kids. There were others of me alone with my shirt open or with no shirt on, and I'm maybe eleven and I'm looking at the camera in this creepy sexy way. On the set, I just did what they told me. But why would they pose kids like that? My mother was shocked once I pointed these things out to her. It was like she'd never seen them before. She admitted that she'd gone along with the shoots because she trusted the photographers, and, of course, the money was good. I think you were smart not getting into that business."

Leo grimaced. "I was too shy to perform in front of anyone, even just a photographer. My mom didn't need any money. I think she just wanted to brag and have people say how beautiful I was because I looked like her."

Asher nodded. "You do look a lot like her."

"Don't rub it in."

"No, that was a compliment," Asher added quickly. "I mean, you're really good-looking."

Embarrassed, Leo glanced down. "Thanks. Uh, was high school any better for you?"

Asher shrugged. "I didn't know how to make friends. Not a clue, really, because I'd never had time to learn. When I got into the film program sophomore year, it was a little better. But I never really got close to anyone until last year, when we made a movie together."

Leo nodded. He understood the no-friends thing. Thankfully, he'd had J.C. or he'd have gone nuts.

"I don't know why I'm telling you all this, Leo," Asher went on, interrupting Leo's thoughts. "I don't think I've ever told anyone my feelings before, not even my mother. I guess… I guess I sense you can understand."

"I think I do."

A heavy silence fell between them.

"Um, Leo."

"Yeah?"

"What did your mom mean about, you know, me and you being a lovely couple? It was kind of random and, well, weird."

Now Leo felt humiliation wash over him. "I'm sorry about that. I think, well, I haven't asked her, but I think my mother wants me to be gay."

Asher pulled a stunned face. "Why?"

Leo shrugged, glad he wasn't making eye contact. "I don't know. She thought J.C. and me were together that way, and when I told her we were just friends, I guess she… I don't know what she thought."

Asher's handsome face lit up with understanding. "That explains what she said on the phone when she invited me to stay."

"Oh no, what did she say?"

Now it was Asher who looked red in the face. "She told me that if I got lonely or nervous by myself in this big house, I could sleep with you because you had such a big bed."

Leo's mouth dropped open. "She didn't!"

Asher nodded.

"What did you tell her?"

He grinned. "I said thank you. I mean, she *is* paying my salary."

Asher's grin was so infectious that Leo lost his anger at his mother. He was used to her inappropriate comments and decided not to let this latest one bother him. Leo had never met anyone as easy to like as Asher, especially in La Costa where most of the kids were self-centered jerks.

Asher's face lit up with a revelation. "You told her to change the script, didn't you?"

Leo felt color return to his face as he nodded. "I told her if she kept the two main characters as boyfriends, me and my friends wouldn't be advisors on the film."

Asher beamed. "Good for you. I hate movies based on real people where the truth is changed to make the story more 'dramatic'." He used air quotes for "dramatic."

Leo relaxed, knowing that Asher would have his back on everything. "I was wondering something."

"What?"

"If you didn't like the modeling, why are you acting in this movie?"

Asher took on a sheepish little smile. "I really wanna be a DP. That's a director of photography, but when Mr. K, the director, asked me to play you, I jumped at the chance."

Now it was Leo's turn to pull a face. "Me? I'm the most boring kid in this town."

Asher's mouth dropped open so wide it looked like he was trying to catch flies. "Are you kidding, Leo? After all the stuff I read about you? How many kids in this town would've almost died to protect their friends?"

"Probably none."

"Exactly. I took the part for two reasons. I wanted to meet you because, well, I really admire you."

"Oh." Tongue-tied, Leo looked down at the plush carpet beneath him. "What was the other reason?"

"I know the character isn't exactly you, but everyone knows it's based on you and I wanna make sure they see what an awesome guy you are."

Now Leo gaped like a fish. "You just met me."

Asher shook his head. "I read everything I could about you before I got here. I'm also really good at sizing people up, you know, who they are inside. And I know you're someone special." He glanced down. "Sorry, I get carried away sometimes."

Leo was speechless for a moment. "It's okay." Needing to change the subject, he added, "Uh, I'm worried about what happened this afternoon."

Asher lost his smile. "What do you mean?"

"You know, that car almost running you down?"

"Yeah, that was freaky. But it showed you up again. You risked your life for total strangers."

"It was just a reflex action," Leo said, feeling under the microscope again. But the chill filling his insides wouldn't go away. "I been thinking about what happened and… I don't think it was an accident or bad driving."

"What do you mean?" Asher's slim eyebrows furrowed.

"I think that driver was trying to kill you guys, or one of you, anyway."

Asher stared a moment in horror, and then cracked up. "Good one, Leo."

"I'm serious, Asher. I have this feeling that won't go away."

Asher studied him intently. "You mean like when you knew J.C. was in trouble?"

Leo flinched and hoped Asher hadn't noticed. "Kind of, yeah. Do you have any enemies that you know about?"

Asher considered a moment. "No, but Robert might. Maybe the boyfriend of some girl he messed with. The new Robert wouldn't do that, but the old Robert was a real player."

Leo lapsed into deep thought. "Maybe, but you need to be careful, Asher. I'm gonna watch over you this whole shoot. Is that okay?"

Asher offered a shy smile. "I can't think of a better bodyguard."

Leo nodded and stifled a yawn. "We have an early call tomorrow, so we better get to bed. In our own rooms."

He grinned, and Asher returned it.

CHAPTER TWO

HE'S GOING TO DIE

Since Donovan didn't have access to a car of his own, Cassie drove them from the San Fernando Valley to their La Costa location. They left extra early to deal with the heavy traffic along the 405 freeway through West LA. The cars moved slowly in spots, but they managed to hit the exit for La Costa with time to spare before they were due on the set.

Donovan gazed with a sense of wonder at the old Victorian and Queen Anne-style homes that seemed to make up most of the town. "These houses are amazing."

Donovan was into everything retro, so old-style architecture was definitely his thing. It had been arranged for cast and crew to park at La Costa High School and take shuttles to and from the location, which happened to be the oldest house in town where the surviving kids had their final confrontation with the killer.

La Costa High was a mix of old and new, especially the ultra-modern metal and glass cafeteria that was clearly visible from the parking lot as they strode hand in hand to the waiting shuttles. Other crew members were arriving, but Cassie didn't see any she knew, nor any of her friends who were acting in the film. She could barely contain the butterflies in her stomach. Her first Hollywood film and she was AD. It was a dream come true.

Donovan didn't seem at all nervous as he scoped out the Art Deco buildings that made up much of the old campus, but then he had something of a photographic memory for details, so script supervisor should be a breeze for him. He wore a red fedora, a checkered shirt, and what looked like '70s bell bottom pants. He didn't like acting much, but she always thought he should be in front of the camera because he was so photogenic.

Her frizzy reddish hair was tied back off her face, revealing all her freckles, and she wore comfortable jeans and a short-sleeve pullover shirt. It would be hot this entire week and she wanted to be comfortable. They settled into their seats on the shuttle, which was populated by chattering crew members clutching cups of coffee. Cassie smiled at the young man across from her who looked only a few years older. His goatee gave him an even older appearance, but he was handsome with his long blond hair tied back in a ponytail poking out of a Dodgers cap. He returned her smile around a sip of coffee and asked what her job was on the film.

"AD," she replied proudly, "and Donovan is script supervisor. I'm Cassie, by the way."

The young man's eyebrows shot up in surprise. "Wow. I'm just a lowly production assistant, but I'm happy to bring you whatever you might need. Stuart's my name, so don't hesitate to ask for anything. I want to make a good impression on this film so I can move up the ranks."

"Thanks, Stuart," Donovan said, offering a smile. "We appreciate any help you can give us. Been on many shoots?"

"This is my second. Eventually, I want to be a gaffer. I took some electrical courses at community college, so I'm not a complete noob."

"We'll definitely need your help," Cassie assured him, "so I appreciate the offer."

Stuart raised his coffee cup like a toast and took a sip. By now, the shuttle was out of the parking lot and onto streets just springing to life with local residents heading to work. She and Stuart chatted while Donovan gazed out the window at the beautiful homes.

"I hear this location is pretty creepy," Stuart told her. "The locals call it the haunted house."

"That's what I heard too," Cassie said. "Some kind of murder there years ago."

Stuart nodded. "No one's lived in it since." He glanced past her out Donovan's window. "There it is now."

Donovan pointed out the window. "See, Cass. Perfect for a horror film, huh?"

Cassie leaned closer and gazed out the smudged shuttle window. They were approaching a house near the end of the street before the beach took over. It was three stories, with a single window on the third floor, peeling blue paint, and overgrown landscaping. It looked haunted all right.

"It's perfect." She squeezed Donovan's hand. Then she froze, gripping Donovan's hand so hard he grunted.

"Cass? What's wrong?"

She practically landed in his lap as she pressed forward to get a better view. The shuttle was slowing as it approached the haunted house, where crew members drifted in and out with various pieces of equipment. But just past the house, almost where the beach began, stood a lone figure all in black watching the approaching shuttle. What sent a small gasp to her lips was the skull mask and black hood worn by the figure, exactly like the one she'd used in their student horror film last spring!

"Donovan, there, do you see him?"

Donovan peered through the window. "That looks like…"

"Like the costume we used in our film."

"Something wrong?"

Cassie turned to find Stuart leaning across the aisle, a concerned look on his face.

"There's somebody out there who…" She trailed off and turned to find Donovan gazing at her with fear in his green eyes. She looked past him and let out another gasp. The figure had disappeared.

Donovan turned back to the window and flinched. "He's gone."

The shuttle was rolling to a stop across the street from the haunted house as Stuart stood and leaned down next to them to peer out the window. "What did you see?"

Donovan was speechless, so Cassie composed herself enough to say, "Somebody wearing a creepy skull mask, staring at us. But he's gone now."

Stuart frowned. "Kind of early for Halloween. Maybe just a local kid playing a prank. They do call this the haunted house, after all."

Cassie smiled. "You're probably right."

But she knew he wasn't. As they all stood to exit the shuttle, she exchanged a worried look with Donovan. It *had* been the same mask from their movie, maybe the same outfit. But how? No one who worked on that film would pull such a prank, and the real killer was in jail. Could there be someone else who'd been involved, someone her dad and the other cops hadn't apprehended?

"Well, I'll see ya on the set," Stuart said as they stepped onto the sidewalk.

"Yeah, see you." Cassie waved as he darted up the stone steps toward the open front door.

Donovan stared at the spot near the beach where they'd seen the figure. "What do you think it means?"

"I don't know. C'mon, we've got a movie to make."

She took his arm and led him up the steps.

Leo, having been around film sets as a child, watched with indifference as crew members flitted here and there like bees, setting up lights and other necessary equipment in the large drawing room. J.C. stepped into the entry hall, his mouth hanging open, and approached Leo, who stood just outside the drawing room to avoid being in the way.

"This place sure looks different than the last time we were here," J.C. exclaimed, gawking at the scads of people and equipment.

"Yeah. Not so scary now, huh?"

"That's for sure."

"So, how's it working out with Diego?"

J.C. shrugged. "He's cool. Got a dad who's worse than my mom. Way worse."

"How?"

J.C. glanced around, but the bustling crew members ignored them. "Diego's in makeup right now, but I don't think he'd mind me telling you. He's pretty open. See, Diego's gay, but not out to his parents because he says his dad'll kill him if he finds out."

Startled, Leo faced him dead on. J.C. was the only person Leo could look in the eye, besides Chet, and he saw that his friend wasn't joking. "For real?"

J.C. nodded. "His dad's a real dick about gay people. Diego says he's gonna move out soon, hopefully with the money he's making on this movie. Anyway, he knows some killer dance moves, so him and me are working on a hip-hop routine together. It's gonna be epic."

"That's great," Leo said, and he meant it too. "Sounds like you two have a lot in common."

J.C. grinned. "Yeah. So, how's Asher?"

"He's a nice guy, real mellow and easy to talk to." Leo was afraid to share the stuff his mother had said about him and Asher, so he left out those details. Fortunately, before J.C. could press him for more information, Laura and Chet entered the large foyer and joined them.

Laura looked around at all the activity, wide-eyed. "This place is really lit up."

Chet's good-looking face was etched with distaste. "I never figured I'd be back here."

"You and me both," J.C. replied, sharing an unusual solidarity moment with the guy who bullied him for so many years.

With all that had happened to the four of them, and everything he'd learned about Chet in the process, Leo had come to realize that people weren't as simple as they seemed on the surface.

"So, what do we do exactly?" Laura studied Leo, since he was the one with the movie experience.

Leo shrugged. "We just hang around and watch, make suggestions, answer questions from the director or actors."

"Pretty easy way to make money," J.C. added with a grin.

"Like we need it." Chet folded his arms across his thick chest and sulked.

"So, Laura," Leo began, "how's Kristen up close?"

"Yeah," J.C. jumped in. "Did she pick your brain."

Laura laughed. "Like I'd let her? She's not so bad, actually. She spends a lot of time in front of mirrors and is very serious about her career, but I think a lot of her act is just for show. Her parents expect a lot from her, like she'll be the next Nicole Kidman or something."

Chet sighed. "Aren't there any parents out there who just let their kids be who they want to be?"

Laura shrugged. "I don't know any like that."

Leo realized he didn't either. Even Asher's mom had put him into modeling because it was what she wanted, not what he wanted. He vowed to let his own kids be themselves, if he ever had any, of course.

"How about Robert? What's he like?"

Chet shrugged his big shoulders. "His dad's an asshole, from what he said. I guess Robert was a jerk for a while. Seems easy going now."

J.C. studied him a moment. "Did he want to know about the club stuff?"

Chet squirmed and glanced around, but the passing crewmembers ignored them. "Yeah, he wanted to know how to play those scenes, if he should be more interested in girls or boys or both the same."

"What did you tell him?" Laura asked.

"I told him he had to show interest in boys but to play it however he wanted. I wasn't into talking about that. It's still a sore spot with my mother and she was home last night."

"Is Asher as cool as he is beautiful?" Laura asked Leo with a wink.

Leo smiled; Laura could always draw one out. "Yeah, he is."

J.C. tossed him an odd look, but before he could say anything, a middle-aged man approached from inside the drawing room. He was dressed in frumpy, comfortable-looking clothes and wore a baseball cap.

"I'm Brian Ketchum, the director." His voice was full and inviting, as was the warm smile he offered them. "You must be Leo, Laura, J.C., and Chet. It's great meeting you at last." He shook hands with each in turn, making eye contact will all but Leo, who focused, as he always did, on the middle of the man's face.

"Nice to meet you, Mr. Ketchum," Leo said.

"I really appreciate your help on this film," Ketchum went on, "and I have an inkling how difficult it might be, given my own experience last March. Feel free to comment on anything that makes you uncomfortable. The last thing I want is to make your lives more difficult."

Leo liked the director. The man's tone and honesty soothed his concerns that his mother might yet muck up the film and, in some way, make him look bad. "Thank you, sir."

Ketchum tossed off another smile and vanished into the back of the house. A trio entering through the open front doors caught Leo's attention. One of the boys was dressed retro and wore a cool-looking fedora. The other guy was tall with a goatee, and the girl had frizzy red hair. The boy in the fedora spotted Leo and smiled, leading the others across the foyer to where he stood.

"You're Leo, right?" The boy had an inviting face.

Leo nodded.

"I'm Donovan and this is Cassie and Stuart." He indicated the other two, who smiled.

Leo introduced the others in his group, swallowing his intense desire to go into one of the vacant rooms and hide.

I can do this.

"We've been looking forward to meeting you all," Donovan gushed, sounding much like Asher had the night before, as though Leo and his friends were celebrities.

"We really have," Cassie echoed.

"What are your jobs on this movie?" Laura asked, and Leo was happy to turn the discussion over to her.

"I'm assistant director," Cassie answered without the slightest bit of haughtiness, "Donovan is script supervisor, and Stuart is a production assistant."

"What does a production assistant do?" J.C. asked.

Stuart grinned. "I'm basically a gofer."

"What's that?" Laura asked.

Stuart pointed at Cassie and Donovan. "Whatever they need, I go for it."

Laura laughed, and even Leo smiled. Stuart had an infectious personality.

Stuart addressed Leo and his friends. "That goes for you too. If you need anything, let me know."

"Thanks," Leo said, again forcing himself to speak up.

"We need to check in, so we'll see you all later," Cassie said with another smile.

They said their goodbyes and the trio vanished into the back of the house.

"I remember them from the news last spring, at least Donovan and Cassie," Laura commented to the others. "Remember, Leo? We talked about it. The media called it the horror film killings."

"I remember," Leo replied.

"It's kind of weird to have them working on this movie," Chet added, as though talking to himself.

"No coincidence. My mom hired Mr. Ketchum because of all the publicity he was getting back then," Leo explained. "He brought along the others because he likes how they work. My mom must've gotten some kind of special provision for them to do their jobs, since they aren't union members."

Laura shook her head. "Your mom sure knows how to play every angle."

Leo nodded, again reflecting on his mom's behavior the previous night with Asher. Thinking of the other boy made him wonder where Asher had gotten to. He'd said he needed to report for makeup and costumes, but he hadn't returned yet. Leo couldn't imagine Asher needing much makeup. He looked fine already.

From the backside of the house, Robert appeared wearing jeans and a long-sleeve pullover shirt that accentuated his muscular chest. He grinned when he spotted Chet and the others.

"Hey, everyone, how's it going? Long time, no see, Chet." He made a fist and Chet bumped it.

Leo noted that Chet seemed pleased to see Robert, which indicated they must have gotten along the previous day.

"Sometime today, I'm gonna shoot the scene where I fall through the floor," Robert went on excitedly. "Did you see how they fixed up the hole in the drawing room?"

Chet shook his head.

Not waiting for the others to respond, Robert grabbed Chet by the arm and pulled him toward the open double doors. "C'mon, check it out."

Leo exchanged a look with Laura and J.C., and then reluctantly followed. The déjà vu was bad enough in the foyer. The drawing room would be murder. The other two trailed after him.

The wide double doors stood open, Leo presumed, for easier access for the camera and other equipment. The massive fireplace was directly across the room, framed in ornate stonework that stretched upward to the fancy wood-paneled ceiling. Old, beat-up chairs lay in front of the fireplace, but not the ones that had been present that horrible night last March.

Several crew members were arranging the furniture as the art director had obviously instructed them. The art director, Leo knew, designed and "dressed" the set, even on location shoots, and was no doubt hovering somewhere in the house approving another setup. The floor-to-ceiling bookcases lined the walls as before, and Leo found his eyes drawn to the secret panel behind which he and J.C. had hidden. It hung slightly ajar, and he figured lights were being set up so filming could take place in there, as well. The ancient grand piano still rested in a corner near the thick, brocaded drapes that blocked out all light from the street. None was needed, however, because lights on stands lay scattered about the room, illuminating key areas.

"Looks a lot less creepy than the last time we were here," Laura commented.

"Busier, too," J.C. added.

Robert had pulled Chet over to a wooden chair where he would be tied up for the scene, and Leo saw that Chet wasn't thrilled to be reliving this moment. Leo hadn't met the actors who were to play the Chet-character's "friends," but it didn't matter to him.

A chubby young guy and an older man were setting up the sound equipment, and another young guy with long bangs covering his face worked with the cameraman to arrange a shot designed to capture the action. Leo caught a movement from the corner of his eye and turned to look back at the secret panel.

A good-looking African American youth, who looked Donovan's age, stepped out of the passage behind the panel pulling an electrical cord, which he proceeded to plug into a generator set off in the corner behind where Leo and his friends stood. The boy had perfect cornrows adorning his head and turned around just in time to catch Leo staring. Rather than look offended, he straightened up and gazed back in recognition. Leo was sure he'd never seen this guy before, but the young man approached with some hesitancy. Laura and J.C. turned away from Robert and Chet to meet the newcomer.

Their turning caused the young man to halt, as though afraid to come closer. "I'm sorry," he said quietly, "but you're Leo, right?"

Leo nodded.

The guy offered a tiny smile. "I'm Jaden. I'm shy too. It's cool to know someone else like me."

He started to turn away when Leo spoke. "Wait, Jaden."

Jaden turned back to face the trio but was unable to keep even momentary eye contact.

Leo stuck out a hand and Jaden inched forward to shake it. "Nice to meet another Shy Boy," Leo offered with a smile. "That's my nickname in this town."

Jaden grinned. "I know what you mean."

"This is Laura and J.C.," Leo went on before Jaden could scuttle away.

Jaden nodded. "Maybe I'll see you all later. Gotta work now."

"See ya," Laura managed to say before the slim young man darted from the room.

"He's shy, all right," J.C. commented dryly. "At least, you're not *that* bad anymore, Leo."

Leo ignored the comment, focusing on Robert and Chet talking over by the chair. He wondered again if that near miss the previous day had been an attempt to kill Robert. Asher seemed to be sure it wasn't aimed at him, but that wasn't established. Still, from what Asher said about how Robert used to treat girls, he was the most likely target.

Leo bit his lower lip and considered whether he could go through with the only way he knew of to learn the truth. Since the car attempt had failed, another attempt would likely be made on Robert's life and only he, Leo, could find out when.

Chet told Robert he had to leave and took off out the open doors and into the foyer. Startled, Robert approach Leo and the others.

"Is Chet okay? We were just talking about how the stunt would be done and he bolted."

Laura spoke for the group. "I think it's just too harsh of a memory."

Robert's face went pale, even through his makeup. "Oh, wow. What a jerk I am."

"It was an honest mistake," Laura went on, glancing at Leo and J.C. as she spoke. "It's just, well, what happened to us is still pretty fresh, especially for Chet. He only got the brace off his leg last month."

"I'm sorry."

Leo believed Robert. He seemed genuinely contrite. Before the awkward moment could get any worse, the young guy who'd been fiddling with the camera and lights approached.

"Hi." Dressed grunge, he swept his long bangs away from his eyes to gaze out at them. "I'm William, one of the assistant camera guys. Could I ask one of you to do me a favor?"

Leo saw that William was addressing them, not Robert, and was about to answer when J.C. said, "What kind of favor?"

"Well, I'm trying to adjust the lighting for this scene, and I was wondering if one of you might squat down in front while Robert's in the chair, so I can get the lighting right."

J.C. uttered a slight gasp of surprise, and Laura opened her mouth to speak, to say no to the request, was Leo's thought. On impulse, he interrupted her.

"I'll do it."

Stunned, Laura turned to him, mouth hanging open, while J.C. stared in horror.

"Are you crazy, Leo?"

"Leo," Laura said, her voice calmer than J.C., "are you sure you want to relive that moment?"

"Oh shit," William exclaimed, his eyes wide with realization. "You're them, the ones this movie is based on."

"That's us," J.C. retorted sarcastically, "the 'thems'."

Laura elbowed him. "J.C., chill. He didn't know."

William put up both hands and stepped back, as though afraid J.C. might attack him. "Listen, I'm sorry. I'll get someone else."

"No." Leo surprised himself with the strength of his response. "I wanna help. C'mon, Robert, let's get in place."

Robert looked confused by Leo's willingness to help, but not nearly so much as Laura. Leo didn't wait for any more arguments, striding across the wooden floor and stopping in front of the chair. Robert followed, while a flustered William returned to the camera, set on a tripod at an angle to frame both boys in profile.

Robert sat in the chair, his large shoulders pressed against the wooden back, and gazed at Leo uncertainly. "You sure you wanna do this, Leo?"

Leo was sure he *didn't* want to do this, but he also knew he had to, for Robert's sake. Despite his anxiety, he nodded and squatted down in front of the chair.

William slipped behind the camera and peeked through the eyepiece. "That's perfect. Just stay there while I make some adjustments." He darted to the key light and adjusted it slightly to the left. Then he scurried past

Robert and Leo to adjust the light behind Robert, who looked down at Leo with a look of understanding on his face.

"I spent a few days in county jail last spring," he said quietly, fixing his gaze on Leo's face, "and I know I never want to even see that place again, so I get how you must feel being back here."

"Yeah, but jail's gotta be worse," Leo muttered, feeling Robert's eyes pinned to him. He knew now was the moment, so he raised his head and locked eyes with Robert. What he saw almost caused him to lurch backward, and he gripped the legs of the chair to keep from toppling from his squat.

Robert furrowed his brows with concern. "What's wrong, man?"

Leo broke eye contact and struggled against the panic welling up in him.

"Okay, guys, I'm done."

William's voice penetrated the fog in Leo's brain, but he still didn't rise or even move.

"Leo?" Robert gently shook his shoulder.

Then Laura's voice intruded. "Leo, are you okay?"

"C'mon, man, snap out of it." J.C.'s sharp retort seemed to do the trick and Leo blinked once before realizing that he was surrounded by Robert, still seated, William behind Robert, with Laura and J.C. on either side. He realized he'd drawn much more attention to himself than he'd intended—he'd have to chalk it up to a flashback.

"Sorry," he said, his voice a bit on the breathy side. "I guess I froze for a sec, thinking back to when all this happened for real. I'm okay, Robert, really."

He stood and stepped back, allowing Robert to rise from the chair, looking concerned but relieved too. "Like I said, if I ever had to go back into county jail even as an actor, I'd probably freak too."

Leo offered a wan smile. "Thanks, man. I think I'll go grab a water."

He felt William and the other crew members staring intently at him, like he might be crazy, but he ignored them and ushered J.C. and Laura to follow, stepping out into the foyer, where Chet stood alone, staring up at the second-floor landing. As he started forward, J.C. grabbed Leo by the arm and tugged him into the hallway to the left of the stairs, since the crew all seemed to be using the hall on the opposite side. Laura and Chet followed.

"Okay, Leo, I know you weren't spooked about this house. Only I'm that wimpy. You saw something, didn't you?"

Leo nodded, glancing at Laura's anxious expression before responding to J.C. "I had a strong feeling yesterday that the speeding car wasn't an accident, that it was trying to kill either Asher or Robert."

"Robert?" Chet looked concerned. "Why would someone wanna kill him? He's cool."

"You told this to Asher?" Laura ignored Chet's interruption, glancing around to make sure they couldn't be overheard.

Leo nodded again. "Asher's a super chill guy, mature and not aggressive at all. He told me that the car might have been after Robert because he used to be a player and messed with every girl he could, even if they had boyfriends."

"So you decided to look into his eyes," Laura said.

J.C. scowled. "Sounds like you got pretty chummy with Asher."

Laura tossed J.C. a harsh look that made him step back. "What did you see, Leo?"

Leo took in a deep breath, recalling the disturbing images he'd seen when he looked into Robert's eyes. "He's going to die. Today."

CHAPTER THREE

QUIET ON THE SET!

LAURA GASPED.

"The hell?" J.C. exclaimed.

"I don't believe it," Chet muttered, but the shocked look on his face proved that he did.

Leo nodded again. "It's that chair rig they have. When they film the scene, the floor's gonna be blown apart so it crumbles and the chair will fall in, except they got it hooked up so the chair only starts to fall. But something goes wrong, and Robert really falls into the basement."

Chet flinched, looking shocked.

"Assuming I even followed what you just said, Leo, how is that gonna kill Robert?" J.C. had that look on his face, the angry one when he wasn't understanding something.

"Somebody tampered with the system, I think," Leo went on, exasperated with J.C. "When the floor goes, Robert goes with it, and I guess they don't have padding in the basement because no one's supposed to fall through."

"So, how does he die?" Chet gazed so intently at him that Leo glanced away.

"He lands on his head. Broken neck." Leo can't face the others after sharing such horrible news.

"We gotta warn him," Chet insisted, his face twisted with anxiety.

"How?" Laura faced Leo. "Are you gonna tell him about you?"

The last thing Leo wanted was for anyone to know about his unique power. "I don't want to."

"Why not talk to Donovan and the girl he was with?" J.C. kept his voice steady, but he was clearly excited by his plan. "Tell them you're nervous or something and maybe they should check the system."

"It could work, Leo," Laura agreed, biting her lower lip thoughtfully. "You could even say you had a feeling about J.C. last spring, and that's how you were able to save him."

"I say go for it, Leo," Chet insisted. "We can't just let Robert die."

"No, we can't." Leo would never forgive himself if there was a chance to save Robert and he didn't take it. He'd learned months ago that his power to know when people would die carried a heavy weight of responsibility. "But let's check out how that chair is rigged up first. If someone messed with it, maybe we can fix it or report it before they film that scene."

"That's a good idea," Chet said. "Laura?"

She nodded. "Yeah, let's see what we can find out."

Just then, Cassie, Donovan, and Asher walked through the foyer engaged in animated conversation.

"Leo." Asher beamed with pleasure.

"Hi, Asher." Leo stepped out into the foyer to join them, Laura and the others right behind him.

Leo stopped in his tracks, suddenly noticing the change in Asher's appearance. He wore a white undershirt tank top that revealed lean, veiny arms, black pants, and he carried a black hoodie. His face had been made up, but subtly, as though his features were too perfect to put beneath much makeup. But the hair was what startled Leo. Gone were Asher's Chia Pet curls. In their place was auburn hair, thick and wavy, with bangs that swept almost across his eyes, and in the back the hair just passed where a shirt collar would be. The hair looked so much like his own that Leo was more speechless than usual.

"What do you think, Leo?" Asher looked pleased by Leo's response. "Diana, the lady in charge of makeup, is talented, and I asked her to match your hair perfectly."

Realizing he had to speak, Leo nodded. "She sure did. 'Cept yours is more neatly brushed." He offered a smile. Seeing Asher made him feel better somehow, even though the problem with Robert still loomed large and imminent.

Asher glanced down, suddenly bashful. "I know it didn't have to look like yours, but I wanted it to. She had some wigs and made this one up special."

"I think you look great, Asher," Laura said, trying for a light tone. "You and Leo could be brothers. Even in the veins department." She pointed at Asher's arms.

Asher blushed. "I, uh, I worked out a lot over the past few months because I knew Leo was a gymnast and all."

Cassie and Donovan had watched the exchange with amusement, and Donovan smiled. "Does it feel weird to have someone playing you, Leo?" he asked.

"Oh, yeah."

Donovan laughed.

"Well, we're going to start soon, so we need to get ready," Cassie said, glancing at her clipboard, as though for reassurance that she had everything she needed.

Laura kicked Leo in the ankle, and he grunted. "Uh, when do you get to the part where the floor drops out?"

"After lunch," Cassie replied, not even consulting her clipboard "We'll film the scenes leading up to that first, so the set guys won't have to rebuild the floor again." With a smile, she vanished into the living room. Donovan tipped his fedora and followed.

"If there's anything about my performance you think I can improve, Leo, please tell me. I want it to be just right."

Leo heard Asher's sincerity and saw the eager look on his handsome face, liking this boy more and more. "I'm sure you'll be perfect. Just make the character your own and it'll work fine."

"Will you be watching?"

Leo glanced at the others. "We'll be in and out."

"Cool. See ya."

Asher hurried into the living room, leaving Laura with a smile on her face and J.C. wearing a scowl.

"Is that guy kissing up to you or what, Leo?" J.C. snorted with disgust.

"I want to play you just right," he said in an exaggerated falsetto voice, much higher than Asher's boyish tone.

Leo felt anger rise within him. "He's a nice guy, J.C., so lay off." His tone was sharper than he'd intended, and J.C. recoiled.

"What's up with you?" J.C. studied him with deep wariness.

"Nothing." He squelched the anger, noting Laura gazing at him with a look of understanding. He didn't want to know what she thought because Laura was preternaturally good at reading people. "So, we have till after lunch to figure out the Robert thing." He paused a moment. "Let's go down to the basement and see how it's set up for that scene."

Without another look at J.C.'s squinting face, Leo turned and hurried past crew members toward the hall leading to the kitchen.

Several crew members were arranging light stands when Leo and his group entered the kitchen. Leo paused a moment, having not been in this room since that horrible night. It looked the same, down to the layers of dust everywhere. He started for the open door leading to the basement.

"Hey, you kids," said a gruff male voice. "Where do you think you're going?"

Leo stopped so suddenly that J.C. crashed into him, causing him to stumble slightly. A short, squat middle-aged man wearing overalls and a threatening look on his swarthy face, stepped in front of Leo, blocking the entrance to the basement.

"You kids can't go down there," the man grunted, his voice sounding like tires on gravel. "Only the crew."

As always, Leo froze, unsure how to respond. But also as always, Laura stepped up to handle the situation.

"Excuse us, sir, but we're part of this production. This kid here"—she pointed at Leo—"is the producer's son. Show him your ID, Leo."

Leo felt like kicking himself. He was wearing a tank top and open button-down shirt combo, and the badge his mother had given him was inside the shirt. He pulled at the lanyard around his neck and slipped out the hard plastic ID, holding it out to the grumpy man.

The man grabbed the badge and squinted at Leo's photo and name. "You're Cassandra Cantrell's kid?"

"Yes, sir," Leo said, forcing strength into his voice. After all, he had as much right to be on these premises as this man. "My mother gave me and my friends the run of the locations and sets."

The small man glowered at him, looking like he was going to argue, and then dropped the badge, where it dangled against Leo's chest. "Yeah, well don't touch anything."

"We won't." Leo offered a smile, but the man just grunted and returned to the light stand he'd been setting up.

"Fun crew," Laura muttered.

"Asshole is more like it," J.C. muttered as he followed Leo to the open basement door.

Chet said nothing but looked even paler than when he'd first arrived. "We gotta go down there?"

"You can stay up here, if you want, Chet," Laura said, placing a hand on his thick forearm.

Chet eyed J.C. "You going down?"

J.C. clearly didn't want to look weak in front of Chet. "Hell yeah."

Chet nodded. "I'll come."

Leo looked down the old wooden steps. The bottom was lit up, unlike the other time he'd been there, so he didn't think it would be too traumatic to re-enter the place where he'd come so close to dying.

"Let's go." He started down the creaky steps, relieved to hear the others following him. When he reached the bottom and looked around the large basement, he spotted electrical equipment and cables, generators, and some lights on stands. Several crew members were tinkering with the equipment but appeared to be awaiting their orders.

He looked across at the ceiling where the floor to the living room would be. The old, splintered wood had been removed and new beams and floorboards installed in their place. He noted thin wires crisscrossing the ceiling that came together into something resembling a game controller resting atop a folding table against the far wall.

"What're you kids doing down here?"

Leo turned to find a man approaching from the other side of the stairs, almost near the entrance to the crawlspace that Leo and the others had used to enter that terrible night. Deciding he had to be more proactive, he held out his badge.

"I'm Leo Cantrell. My mom is the producer."

The man was tall and lanky, maybe in his thirties, with dark hair and a thin moustache. He peered at Leo's badge and nodded. "So you are. How can I help the producer's son?"

Leo's mind spun with uncertainty. He hadn't thought of a good reason to be down there. Then it hit him. "Uh, my mother likes me to know all about her job, so I'm trying to learn as much as I can about a film shoot."

The man accepted that. "Makes sense. What can I show you?"

"Well, uh, I know there's going to be a stunt with a chair in the living room, when the floor drops out? I was wondering how it will work."

"C'mon, I'll show you."

The man walked past him toward the opposite side of the basement. Leo glanced at the others. Laura whispered, "Good job," while J.C. tossed him a thumbs-up and Chet just stared at the cellar floor as though looking for the exact spot where he landed when he fell through. Leo hurried after the tall man.

He caught up with him at the folding table that Leo had noticed before. The man picked up the object that resembled a game controller and held it out. The controller had numerous buttons of different colors and the cables snaked away from it to connect with the wires running up the wall and across the ceiling.

"This is pretty sophisticated stuff, if you ask me," the man commented, as Leo leaned closer to examine the device. "The floor/ceiling combo above is made of breakaway wood, but solid enough to walk on. Each of these buttons will set off a tiny explosion at key spots along the ceiling, causing a section of the floor to collapse. The first area to explode is underneath the chair you mentioned. The chair is attached to a solid section of the floor by a hinge that will only allow it to tip a few degrees. They stop filming and replace all the actors with stuntmen before blowing the entire floor and toppling the chair down here. By then, this floor will be covered with big air mattresses for the guys to land on. Pretty nifty, huh?"

Leo nodded, thinking about what he'd seen in Robert's eyes. "Is it only a hinge that keeps the chair from falling the first time?"

"No. There's thin but strong wires from the wall to the chair. That boy'll be perfectly safe."

"Pretty cool," J.C. commented, nodding with admiration.

"Is everything checked right before shooting, just to make sure it still works?" Leo asked.

"Well, we only get one shot at blowing the floor, so the stunt coordinator will check out the chair up top to make sure it's secure for the actor. Safety is our motto. If you're gonna be a big-time producer like your mom, Leo, you'd best remember that mantra."

"Yes, sir. Thank you very much for explaining how it works."

"My pleasure. You let me know if you need anything else."

"I will."

Leo offered the best smile he could muster and then waved the others to follow.

As he stepped out the door into the kitchen, Leo nearly bumped into Stuart carrying four cups of coffee in a cardboard carrier.

"Oh, sorry, man, I didn't see you," Leo blurted, lurching to one side to avoid the collision.

Stuart grinned. "No worries. I gotta drop these off in the drawing room. Can I get any of you anything?"

By now, Laura, J.C., and Chet had emerged from the cellar.

"Nothing for me," Leo said, glancing back at the others.

"No, thanks," Laura replied, and the two boys shook their heads.

"Well, let me know if you need something." He started to leave, then turned back. "Oh, almost forgot. Asher said to tell you, if I saw you, that they're going to start filming soon, if you wanna watch." He smiled and left the kitchen.

Leo felt eyes on him and noticed the short, stocky guy glaring at him from an area near the sink, so he darted out of the kitchen and into the hallway. The others followed.

As he moved back toward the foyer, he felt more eyes burning into his back and glanced around to find J.C. glowering. He knew it was because of what Stuart said about Asher, but he decided not to be argumentative.

"What's up, J.C.?"

"Nothing. But I'm getting tired of Asher, and I don't even know the jerk."

Laura exchanged a look with Leo and told J.C., "He seems nice and he's excited about this film. What's it to you?"

Chet grumbled from behind them, "Rivera sounds jealous to me."

J.C. snapped, "You stay out of it, Hamilton."

Laura stopped them in the foyer. "Look, guys, being back in this house has all of us a little freaked. What Leo saw with Robert makes it worse. We've gotta keep our heads on straight."

"You're right," admitted Chet. "Sorry, Rivera."

J.C. grunted but otherwise ignored the apology.

"J.C., let's talk a minute," Leo said, feeling the need to address J.C.'s jealousy, which he knew to be real. He waved his friend into an alcove beneath the stairs, and J.C. reluctantly followed.

"What?" J.C. glowered at him.

Making eye contact, Leo said, "Look, J.C., you've been all excited about how much you have in common with Diego, especially the dancing. I'm happy for you that you finally have someone to share that stuff with, and I'm not jealous at all. Why should you be of Asher? He and I just fit together, like you and Diego."

J.C. bowed his head in shame. "I'm sorry. I guess 'cause for so long it was just you and me, I forget it's okay for us to have other friends."

Leo offered a little smile. "We'll always be best buds, J.C., no matter what."

J.C. returned the smile, and they did a fist bump.

"Now, c'mon, we gotta figure out how to save Robert."

J.C. silently followed as Leo rejoined the others and they all entered the drawing room, which was bustling with activity.

Chattering crew members were everywhere, tweaking lights, shifting cables, moving furniture, touching up cobwebs, and otherwise dressing the set to look like the place had been abandoned for decades, which it had been.

Leo spotted Asher and the other actors gathered around a woman he'd not seen before. She was middle-aged with short, dark, curly hair and a round pleasant face. She was touching up Diego's makeup as Kristen watched with amusement.

"Leo, we're almost ready," Asher announced breathily. "I want you to meet Diana."

Leo glanced back at the others. Laura shrugged, but the two boys looked noncommittal. Asher waved Leo forward, and not wanting to insult his new friend, Leo followed.

Kristen greeted Leo with a dazzling smile, while Robert offered the chin raise. The lady touching up Diego's makeup finished, and Diego stepped back, tossing J.C. a smile.

"Not my favorite part of the biz, but Diana makes it fun," Diego said.

"Diana," Asher said, "this is Leo and those are his friends back there. Leo, this is Diana. She did the amazing job on my hair."

Diana offered a warm, toothy smile that Leo immediately liked. She reminded him of Mrs. Santini, the school librarian. "So you're Leo," she said, her voice soft and feminine. "I've heard a lot about you, mostly from Asher, who's quite the fan."

Asher glanced down but didn't deny her comment.

Diana looked over Leo's friends, clearly awaiting an introduction.

"Oh, uh, nice to meet you, Diana," Leo blurted, still thinking about Asher talking him up so much. "This is J.C., Laura, and Chet."

She shook each of their hands and studied them as though they were fine works of art. "Each of you has a face that belongs on camera, especially you, Leo. Trust me, a makeup artist knows these things."

Laura laughed. "Thanks, but we prefer staying behind the camera."

J.C. was clearly flattered. "You really think so, Diana?"

"Absolutely, J.C.," Diana replied. "I do headshots on the side and make my subjects look stunning. Let me know if you want to try a few photos."

J.C. grinned. "See, Leo, you're not the only one who could be a model here."

Leo reddened. "J.C., I don't wanna be a model. You can if you want."

J.C. tossed him a smug look. "I just might."

Diana glanced at Chet, but he shrugged. "I never thought about it before. I'm no actor, I know that much."

She smiled and fixed her gaze on Leo to the point he almost blushed. "I've known your mother for years, Leo, and she was right to try to get you before the camera. Such soft, photogenic features and gorgeous hair." She sighed, as though greatly disappointed. "Alas, it's not for everyone."

Leo glanced down. "No, ma'am."

Cassie's voice rang out across the room. "Places everyone for the first shot."

Asher offered him such a warm smile that Leo felt his heartbeat accelerate. Then the other boy turned away and he and his fellow actors disbursed to their assigned spots.

Unnerved by his reaction to Asher, Leo said, "Let's get behind the camera crew so we're out of the way."

Without awaiting an answer, he strode across the room and ducked behind the chubby kid holding the boom mic, finding himself next to Jaden, the shy African American guy. Jaden nodded at him as Laura, J.C., and Chet joined them. To Leo's surprise, the chair Robert would use to fall through the floor had been moved to a different location.

Cassie placed all the actors in their assigned spots around the room, stirring uncomfortable memories in Leo's mind. Asher, Diego, Kristen, and Robert were standing inside the door as though scoping out the room, just as Leo and the others had done on that fateful night. He knew the dialogue wouldn't be the same as what had really happened because he and his friends had only given the screenwriter a basic description of what they'd said and done. The finished script was highly fictionalized, especially in how the four main characters talked. In real life, none of them cussed much at all, but in typical Hollywood fashion, they all used profanity in the film, further proof that Hollywood cared little for honesty.

"Quiet on the set!" Cassie called out, and all movement ceased.

Mr. Ketchum looked at the actors. "Just like we rehearsed. We play the scene until Asher and Diego leave the room."

The four young actors nodded.

Mr. Ketchum, standing beside the camera, told the camera operator, "Roll camera."

The operator, a middle-aged guy with thinning blond hair said, "Rolling. Speed."

"Action!" barked Mr. Ketchum.

Leo exchanged a look with J.C., knowing his friend was uncomfortable reliving these events. He offered a reassuring smile and watched as the four actors examined the drawing room a moment before Asher announced he would search the rest of the house, to make sure it was safe. A terrified Diego insisted on going too, not willing to stay in the room with Robert's character. Kristen held up a gun and said she would secure the downstairs, insisting that she had experience with guns through her father. Asher and Diego left the room.

"Cut!" Mr. Ketchum announced. He called the two boys back in. "The master is perfect. All of you were spot on. We'll shoot it once more for safety and then get the closeups and reverses."

The four actors looked pleased by the praise, and Leo found himself in agreement with Mr. Ketchum. They were all terrific actors. He could see bits and pieces of J.C., Laura, and Chet, and a lot of himself, amazed that Asher had managed to channel so many of his mannerisms and body language from the short time they'd spent together. For example, despite being in great shape, Leo tended to slouch a bit to not call attention to his pronounced chest and shoulder muscles, and Asher imitated that perfectly.

The master was repeated, also without mistakes. Then, the camera was moved around to film the same scene from different angles until Mr. Ketchum was satisfied. Each time, the actors repeated their performance with precision, which, Leo knew, would really help the editor piece the footage together. Chairs were moved for the next scene, avoiding proximity to the fireplace where the floor was supposed to be weak and unstable.

Chet squirmed and shifted during the next sequence when the four characters learned more about each other, and certain misconceptions were cleared up. Laura placed a hand on his arm and gave a supportive squeeze during the dialogue regarding his character's behavior at some dance clubs.

Once again, Leo was impressed by everyone's acting but noticed that Diego's character seemed jealous that some guy in a club was interested in Asher's character, which wasn't the way it had really gone down. Had it? He considered that night when he'd sat beside J.C. and they'd peeled back layers of themselves while learning more about Chet than they'd ever suspected. Had J.C. been jealous because a friend of his at the club always talked about Leo while they were hanging out? He didn't think so, but then, given J.C.'s jealousy toward Asher, it was possible.

Maybe Diego, as an actor, thought it would add an extra level to his performance. Or maybe he'd read the previous draft of the script that Leo insisted be changed. In any case, his performance was terrific. Equally strong was Kristen as the cool-headed Laura, who always stayed calm and composed no matter what.

Looking around the "set," Leo noticed a chandelier hanging over the spot where the floor would collapse. There had been no chandelier when he and the others went through their ordeal, so he knew the filmmakers had hung it there. As he stared at it, an idea began to form. Not a great idea, but one that might be his only option for saving Robert.

As the morning dragged on, the filmmakers finally got to the scene when Robert's so-called friends entrap Robert, Kristen, Asher, and Diego and torment them. Chet gasped when he saw the snake jacket for the first time, draping the shoulders of a young actor Leo hadn't met. That jacket had been both a major clue and a major source of confusion during their real-life experience, and Chet, not wanting to be reminded of those days, had given it to Laura, who'd created the design in the first place.

Laura leaned into Chet and whispered, "I told you I was letting them use it for the film, remember?"

He nodded but looked whiter than a tee shirt as he gazed with distaste at the black leather jacket with its massive spitting cobra adorning the back, tail twisting around to the front.

J.C. looked his way and Leo nodded, knowing his friend was recalling every frightening moment. Leo flashed back on the vision he'd had of J.C.'s murder, and the clear image of the snake jacket that helped him search for the killer. He shivered at the memory, despite the hot air in the room generated by all the studio lights.

Leo glanced at his phone frequently to check the time, not knowing when the lunch break would be called. Watching all this action play out, his insides roiled with discomfort. The physical wounds had healed, but the psychological scars were very much present. It didn't help that the actors were so accomplished. He sat there reliving, through Asher, his fear and humiliation and yet, like at a train wreck, he couldn't look away. It was a distasteful out-of-body experience.

And this is only the first day.

He glanced at J.C., who winced when one of the actors kicked Diego in the stomach to humble him. Leo placed a hand on J.C.'s arm and his friend looked at him. Leo offered what he hoped was a sympathetic expression, and J.C. nodded.

Finally, Cassie called out, "Lunch, everyone. Craft services has tables set up outside on the street with hot food ready to be served. It's one o'clock now, so everyone be back at two-thirty. Thanks."

J.C. expelled a deep sigh of relief, and Leo felt the same. He was anxious to get out of that house and away from his past. He stood to stretch as the crew scrambled to turn off lights, while William secured the camera. J.C., Laura, and Chet also stood, but before any of them could get out of the room, Robert, Kristen, Diego, and Asher popped up in front of them asking, at the same time, how they did, performance-wise.

Laura spoke first, praising Kristen for her acting and for making her look glamorous. Kristen laughed. "The glamorous part comes easily."

Chet said, "You were great, Robert. You make a better me than I do."

Robert laughed and punched Chet on the shoulder.

J.C. eyed Diego as though he was going to say something critical. But then he just nodded. "You did good, Diego. Made me look strong. Thanks."

The way J.C. gazed at Diego caught Leo's attention because Diego gazed right back at him, both locking eyes and holding for a long moment.

"Thanks, J.C.," Diego replied with a grin, his teeth so white they were almost blinding. "I want to make you look good."

"How 'bout me, Leo?"

Leo looked at Asher's eager expression, avoiding direct eye contact because the other boy was so close. What could he say but the truth? "You were fantastic. I felt like I was watching myself. Weird feeling."

"Thanks, man." Asher looked like nothing else could make his day better.

"Everyone ready for lunch?" Diego asked. "I'm starved."

"Me too," Robert echoed.

Leo would've preferred to eat with just his crew so they could talk about the Robert situation, but he didn't want to be rude. "You lead, and we'll follow."

Diego led the way.

Laura held Leo back as the four actors stepped through the front door and into the bright summer sunshine. She leaned in and whispered, "Any idea what to do about Robert?"

Chet and J.C. both stopped to listen.

Leo made sure no one was near them as they stepped out onto the front porch. "I have an idea."

Laura eyed him with raised eyebrows. "Is it a good one?"

Leo tossed her a look. "No, it sucks, but it's the best I can come up with."

CHAPTER FOUR

I'M GOING TO FIND OUT HOW THEY KNEW

Cassie's mind whirled with anticipation over all she needed to do that afternoon, and she barely nibbled at the lasagna on the plate in front of her.

Donovan nudged her arm. "Eat, Cass, we have a long day to go."

She eyed his soft, gentle smile beneath the fedora shading his face, and couldn't help but relax. "Just thinking about everything I have to do." She took another bite of her food.

"And you'll do it perfectly, just like you did this morning," he said, swigging from a can of Coke.

"Thanks. I just don't want to make any mistakes."

"I know you think because you're female, any mistakes will look worse than if I was AD, but don't forget the producer is a female."

She grimaced. "That might be worse. She might expect even more from me than a man would."

He took one of her hands in his and held it up to his heart. "You're the most organized person on this set. And don't forget I'm always here for you."

She broke into a smile, and her worries eased. "I could never forget that." She squeezed his hand, and they resumed eating.

A shadow fell across them. Cassie looked up to see Ms. Cantrell, the producer, eyeing her and Donovan, and almost choked on her food.

"Ms. Cantrell," she blustered, trying to recover her aplomb.

Fortunately, Donovan came to her rescue. "Hi, Ms. Cantrell. This lunch is great."

"I'm glad you like it." She tilted her head, studying him for a long moment. "You have beautiful features, Donovan. Do you ever do any acting?"

That was Cassie's cue to recover herself and speak up for the man she loved. "He has, Ms. Cantrell, and he's great. Looks amazing on camera too."

She nodded, appraising them both.

Donovan glanced down, embarrassed. "I like behind the camera better."

"I fully understand," Ms. Cantrell said, her voice sounding like a sigh as she glanced across at another large table where Leo sat quietly, while his friends and the actors talked animatedly. "My beautiful son has steadfastly refused to step in front of a camera for me." She studied Donovan once more. "With your looks, you'll have tongues wagging. There's a small part in this film, a walk-on really, that just opened up. The actor I hired stupidly broke his leg skateboarding. I'd like you in that role."

Cassie grinned, but Donovan blanched. "Uh, I don't know, Ms. Cantrell."

"Of course, I'll pay you for the acting in addition to your current job, and since you have several lines, the money is good."

Cassie elbowed Donovan and he nearly dropped the Coke in his hand. "Come on, D-Boy. You know I love seeing your face on the big screen." She offered her most loving expression and he quickly gave in.

"Sure, Ms. Cantrell," he said to the waiting producer. "I appreciate you thinking of me."

She beamed for the first time. "Splendid. I'll make sure Mr. Ketchum gets you those pages." She started to leave, but then turned back to face Cassie. "Oh, and Cassie. I must compliment you on a job well done. You've kept everything on time and running like clockwork. Keep it up, girl." She offered a reassuring smile and then strode off toward Mr. Ketchum's table, where he sat with William, Baxter, and Jaden.

"See?" Donovan said. "I told you she'd be happy with you. But I wish you hadn't given me that look about the acting job. You know I can't resist it."

She smirked. "I can't help wanting to show you off to the world."

"Very funny." But he flashed the smile she loved, and they focused on finishing their lunch.

They headed back to the house before lunch officially ended because Cassie wanted to check that everything was ready for the next scene. By the time the actors and crew members began trickling in, she had her clipboard and was ready to put everyone through their paces. Quelling the butterflies in her stomach, she sent the actors off for makeup retouching, while William and Baxter assisted their respective crewmembers to arrange the camera and sound equipment for the first setup.

As Mr. Ketchum joined them, chatting with the DP, Stuart drifted around the room offering cups of coffee. When he arrived at her side, Cassie smiled.

"You read my mind, Stuart," she said, reaching for a Styrofoam cup of steaming coffee. "Even though it's hot in here, I need a caffeine boost."

He offered a pleasant smile, his goatee wrapping itself around his mouth and adding to his attractiveness. "I aim to please, Cassie." He moved on to Mr. Ketchum and she consulted her clipboard for upcoming tasks.

She noted that Leo and his crew hung out in one corner. They had their heads together conversing about something, with Leo occasionally pointing at the overhead chandelier and then at Chet and J.C., like he was blocking out a scene for the movie. She thought their behavior curious but didn't have time to think about it because Mr. K was ready to shoot, so she called the actors to their places.

The afternoon seemed to fly by as the filming proceeded without incident. The actors were spot on, and Mr. K waved his arms with glee at the footage he was acquiring. Finally, it came time for the first of the "floor-dropping" scenes, as Cassie called them, this one involving the chair Robert would be sitting in. She observed the crew members rigging the chair in its place with a strong but barely visible hinge at the base of one front leg, attaching it to the floor. Then they secured the chair to the wall via wires that would be erased from the final print, thereby making certain the chair would only tilt a few degrees before stopping, to ensure Robert didn't fall down the hole. For the shot of the entire floor collapsing, stunt doubles would step in for all the characters who needed to fall into the basement.

Robert was already in the chair from the previous shots, as this was a continuation of the same scene. Mr. K walked over to talk with him, while

Cassie took note that everyone else was in place, and Donovan jotted down details to replicate should any of this scene have to be repeated. Cassie thought it odd that Leo left his crew and walked across the room to stand on the opposite side, so that he was now facing Robert, rather than behind him. Two of his friends, J.C. and Chet, split up and moved around behind Robert, somewhat to either side of him. Laura stayed where she was. All of them remained out of camera range, but their behavior was puzzling.

Forcing herself to focus on the job, she did a last-minute check of her notes and then said, "We're ready to shoot, Mr. K."

Mr. K and Tank, the stunt coordinator, checked the tautness of the wire holding the chair to the wall. There was a slight give to allow the chair to tilt a few inches, but they seemed satisfied that it was secure. Then Tank, bald, beefy, and middle-aged, squatted down behind Robert and loosely tied some cord around his wrists and secured his ankles in the same way.

"Not too tight?" Tank's voice boomed out of him like a bullhorn.

"I'm good, Tank," Robert said.

Tank stepped back out of camera range, folding his thick arms across his barrel chest, waiting for the action to commence.

Cassie stood beside Donovan, directly behind Mr. K as he looked through the camera eyepiece to check the framing of the shot.

"Looks good," Mr. K announced to the actors and crew.

Chet stepped forward, surprising everyone. "Uh, Mr. Ketchum, can I tell Robert something before you shoot?"

Mr. K looked curious, but said, "Certainly, Chet."

Chet hurried over and squatted down beside Robert, whispering something to the actor. His body blocked Cassie's view of Robert's face, though she couldn't make out the whispering in any case. They remained that way for a few moments, with Chet almost hugging the back of the chair as he shared whatever he was telling Robert. When he stood, Robert looked confused, but nothing more was said.

"Thank you, Mr. K," Chet said politely before returning to his previous spot to one side of Robert's back. J.C. remained at the opposite side, both far enough to be out of camera range.

What was that all about?

Mr. K's voice brought her back to the moment. "We're ready, Cassie."

Ignoring her uncertainty, Cassie waved over Asher and the actor playing Wayne. Asher bounded forward and squatted down in front of Robert, placing his hands on Robert's knees. The other actor, cell phone in hand, squatted to Robert's right side, holding up the camera as though to film the other two boys. The dialogue portion had already been shot, as had much of the action.

Cassie glanced at Leo on her side of the room but opposite Robert. Leo looked taut as a panther, like he was ready to spring into action any moment.

"Okay, everyone, this is a take," Mr. K announced. "Roll camera."

The cameraman said, "Camera rolling. Speed."

"Action," called out Mr. K.

Asher swung out one foot and looped it around Wayne's ankle, pulling back hard and flipping Wayne onto his back. Wayne scrabbled away as a loud cracking sound filled the room. Asher leaped past Robert just as the floor beneath the chair splintered and pieces broke away. Robert looked suitably terrified as his chair began to tilt toward the opening in the floor.

Snap!

Leo sprang into action, pelting forward and leaping upward. He grabbed the overhead chandelier, then swung across the widening hole in the floor.

Robert cried out in fear as his chair tilted more than it was supposed to. Frozen in place, Cassie watched, terrified, as Leo swung closer to Robert, while J.C. and Chet bolted forward.

"Grab on, Robert!" Leo called out as his dangling legs reached the other boy.

Already falling, Robert reached out and grabbed hold of Leo's legs.

Wait, Cassie thought. *His hands were tied. Weren't they?*

With Robert gripping hard to Leo's legs, the chair beneath him tumbled away down the hole into the basement. Leo's swinging momentum was enough to bring Robert close to the edge of the hole, where Chet and J.C. grabbed him and yanked backward. The three of them tumbled into a heap on the floor as Leo swung back over the hole and then kicked out with his legs to return him to the side where Chet, J.C., Robert, and now Laura huddled together.

Then Leo did something that astonished Cassie even more. He let go of the chandelier, did a flip in the air, and came down onto his feet, knees bent, maintaining his balance, just like an Olympic gymnast. For a second, she didn't know whether she should clap or give him a score.

Everything had happened so fast that the entire crew remained frozen. Mr. K yelled, "Cut!" and then Tank lunged forward, checking Robert for injuries.

"You okay, kid?"

Robert nodded, breathing heavily, and looking stunned.

Mr. K quickly followed, while Cassie glanced at Donovan beside her. He looked stunned, exactly how she felt. Heart pounding with the adrenaline rush, she stepped closer to the edge of the hole, which was only five feet in diameter, and looked down into the basement. The chair had shattered when it struck a large generator below. Several crew members stared at the broken chair in disbelief.

"Is everyone okay down there?" Cassie called out.

One of the crew tossed her a thumbs-up. "We're all good here. What happened up there?"

"We don't know."

She turned away from the hole as Mr. K approached her and Donovan.

"Is Robert okay?" Donovan asked, his voice laced with concern.

Looking rattled, Mr. K replied, "Thankfully, yes. I don't know what happened. I'm sure that chair was secure. Tank was sure."

"Mr. Ketchum," came a female voice from the doorway behind them.

The three of them turned in surprise to face Ms. Cantrell, looking quite unhappy, standing in the open doorway.

When did she show up? Cassie wondered.

"Once Tank and his crew have determined the cause of this unnecessary accident, have them report to me, along with yourself, for a full report. I'll be in my temp office at the back of the house."

Mr. K looked like he might faint. "Yes, Ms. Cantrell. We'll get to the bottom of it."

Her eyes glittered with anger. "I sincerely hope so. Are you prepared to shoot other scenes in this house?"

Mr. K glanced at Cassie, and she consulted her notes. "Yes, the kitchen is ready."

Ms. Cantrell lifted her chin and gazed firmly at Mr. K. "Then I suggest you move on to the kitchen until the fault in this stunt can be rectified."

With that, she looked away as though dismissing him and fixed her piercing gaze on Leo, who was trying to be invisible behind his friends in the corner. "Leonardo."

Leo gingerly stepped out from behind Chet. "Yes, Mother?"

"A private chat. Now."

Leo glanced at J.C., who nodded his support, and then started across the room, head bowed like a child who was about to be spanked. Everyone stared at him in silence.

Robert stepped away from Tank and grabbed Leo's arm. "I owe you again, Leo. Thanks, man."

Leo offered a weak smile before continuing past Asher, who offered him a grin of encouragement. Looking down at the floor, he followed his mother out of the living room.

The silence erupted with activity as everyone prepared to pull up stakes and head into the kitchen.

Donovan shook his head in amazement. "That was crazy, wasn't it?"

Cassie faced him, brows furrowed with uncertainty. "Did you notice how Leo and his friends were acting before we started shooting?"

He nodded. "Especially Chet talking to Robert. It was almost like they knew it was gonna happen."

"Exactly. And I'm going to find out how they knew."

CHAPTER FIVE

BE CAREFUL AROUND HER

LEO COULDN'T LOOK AT HIS mother, but then, he never could, even before he'd acquired his strange power. When he used to watch for her admiration as a child, he'd always been disappointed to find her wearing a scowl of disapproval. She was a hard woman to please, and he knew Tank and Mr. Ketchum were in for a serious chewing out later on. Right now, it was his turn.

She led him to an alcove under the main stairs, where they would not be overheard by crew members in the foyer.

"That was quite a performance you put on in there, Leonardo," she said dryly, scrutinizing him sharply. "Nice dismount, though."

Leo didn't respond. He didn't even look up. He felt the power of her withering gaze and didn't need to see it up close.

"I'd like an explanation," she went on, her tone commanding.

Leo hadn't exactly thought through what he'd tell his mother. He was a terrible liar at the best of times, and she always saw through him. "I, uh, I just reacted, like I've been taught in aikido. I saw the chair starting to fall for real and, well, I noticed the chandelier before, so I just jumped without thinking."

"I see." There was a moment of tense quiet, with the only sounds being the crew passing back and forth in the foyer. "Leonardo, I watched the entire episode and it clearly looked like you and your friends knew this was going to happen."

Now he did look up—not into her eyes but so she could see his—and hoped he sounded sincere. "How could we know that? J.C. and Chet have never watched a stunt before. I guess they were worried Robert might get hurt somehow."

"I see," she repeated. "It should be interesting, when I speak with them one-on-one, to see if they corroborate your story."

Leo's stomach dropped in fear. What if he and the others couldn't talk before she got to them?

"Another thing, Leonardo," she went on, her tone suspicious. "Several of the crew have mentioned you using my name to ask questions and check on their work."

Leo relaxed, having already planned a story for this. "I'm sorry, Mom, I didn't think you'd mind. It's just, well, if I ever wanna be a producer like you someday, I figured I needed to know everything that happens on a film shoot."

Her face shifted, the suspicion morphing into a look of surprise. "You're interested in producing?"

Leo shrugged. "Well, sure, I mean, why not? I've got the best teacher to learn from. I also thought maybe it could help my shyness to talk to more people."

Her mouth formed into a genuine smile. "I must say I'm impressed with your thinking. I will let Mr. Ketchum and the crew know that you have my authorization to watch, learn, and ask questions." Her smile dipped into a frown. "So long as you don't disrupt shooting."

"Mother, I'm seventeen, not seven."

She gave him an appraising look, as though seeing him for the first time. "Yes, I suppose you are."

"May I go now?" He was desperate to get away from her before he gave anything away.

She nodded. "But Leonardo, this isn't the last time we'll discuss what happened with Robert. Count on that."

"I understand." He left the alcove and hurried up the short hallway into the foyer, where he nearly ran into Donovan. Most everyone had already cleared out of the drawing room and were headed for the kitchen on the opposite side of the stairs.

"Sorry, Donovan," Leo blurted, reaching down to retrieve the notebook he'd knocked from the other guy's hand.

Donovan offered an understanding smile as he took the notebook from Leo. "It's okay. My mom is a lot like yours."

That caught Leo by surprise. "Yeah?"

"Yeah. She's mellowed a little since she got attacked at work last spring, but she's still rough around the edges. I love her, but I do look forward to moving out."

Leo smiled. "I know what you mean. Thanks for telling me. I always figured my mom just didn't like me, but now that I'm older I think maybe it's not that simple."

Donovan offered an infectious grin from beneath the fedora. "We should kick it some time."

"Yeah, that'd be cool." Leo found himself liking that idea immensely.

"I gotta go now. See ya."

Donovan took off across the foyer, working his way between other crew members toward the kitchen hallway.

A hand on his arm made Leo whirl in surprise, only to relax when he realized it was Laura.

"Let's talk," she said and led him toward the open front door.

Once outside on the creaky wooden steps, she led him into the desiccated ruins of the front yard. Where once existed a lawn, now only a rectangular stretch of dirt remained. Flower beds lay empty and forlorn, and weeds practically strangled each other to dominate the landscape.

Once they were far enough away from the comings and goings at the front door, Leo asked, "Where's J.C. and Chet?"

"Your mother," Laura answered, looking somber.

Leo gasped, fearful that they would contradict what he'd told her.

"What did you tell her?"

Glancing away from the blinding sunlight, he answered, "I, uh, I just told her I reacted instinctively, like I learned in aikido, and that J.C. and Chet must've been ready to help 'cause they were worried about the stunt going bad."

She rubbed a hand through her pixie-cut hair and looked thoughtful. "That's kind of what I told them to say, so we might be okay, but..."

He squinted, putting a hand over his eyes to shade them. "But what?"

"Have you thought about telling her the truth? About you, I mean?"

Leo's heart hammered in his chest just thinking about telling his mother. He shook his head. "No, I can't. I don't know what she'd do with that information."

She studied him in that way he hated but at the same time liked, because he knew she cared about him. "What do you think she'd *do* with that information?"

He walked away, still feeling her gaze piercing his soul. "I don't know, but..."

She approached and placed a gentle hand on his shoulder. "But what?"

Leo didn't respond.

"Is this about your mother thinking you and J.C. are boyfriends?"

Leo whirled around, startled. Then he offered a rueful smile. "No, she's moved on from there. Now she's trying to get me and Asher together."

Laura guffawed in shock. "No way!"

"Way. She even suggested we sleep in my king-sized bed because that way Asher wouldn't feel lonely."

She shook her head in consternation. "Okay, you got me there." She paused a moment, her expression becoming thoughtful. "But I have noticed that you..."

When she trailed off, Leo asked, "That I what?"

She shrugged in a dismissive way. "It's not important now. But your mom is trippy. Forget my suggestion."

He grinned. "It's already forgotten." Though he did wonder what she'd stopped herself from saying.

"Let's go back in and find out what's happening," she said. "'Sides, it's hot out here and we're not on the beach."

The moment they entered the house, J.C. and Chet pounced on Leo like tigers on their prey.

"Oh my God, Leo," J.C. blurted. "Your mom made me feel like a mass murderer."

"Hell, yeah," echoed Chet, wiping perspiration from his brow. "My mom could take interrogation lessons from her."

J.C. nodded. "And your mom's police chief too."

"Exactly."

Laura held up her hands. "Whoa, slow down. What did you tell her?"

"Exactly what you told us to," J.C. insisted.

"But she didn't believe us.," Chet added, and J.C. nodded.

Leo stared at his two friends in amazement, never having seen them so in sync before. *Yeah, my mother has that effect on people.*

"Did she call you liars?" Laura looked from one to the other awaiting an answer.

"Not exactly," J.C. admitted.

"But you know that look adults give you when they think you're lying?" Chet asked.

Leo and Laura nodded.

"Well, your mom was wearing it like a Halloween mask," J.C. asserted.

Leo felt he needed to say something, so he said, "I'm sorry for the way she acted."

"Look, she can't prove any of us are lying unless we mess up," Laura added in a low voice, making sure passing crew members couldn't overhear.

Leo spotted the massive Tank leaving the living room and whispered to the others, "Be right back." Then he hurried up to the man before Tank could head down the back hallway toward the temporary office his mother had set up. "Uh, Mr. Tank."

Tank turned, his thick chest and arms making Leo feel puny by comparison. "It's just Tank, Mr. Cantrell."

"It's just Leo, Tank."

Tank offered a tight smile. "Okay, Leo. What can I do ya for?"

"I, uh, I was wondering if you, you know, figured out what happened with the chair."

Tank fixed intense brown eyes on him, and Leo forced himself not to squirm.

"All I can determine is that a small section of the wire was thinner than the rest, causing it to break. There are chemicals that can weaken wire, but it'll have to be tested for that. Could just have been poorly manufactured. In any case, I'm in for a tongue-lashing from your mother."

Leo reddened. "Sorry about that."

"No, I deserve it. The lives of every actor and stuntman are my responsibility and if it wasn't for you, Robert could've been seriously hurt."

Dead, actually, Leo thought, but he didn't say that.

"You have quick reflexes, Leo," Tank went on, giving him a once-over. "You're strong from all your gymnastics. Ever thought of being a stuntman? With your looks, you'd double all the young leading man types."

"Uh, no, I don't think stunt work is my thing," Leo mumbled. "But thanks for the compliment."

Tank gazed at him long and hard, but not in a negative or suspicious way. "I've worked on a lot of your mom's films, so I've seen you from the time you were little. You're shy, but you always do things your own way. I respect that in a man. Keep it up, Leo."

"Yes, sir."

Tank turned and strode past crew members down the hall, out of sight. Leo hurried back to his friends.

"Did you find out anything?" J.C. asked, glancing side to side like they were sharing national secrets.

Leo wasn't sure how he felt about Tank's news. Could it have been an accident after all? "He isn't sure. Could've been an accident."

"That's not what you said before, after you looked in Robert's eyes," Laura reminded him.

"Yeah, you said it was murder," Chet added, keeping his deep voice low.

Leo thought back on what he recalled of his "vision," scrunching his brows in concentration. Had he actually seen anyone tampering with the attachment? No, just the wire snapping and Robert falling. But he'd felt a presence, hadn't he?

"I felt someone was there in the background, causing the chair to fall."

"But you didn't see anyone?" J.C. fixed his hard brown eyes on him.

Leo shook his head. "But I'm sure it was on purpose."

"I hate to say this, Leo, but there's only one way to find out," Laura said, her tone one of resignation. "You have to look in his eyes again."

Leo looked up, but quickly averted his gaze from hers. "I know."

Nothing more was said as they crossed the busy foyer and trudged down to the kitchen to see what was happening. As they skirted crew members carrying lights or other equipment, Leo almost bumped into Stuart again, who was carrying some sandbags this time.

"Sorry, Stuart," Leo said, dodging to one side so his shoulder wouldn't collide with Stuart's. "I keep bumping into you."

Stuart only grinned. "No worries, man. I hear you're the big hero. Wish I could've been there to see you swing into action. Sounded better than a Spiderman flick."

Leo's stomach tightened. "You heard, huh?"

"'Course. The whole crew knows by now."

Leo frowned but wasn't surprised by the news.

"Any of 'em say anything about it?" Laura asked, her tone casual.

Stuart shrugged. "Dunno. I been busy running around. Gotta get these bags into the drawing room. See ya." Then he was gone, swallowed up by other milling crew members.

Stealing himself for more questions, Leo made his way into the bustling kitchen, his friends trailing after. Lights blazed as William worked with the Director of Photography to set up camera angles. Cassie and Donovan stood to one side, both checking the notebook each of them held. Cassie looked up and spotted Leo, closed her notebook and weaved through the lighting crew to his side.

"Hey, Leo," she began, "that was crazy, what you did. Robert can't stop talking about it."

Leo's heart raced. *You can do this, Leo.* "Well, I'm just glad I could help."

She offered a smile and turned to Chet, who looked like he might bolt any moment. "I wondered why Robert's hands weren't tied when it happened, but he told me you untied them, Chet. And told him to be ready in case anything happened. Why did you do that?"

Chet looked flummoxed, and Leo shocked himself by speaking up. "It was my fault, Cassie. I get these, I don't what you call them…"

"Premonitions," Laura put in smoothly, as though it was her turn to speak.

"Yeah, that's the word," Leo went on, avoiding Cassie's eyes but letting her see his. "I had a bad feeling about that chair thing, so I told Chet to warn him. It was like the feeling I had about J.C. being killed last March, when this movie happened for real."

Cassie studied him as though searching for guile, but Leo could see she was seriously considering his answer.

"That was the main problem with the script when we came on board," she said, glancing from Leo to the others and back. "There seemed to be no reason for Asher's character to want to protect Diego's. That's why we wrote in the dream sequence."

Leo wasn't sure what to say, so he remained silent.

"That works too," Laura said with a smile. "But I was there both times Leo had these premonitions, and they were real."

"Thanks for telling me, Leo," Cassie said, looking less suspicious than she had only moments before. "Now it makes a little more sense."

"Hey, Cass!"

She turned to find Donovan waving her over to where he stood beside the camera, then excused herself to join him.

Leo allowed himself to relax. "That was close."

"Cassie's sharp," Laura commented. "Be careful around her."

Leo leaned closer. "I think I should keep a low pro for a while."

"Good idea," she whispered back. "We can wander around and check out the crew, look for anything sketch."

He nodded and waved at the others to follow him out of the kitchen. Walking back up the hall toward the foyer, they nearly collided with Asher and Diana heading for the kitchen. Diana gripped a large wooden box that Leo presumed contained her makeup supplies. Asher broke into such a grin upon seeing him that Leo was embarrassed.

"Hi, Leo." Suddenly Asher seemed shy, not quite so exuberant.

"Well, Leo," Diana said to fill the awkward silence, "I hear you're quite the superhero, swinging from chandeliers and all."

Leo felt his cheeks redden. "I, uh, I just saw Robert in trouble and jumped in to help."

Asher turned to Diana. "See what I mean? He saves a guy's life and acts like it's nothing."

Diana beamed. "Humility is so rare these days. Coupled with your gorgeous looks, it's a powerful combination, Leo."

J.C. laughed. "Careful, Diana, you'll give him a big, fat head."

Leo chuckled and elbowed J.C. while Diana grinned.

"We, uh, gotta get to work, Leo," Asher said, again eyeing Leo shyly. "See you later."

Diana nodded and they hurried on down the hallway.

J.C. smirked. "Coupled with your gorgeous looks. Yeah, right."

"Somebody sounds jealous," Chet muttered from behind, and Laura laughed.

J.C. scowled and Leo led them out the front door where they could observe the crew coming and going without interruption.

CHAPTER SIX

YOU READY TO DIE?

Cassie hadn't believed Leo's premonition story, but she didn't have a clear reason why she didn't. A gut feeling was all she could come up with. For now, she needed to focus on getting everyone in place to shoot these kitchen scenes, which didn't involve many camera setups and should go smoothly.

Once Mr. K took charge and ran the actors through their paces, she set aside the Robert incident and did her job to everyone's satisfaction. The kitchen scenes took less than two hours, which was better than expected. The four actors didn't miss a beat and Mr. K went for only a few takes, apparently satisfied with what he was seeing.

Once these scenes wrapped up, the camera and lights were moved to the foyer to capture all the scenes that took place in that location, which Cassie suspected might take more than a few hours. They had the house until ten p.m., if needed, and she knew Mr. K wanted to use every moment he had available.

She did notice that Leo and his crew did not reappear, which was good because the small kitchen was hard-pressed to hold everyone who was needed for the shots. She released the actors for a short break while lights and camera were set up in the foyer, and then she and Donovan followed Mr. K down the hallway to the new location.

"My job's been pretty easy so far," Donovan commented as they looked around the spacious foyer and up at the second-floor landing. "The cast wears all the same clothes, so it's really a matter of keeping track of extreme variations of movement during takes that might not cut."

She tossed him a grin. "You the editor now too?"

He laughed. "No, but continuity is part of my job."

"True."

She noticed Robert heading out the front door just as Leo was entering. Leo must've been lost in thought because he looked up into Robert's face in surprise, as though he had no idea the other was there. Then she stopped in her tracks and grabbed Donovan's arm, indicating the two boys.

Leo was staring at Robert with wide, almost horrified eyes, as though seeing something grisly and unbearable.

"Leo, you okay?"

Robert sounded concerned, but he was sideways to Cassie, so she couldn't see his face.

Leo retained his stunned expression as he stepped back and collided with Laura, who been following him inside.

"Leo?" Robert said again. "What's wrong?"

Leo seemed to recover himself, at least enough to lose the horrified expression and look down at the floor. "Nothing, Robert. I'm good, man. You just startled me, is all. I was thinking."

Robert chuckled. "You must be a real deep thinker. I'm heading out for a snack. You want anything?"

Leo shook his head. "Thanks, anyway."

Robert smiled and stepped around J.C. and Chet to exit the house. Leo turned to Laura and opened his mouth as if to speak, but she shook her head and indicated he turn around. He did and Cassie stared at him, brows furrowed with confusion. Whatever he might've said to Laura remained unsaid as he offered a nervous smile and then exited the house. Laura followed, but J.C. looked confused.

"Uh, Leo, we just came from outside." He glanced at Chet, who shrugged, and then they followed the others back into the bright sunlight.

Cassie looked at Donovan and saw her own puzzlement mirrored in his eyes.

"That was weird," he said, tilting his fedora back off his forehead.

"Very," she agreed. "Did you see the look on Leo's face? Like he saw a ghost."

"Yeah. He could just have been startled, like he said. I was watching him when he came in because he looked so focused on something."

She considered that possibility. "Maybe. But I didn't believe his story about having premonitions, even though it's better than the dream idea we wrote into the script. There's something going on with Leo, and I'm gonna find out what it is."

"What did you see, Leo?"

Laura's voice penetrated Leo's flustered mind as he realized they had left the haunted house and moved off down the street, away from the shoot.

"Yeah, Leo, what was it?" J.C.'s face floated in front of his and he fought his initial panic to focus on what he'd seen in Robert's eyes.

Leo stopped to catch his breath, not because he was winded, but because he needed to process everything before answering. His three friends surrounded him, anxious, gazing at him with expectant expressions. Leo glanced around. The film crew were half a block down at the house, though some members walked from there to trucks parked along both sides of the street and back again.

Leo considered the horrific scene he witnessed in the brief glimpse he'd gotten of Robert's eyes. "He's, uh, he's gonna be…murdered. Next week, on Wednesday."

"Oh God," muttered Chet.

"How?" J.C. asked, his brown skin paling.

Leo tried to replay the vision in his mind. "I only saw it for a second, but it looked like someone was pinning him to a wall with knives, like in a horror movie."

"You're sure he was dead?" Laura twisted her face with worry.

Leo nodded. "There was blood all over him, like maybe he'd been stabbed a bunch of times. It was horrible."

"Least now we know that chair wasn't an accident," Chet commented.

"Could you see where he was?" J.C. asked. "It wasn't in the haunted house, was it?"

Leo shook his head. "It was dark all around him, maybe the outside of a house. Not the haunted house, though. 'Sides, they'll be filming on the studio lot next Wednesday."

J.C. shook his head. "Somebody sure has it in for that guy."

Laura glared at him. "Like somebody had it in for you last spring?"

J.C. looked abashed. "Well, yeah."

"We don't know if Robert did anything to make somebody wanna kill him," Chet said, his tone defensive. "He's a cool guy who told me about his jerk days. We compared notes, since both of us were assholes before we changed. We gotta do something to help him."

"We will," Leo said firmly, with conviction.

"At least we have a week to figure it out," Laura added, her voice far calmer than Leo felt. "But where do we start?"

Leo noted all their eyes on him and once again realized that he was the point man, despite his social anxiety. "Well, um… I think I'll talk to Mr. Ketchum, the director. I wanna know if he hired all the crew or if not, who did."

"Diego told me Mr. K—that's what he calls him—hired him and the others who went to the high school where he used to teach," J.C. put in as he adjusted his styled black hair, which had slipped out of place under the hot breeze.

"Did Diego talk about anyone hating on Robert from that school?" Leo asked.

J.C. shrugged. "Cassie hated him, but then they made up after Robert went to jail."

"Robert was in jail?" Laura's face lit up with excitement.

Everyone looked at Chet, who nodded. "Yeah, he spent a few days in county," he said. "He told me jail is what changed him."

"Did he talk about anyone in jail who might've messed with him or even threatened him?" Laura asked, her voice rising in pitch.

Leo understood her excitement. It could be a valuable lead.

Chet shook his head. "He said he kept a low pro and didn't talk to anyone."

"Still," Leo said to Chet, "it's worth finding out more. I don't wanna tell him yet what I saw, but maybe tonight at your house you can ask him more about jail."

Chet agreed. "He and I have a lot in common, so I think he'll tell me almost anything."

"That's how Diego is with me," J.C. added, his voice taking on a musing tone. "I thought my mom and yours, Leo, were hardasses, but Diego's dad sounds a lot worse. I don't think anybody ever opened up that much to me before. He's a good guy."

"I thought my dad was bad," Laura said. "He refuses to accept me having a girlfriend, but the worst he ever did was lock me in my room."

"Well," Leo said when he realized the others were waiting for him to speak, "at least now we have two things to investigate. I'll check out the crew, and Chet can find out more about people who might have it in for Robert."

"J.C. and I can also ask Kristen and Diego if they remember anyone from high school who hated Robert," Laura added. "Can't hurt to cover all the bases."

"That sounds like a plan," Leo declared, feeling a powerful determination to keep Robert alive. "Nothing'll happen to Robert while we're around."

"You got that right," Chet vowed, his voice solid with conviction.

By the time shooting wrapped for the day, it was nearly ten p.m. and Cassie was burned out. She'd known the days would be long but knowing that fact and living through it were two different things. The sagging Donovan, she knew, was equally exhausted.

Shooting had gone well. They had completed all the scenes that took place on the first floor except the big stunt when the floor collapsed in the drawing room. Because of what happened with Robert, it was decided to film that scene the following day, along with the scenes of Asher attempting to lower himself down through the hole.

Tank wanted extra time to make certain the stunt would be safe and go off without a hitch, so he and his crew had been getting everything set up while Mr. K filmed scenes in other rooms. Ms. Cantrell had floated in and out, observing, never commenting, but Cassie hadn't seen much of Leo and his crew since the kitchen. They'd wandered around chatting with idle crew members, but once the filming started, they were nowhere to be seen.

Asher had seemed disappointed, probably, Cassie thought, because Leo wasn't there to watch his acting, but once the camera started rolling, he fell right into character and gave a great performance. He really was a fine actor, in addition to being a budding director of photography.

As the shooting wrapped for the night, she spotted Leo chatting with Mr. K. It wasn't her business to eavesdrop, so she made no attempt to do so, but she did hear Mr. K say, "The only crew I specifically hired were the kids I used to teach. You'd have to ask your mother about the others."

"Hey, Cass, hand me my bag," Donovan said, pointing to a worn brown messenger bag tossed into the corner behind her.

Pulling her attention away from Mr. K, she faced Donovan. "Huh?"

He smiled wanly. "My bag?" He pointed again.

Slowly, she turned and snatched up the bag by its strap, handing it to him. He slipped the strap over his shoulder, letting the bag dangle against his right side.

"I'm ready for tomorrow," he offered, stifling a yawn. "I'm even more ready for sleep."

"Me too," she agreed, glancing once more at where she'd seen Mr. K and Leo, but they were gone. The foyer was thinning out as crew evacuated for the night, securing equipment before they left. Security guards would remain on duty to watch over everything.

He offered her his hand. "Shall we?"

She took it and smiled, a feeling of warmth and safety flooding through her at the touch. As they descended the outside front steps to the sidewalk, Cassie noticed how chilly it'd gotten. A fog bank had rolled in from the sea, and the street looked like London in old horror films. As they started toward the brightly lit shuttle filling up with crew members, something in the fog caught Cassie's eye and she turned.

A figure seemed to float in the fog down by the beach, most of its lower half obscured in the swirling mist, but the face reflected light from an overhead streetlamp, and Cassie gasped. It was the masked figure she'd seen before. And the mask *was* the same as the one from their aborted horror film!

"Donovan," she hissed, and felt his body shift position as he turned. "Look!"

"The hell!" came Donovan's voice.

The masked figure stepped back, lost in the fog.

"You saw it, right?" Cassie, heart pounding, faced her boyfriend.

"Yeah." He sounded angry. "Somebody's messing with us. C'mon."

He pulled her along the sidewalk to the spot where they'd seen the figure.

"Be careful, Donovan," she whispered, clutching ever more tightly to his hand. She had a rep for being pretty ballsy, but this fog unnerved her more than she'd care to admit.

"Can you see anything?" Donovan asked.

"I can't even see you." Despite being right beside her, he was lost in the fog. "Don't let go."

"I won't." His voice comforted her, and she stared into the thick fog, looking down for her bearings. The mist was thinner around her feet, and she made out the sidewalk.

The sound of retreating footsteps came from up ahead.

"C'mon," Donovan whispered, and Cassie felt herself pulled through the pea soup, focusing on her footing.

Running footsteps came at them in the fog, but Cassie couldn't tell from where. She was completely disoriented and had lost all sense of direction. Donovan grunted beside her and then his hand slipped from her grasp.

"Donovan!"

His only response was a groan, as though he was in pain. Before Cassie could move in his direction, something touched her arm. She cried out, pelting headlong through the fog. The ground beneath her feet went from concrete to sand and she realized she'd stumbled out onto the beach. She stopped to listen, but the only sound in the swirling mist was her own erratic breathing and waves lapping against the beach.

What was happening and where was Donovan?

"Donovan?" Her voice came out a whisper, her heart pounding in her chest like a blacksmith's hammer.

She heard heavy breathing and then a rough voice to her left. "You ready to die, bitch?"

She screamed and ran, nearly colliding with a thick pole that loomed over her in the fog. She grabbed the pole and scooted around it, peering back the way she'd come, fighting to quiet her frantic breathing.

She waited.

Nothing moved in the swirling white soup that engulfed her in a co-

coon of silence, broken only by the sound of her racing heart. Then she heard a whispering voice, not the same one, but one that sounded frantic.

"Not now! You'll have your fun next week."

The voice sounded male, but high-pitched with fear. She strained to hear more, but nothing moved, and no one spoke again. She thought she heard… Were those footsteps moving away? If so, they had to be on the sidewalk, which meant she was hopefully close to where she'd left Donovan.

Choosing her steps with care in case the person who'd touched her was still out there, she felt her way along the sand until her feet met solid ground. The sidewalk! She looked around, trying to get her bearings. From which direction had she run? She heard groaning behind her and spun around.

"Donovan?"

"Here, Cass."

His voice sounded strained, but close. She hurried forward and cried out when her shins collided with something, and she nearly toppled over. Looking down, she saw him, struggling to push himself up off the sidewalk.

"Donovan!" She bent and grabbed him by one arm, tugging him to his feet and holding him steady against her body. "What happened to you?"

His face became visible in the gloom, one hand rubbing his forehead. "Why am I always the one who gets hit?"

His attempt at a joke reassured her he was all right, and she pulled him into a tight hug, feeling the pounding of his heart mixing with hers. "There was somebody out there. He touched me and I ran."

"Did he hurt you?"

"No. Somebody stopped him. I think."

"Huh?"

She released him but kept one hand tight on his arm so he wouldn't fall. "We'll figure it out later. Let's go."

She led him along the sidewalk back to the end of the street, where the familiar lights of the location shoot came into view. The fog lessened somewhat as they approached the house and the shuttles parked in front. Not wasting another minute, she guided him to the nearest shuttle and helped him up the steps. Once inside, she found two empty seats among a smattering of remaining crew members and eased him into it.

"Let me look at your head." She leaned in and examined his forehead, gently pushing aside his thick mop of hair to feel the obvious bump.

"Ouch," he grunted when she touched it.

She pulled her hands back, feeling relieved. "There's no blood, but keep rubbing your fingers over the bump as much as you can. My dad says it can prevent clotting."

He offered her that sweet smile she adored. "Thanks, doc." He glanced at the chattering crew members around them and leaned closer to her. "Any idea what went down out there?"

Cassie's mind raced with all that had happened, and she focused on putting the pieces together. She didn't want the crew to overhear them, so she whispered, "Let's talk in the car."

That seemed to satisfy him, and he leaned back into his thick seat.

CHAPTER SEVEN

YOU SAW SOMETHING, DIDN'T YOU?

LEO HAD TAKEN HIS SHOWER and was waiting for Asher to finish in the bathroom. The second floor of the house was warm, so he only wore workout shorts in preparation for bed. He was tired after such a long day and looked forward to a good night's sleep. Having never been on set for such a prolonged time, he'd come to a better understanding of how much effort went into making movies.

He noticed Asher's messenger bag tossed onto his bed and picked it up to give it to the other boy when he finished showering. An open manila envelope slipped out onto the floor and scattered some glossy 8x10 photos. Curious, Leo picked them up and found they were all headshots of Asher. Most were in black and white and autographed, but a few were in color. Noting the shower water still running in the bathroom, he sat on his bed and riffled through the photos. He couldn't take his eyes off the color ones.

Because of his power, he'd not studied Asher's face in any detail, and now he could. The other boy was incredibly photogenic. His soft features and curly brown hair fit with his small nose and full lips. But it was the eyes that held Leo's attention and quickened his heartbeat. They were hazel in color and looked like a kaleidoscope he'd had as a kid, almost sparkling with life and joy, and seeming to look right through him. Asher wore a smile in this image that filled Leo with happiness for reasons he didn't understand. Everything else melted away as he stared at that photo.

Suddenly, Asher sat beside him on the bed and tapped him on the shoulder. Startled, Leo looked over at the smiling boy and saw the same amazing face as in the photo, topped with damp curly hair. He felt an intense compulsion to look at those incredible eyes and threw caution to the wind. He raised his eyes and locked onto Asher's. For a moment he saw the kaleidoscope in those eyes, but it was quickly replaced by Asher's bloodied face, those eyes open and empty in death. Leo jerked back and broke eye contact, his body trembling, his breathing on hold.

"Leo, what's wrong?" Asher's smile vanished into a look of concern.

Leo didn't answer. He couldn't. It wasn't possible. Not Asher too!

"I'm gonna get your mom."

As Asher rose from the bed, Leo grabbed his arm. "No, not Mom."

Asher slowly reseated himself but said nothing more, just waited.

Leo gave him a sideways glance, vaguely aware that, like him, the other boy wore shorts and no shirt. But Asher's face was twisted with worry and Leo knew he had to tell his friend the truth.

"You said you read all about me last spring when everything went down, right?"

Asher nodded.

"Did you ever wonder how I happened to be in the right place at the right time to save J.C.?"

Asher's face froze, and then looked like a light had just come on. "Yeah, I did, but there was never anything about that in the media."

"That's 'cause nobody but J.C., Chet, and Laura know." Leo paused, collecting his thoughts, hoping this boy he felt so comfortable with would not think him crazy. "I like volunteering at homeless shelters in LA," he continued, sucking in a deep breath and expelling it. "Last spring, before the stuff with J.C., I met an old man at one of the shelters who…" He trailed off.

Asher leaned closer, all ears. "Yeah?"

"It's gonna sound nutty."

"Try me."

Leo gazed at his face and caught a glimpse of those earnest eyes. "He… he got me to look into his eyes and…gave me the power to know when people were gonna die. Said he'd had it for a long time and had to pass it on before he died."

Asher's mouth hung open. "And did he die?"

Leo nodded. "Right in front of me."

Asher looked as though a great mystery had been solved. "Now it makes sense. Cassie and Donovan did a polish on the script and struggled to explain how your character knew ahead of time." He stood and paced in front of Leo, who sat in silence trying not to stare at Asher's toned physique. Asher stopped and snapped his fingers. "That's how you knew about Robert."

Leo nodded again.

Asher paused, staring at Leo uncertainly. "What did you see when you looked in my eyes? You saw something, didn't you? That's why you freaked."

Leo felt cold all over and wished for the warmth of his thick bedcover. "Someone's…gonna…kill you. Next Wednesday."

Asher's face collapsed, and he dropped back onto the bed in shock, his arm brushing against Leo's. Leo pulled away like he'd been electrocuted.

"There's more," he went on, wondering if the shock was static electricity or something else.

Asher, his face drained of color, looked at him. "What?"

"Robert's gonna be murdered the same day. By the same guy."

Asher's eyes bulged to the size of boiled eggs. "That's crazy!"

"I know."

Asher looked ready to swoon and Leo scooted closer to wrap one arm over his shoulders. "You gonna faint?"

Asher's body trembled and Leo pulled him closer, despite the awkwardness of feeling Asher's warm flesh against his own. "I won't let it happen. Just like before. I'll stop it."

Asher met his gaze and seemed to realize something. "You saw the killer?"

"No, just a hand with a bloody knife. But there was a tattoo on the wrist. I saw it in Robert's eyes too. A tattoo of Chucky, that killer doll."

Looking devastated, Asher laid his head on Leo's shoulder. "Why me? I'm cool with everyone."

At first, Leo wasn't sure what to say. Asher's closeness was unnerving, and he couldn't think straight. Then he asked, "Did you piss off any of your girlfriends' exes?"

Asher lifted his head and fought to gain control over his emotions. He shook his head. "I never had any girlfriends. I dated a few girls in high school, but they all asked me out and it only lasted one date. I didn't have anything in common with them. No ex ever got in my face or anything."

Leo paused to think some more. "It's not just you. It's you and Robert. That's the big why. Were you guys friends or enemies?"

Asher pulled away, looking uncomfortable. "Robert was a jerk in high school, and I avoided him. We have nothing in common except we went to the same school."

An idea struck Leo. "And you both worked on that horror film Cassie and Donovan were directing, right?"

Asher furrowed his brows. "You think there's a connection?"

Leo shrugged. "I don't know. We have to tell J.C. and the others tomorrow. Maybe they can come up with something. Laura's smart. She really helped the last time this happened."

Asher nodded, but still looked disturbed, and Leo couldn't blame him. "Uh, Leo."

"Yeah?"

"I know it sounds wimpy, but I don't feel like being alone tonight. Can I sleep in here, on the floor?"

Leo studied his new friend and felt the fear loud and clear. "I got this big-ass king-size bed that can hold four people. I don't wanna sound like my mother, but you can have the other side."

The relief washing over Asher's face sent Leo's heart into overdrive. He didn't understand his reaction to Asher because he'd never felt this way around any guys before. Maybe it was Asher's eyes, that photo he'd stared at so intently?

"Thanks, Leo," Asher said quietly. "I really appreciate it."

Leo smiled and stood, feeling unsteady but needing some distance. He scooped up the photos and Asher's messenger bag and strode to his dresser, setting them on top. Wanting to change the subject, he asked, "You don't seem like the kind of guy who hands out his picture to people."

Asher's face reddened. "I'm not. That was Mr. K's idea. He told all us actors to have some signed photos handy for the location shoot in case anyone asks for one. You know people, they'll ask even nobody actors like me for autographs." He shrugged.

"You're not nobody," Leo said before he could stop himself. "And those photos are dope."

Asher grinned. "You can have any of 'em, if you want."

Leo realized he did want that color picture he'd been staring at, so he pulled it out of the messenger bag, holding it up. "I like this one."

"It's yours."

"Thanks, man." Leo set the photo down next to the messenger bag. As he turned back, he found Asher staring at him so intently he squirmed.

"You okay?"

As though emerging from a trance, Asher flinched and then nodded. "Yeah. Looking at you now, I was remembering how intimidated I was to play this part 'cause of when I had to take off my shirt in the basement scenes."

Leo felt color rise to his cheeks as always seemed to happen if someone complimented him. He just didn't know what to say. "Well, uh, you're ripped as hell. You'll look great."

"You think? When I read that you were a gymnast, I worked out like a madman so I wouldn't be embarrassed."

"Trust me, you won't be." He wanted to end the uncomfortable conversation. "We better get some sleep. Another long day tomorrow."

"You're right." Offering one of those angelic smiles like the one in his headshots, Asher pulled back the bedcovers and slipped beneath, pulling them up over his stomach, leaving his chest exposed.

Odd, Leo thought as he made his way around to the other side of the bed and did the same. *I sleep the same way, with my chest outside the covers to keep cool.*

He and Asher seemed alike in more ways than just personality. He reached up to switch off the night table lamp, plunging the room into darkness.

He looked across the wide bed and could make out Asher's shape. "Good night, Asher. And don't worry. I won't let anything happen to you."

"Thanks, Leo. I know you mean it."

Then both boys fell silent, and before long, Leo drifted into a fitful sleep.

Cassie could think of nothing else on the drive home except the attack on them in the fog. Or had it really been an attack? Donovan insisted he'd felt no one near him when he'd hit his head. Could he have simply bumped into something in all that fog? But what about the voices she'd clearly heard? She supposed they might not have been talking about her and Donovan, but what if they had been? Was she just being paranoid?

As they neared Donovan's house where she'd drop him off, he asked, "So, you gonna tell your dad what happened?"

She glanced over at his shadowed face. "I don't know. I mean, it's possible you ran into that pole I felt, and those voices I heard could've been talking about something else."

"What about the guy we saw in the skull mask?"

"Yeah, there is that." She paused a moment to collect her thoughts. "I'm not sure if any of it adds up to a threat, but I'll talk to my dad about it."

"Good. I'll sleep better that way."

They shared a long, lingering kiss that washed away all her worries. But then he was gone, into his silent house and she was alone. The worries returned.

Dad will know what to do.

Thankfully, her dad was up waiting for her, which made her feel both protected and like she was still a child, rather than an eighteen-year-old young woman.

"How was your day, Cass?"

He was sitting on the living room couch nursing a beer and watching TV. He clicked off the television and awaited her answer.

"Long," she replied, plopping down beside him, suddenly realizing how exhausted she was. These long shooting days were tough, but she wouldn't trade them for anything in the world. He didn't reply because she knew he'd pulled extensive overtime as a cop and understood working long hours.

"How's Donovan?" he asked.

She smiled, as she always did upon hearing his name. "Awesome, like always."

He smiled. "Good. I love that kid."

"He loves you, too, Dad, you know that."

He nodded.

"Uh, Dad…"

He lost his smile. "Something wrong?"

She decided to go for it, filling him in on the masked figure showing up over the past few days and the incident in the fog that night. As always, he listened intently and didn't interrupt.

"It may all be nothing," she concluded. "Maybe one of the crew, like Baxter, pranking me with that mask."

"Do you believe that?"

She only considered a moment. "No." Baxter, like all of them, was still spooked by what had happened during their student film last spring.

"What you've told me is concerning, but not necessarily evidence of a direct threat. It's likely Donovan bumped into something, like he said." He paused a moment, rubbing his beard stubble in thought. "I can contact the La Costa PD, if you'd like, to look into these incidents."

"I know Chet, the police chief's son," she answered. "So that's easy enough to do. I'll talk to him tomorrow. And Donovan wants to go back in daylight to where we were tonight, just to see if he might have hit his head on that pole I felt."

"Those are both sound, mature ideas," he said, though his tone screamed worry. "I'll check in with you tomorrow to make sure everything's good. If you need me, I'm a text away."

"I know, Dad." She threw an arm over his burly shoulders and leaned in close, relishing the feeling of security his presence had always given her. They sat together for a time, just enjoying each other's company, before going to bed.

As Leo opened his eyes, he was surprised to find Asher had rolled closer during the night. Rather than freak out, he glanced at Asher's face and noted the peaceful expression. He turned to the clock on his night table and saw that it was already seven o'clock. They needed to be on set by eight thirty.

Not wanting to startle Asher, Leo sat up and lowered his feet to the floor, realizing that he needed to duck into the bathroom. As he stepped away from the bed, he happened to glance at his bedroom door. It stood ajar. He'd closed it firmly the night before, and Sylvia, the housekeeper, would never enter his room uninvited.

Oh no, he thought, a lump of fear forming in his stomach. *Mom!*

He needed to take care of his bathroom issue first and then he had to warn Asher what to expect when they got downstairs. He'd try talking to his mom first, but he already knew what she'd say.

Crap!

While Asher, dressed in his wardrobe for the day—white tank top undershirt, black hoodie, sweatpants, and sneakers—eagerly dug into the scrambled eggs, bacon, and sausage that Sylvia had so lovingly prepared, Leo ate what he could and then went in search of his mother, hoping she hadn't left for the haunted house yet.

He found her in her office, answering emails on the computer. The room was large, dominated by a huge wooden desk atop which sat her twenty-seven-inch monitor and lots of papers. The walls were covered with posters of movies she'd produced, mostly rom-coms that bored Leo to tears.

"Mom, can I talk to you before you leave?"

She turned from the computer and removed her fingers from the keyboard. No smile, but then she seldom did when she saw him. "Ah, Leonardo, I'm glad you're here. There's something I want to talk to you about."

Here it comes, he thought, leaden butterflies slamming into his stomach with wild abandon.

"Let me preface by saying, I think you and Asher are a beautiful couple and I'm actually happy that you've found one another."

Leo opened his mouth to protest, but she held up a hand like she was stopping cars at a school crossing.

"I'm not finished. Asher is the lead actor in my film, and I need him fresh and energetic every working day."

Leo's passive aggressive nature was about to turn explosive. "Mom." He gritted his teeth to keep from shouting. "Asher and I didn't do anything last night except fall asleep. We were talking and he got tired, so I just let him stay on the other side of the bed."

Her poker face didn't react. "That's not how it looked to me when I peeked in this morning."

"Which you had no right to do! And for your information, I would never have sex with somebody I just met. I do have self-control, you know."

Her brown eyes fixed on him, and she said nothing for a long moment, so he plunged on. "And I don't know why you want me to be gay, anyway, unless it's some trendy thing in Hollywood these days."

She offered a slight smile of amusement at his exasperation. "Well, if you're gay that means I won't have to suffer the indignity of little humans calling me 'grandma'."

It took Leo a moment to understand her meaning. Then he almost laughed. Yes, she was vain to the max. "Grandma" would make her feel old at any age, he supposed.

"For your information, gay guys can get girls pregnant, and I could always adopt *little humans*."

She shrugged. "Possibly. But that's a more complicated process."

He needed to end this conversation and get back to Asher before he said something he might regret. "Asher and I are not having sex. And since you're so nosy, I'm not having sex with anyone."

He turned and stormed from the room, slamming the door behind him.

Once he and Asher were inside his car, Leo told him about the conversation he'd had with his mother. At the notion that they'd been having sex, Asher almost gagged.

"The hell?"

Leo was happy he couldn't see the look of disbelief on Asher's face. "That's my mom, jumping to conclusions."

Asher nodded but said nothing.

Approaching the entrance to the school parking lot, Leo felt a hand lightly rest on his shoulder. He glanced over. Asher looked concerned.

"She's not important right now, Leo. We got bigger problems to solve. Like Robert's murder. And mine."

His words felt like a bucket of ice water thrown into Leo's face. Of course, this business with his mother was meaningless compared to the impending murders.

"You're right. And I'll keep my promise to protect you."

Asher smiled wanly. "I appreciate the help, but we're in this together."

Leo nodded and steered his Prius into the lot.

CHAPTER EIGHT

WHAT DID YOU SEE?

Cassie and Donovan arrived at the location thirty minutes early so they could snoop around the beach area where they may or may not have been attacked. The sun was already bright and warm, despite the early hour, and the dense fog of the night before was nothing but a bad memory.

The white sands of the beach stretched invitingly from the path on which they walked, ending at the calm ocean water, slipping up and down the sand with smooth abandon. They stood at the corner, where the side-walk met the path, looking around. Other than the film crew behind them, the only activity on the beach was a lady running with her dog.

Cassie glanced at Donovan and pointed to her right. "We turned this way. I know that much. Let's walk a little ways."

"Okay, but I think I already see what happened to me." He outpaced her and stopped before the thick post of a tall streetlight. "I don't know about you, but I sure didn't see this last night."

She examined the post. It could have caused the lump on Donovan's forehead, which he covered up this morning by tilting his royal blue fedora down over that side at a rakish angle. She rather liked the look. Made him sexier than usual.

"I didn't see anything last night, but I did grab onto to something, so this could be the culprit all right."

She glanced around and spotted a bench a short way beyond the light post. Could the voices she'd heard have come from two people sitting on that bench? It was possible, though sketchy to find two people sitting on a bench in fog so thick they couldn't see a foot in front of them.

"The voices I heard could've come from that bench," she grudgingly acknowledged.

Donovan nodded. "Kinda creepy, people sitting in thick fog like that."

"I agree. But as of now, there's no evidence you were attacked, or we were stalked."

He faced her and shrugged. "Overactive imaginations, I guess. That's what we get for watching all those horror movies."

She offered a tiny smile. "Probably."

Something in the pit of her stomach told her it wasn't so simple, but without any proof, what could she do? There was no connection between the guy in the mask and Donovan's injury, so she was forced to let it go for now and focus on the day ahead.

"Let's check in and get ready to work."

He smiled. "Lead on, Madame Assistant Director."

She punched him on the arm and then took his hand for the walk back.

Leo had texted his friends before leaving home and asked them to meet in front of the haunted house. As he and Asher strolled past crew personnel pulling equipment from large trucks, he spotted them on the sidewalk. J.C. stood out in a bright fancy shirt and long pants, while the others wore shorts and tee shirts.

Leo glanced at Asher beside him and then hurried forward to join his friends.

"Where's the fire?" J.C. asked, his snark in full force.

Leo furrowed his brows in confusion. "Huh?"

Laura said, "He means, what's the big emergency?"

Leo glanced around. The number of crew members entering and leaving the house was increasing. "Let's walk toward the beach. Fewer people there."

Without awaiting a reply, he started down the sidewalk toward the beach, Asher still at his side. He heard the others following, but something ahead caught his eye. Cassie and Donovan were headed their way, probably after a morning walk on the beach, he guessed. Both smiled upon seeing him and the others.

"Morning all," Cassie said with a grin. "Ready for another day of movie magic?"

"Uh, sure," Leo said.

"Just tell me where to stand," Asher added with a grin, and Leo was impressed by how calm he sounded.

Cassie laughed.

Donovan eyed Leo with envy. "It must be so cool to live this close to a beach. I love it here."

"You wouldn't love Costa High," J.C. put in, scowling.

Donovan shrugged. "School is school. It's the friends that make it good or bad, and I think hanging with you all would be dope."

Chet looked especially surprised. "Thanks, man."

Cassie eyed Laura curiously. "So, how are you and Kristen getting along?"

"We're pretty different," Laura answered, "but so far it's all good."

Leo studied Donovan. Something was different, but it was hard to figure out what. Then he had it. The fedora was tilted at an odd angle and almost covered one eye. Looking more carefully, Leo saw it. A lump on the other boy's forehead.

"What happened, Donovan?" Leo pointed to his own forehead.

Donovan looked embarrassed. "Me and the lamppost back there"—he pointed back toward the beach—"had a run-in last night in the fog. I'm okay. Just clumsy."

"You're not clumsy," Cassie put in. "That fog was thick as soup. Anyway, we've gotta get inside. Asher, you're due in makeup in ten."

Asher saluted. "Yes, ma'am."

Cassie laughed and started toward the house. Donovan faced Leo and the others. "See you later." He began to follow but must have felt Leo's intense gaze because he turned back.

Leo had been thinking about the fog incident and didn't expect Donovan to turn, but their eyes met, and he saw it. Blood. The knife. That Chucky tattoo on the wrist. Donovan with his throat slit from ear to ear. He gasped and lurched back a step.

Donovan frowned. "You okay, Leo?"

Leo nodded. "Uh, yeah. Um, see you later."

Donovan looked mystified as he turned to follow Cassie.

Asher was at Leo's side. "What did you see?"

Now J.C. was there, sounding confused and angry. "What, you told him what you can do?"

Leo didn't answer, so Asher turned to J.C. "He told me last night."

"Why?" J.C. sounded like a mountain lion about to strike.

"Chill, J.C.," Laura said, stepping closer to Leo and taking his hand. She rubbed it gently. "Your hand is like ice, Leo. Can you tell us what you saw?"

"Donovan's gonna die, too, isn't he?" That was Chet.

Leo nodded. "And Asher. Next Wednesday."

Laura looked stunned. "All next Wednesday?"

"By the same killer?" J.C. had lost the anger by now.

"Yeah."

When Leo couldn't think what else to say, Asher came to his rescue. "Leo looked in my eyes last night and saw...well, you know."

J.C. squinted dangerously. "Why was he looking in your eyes?"

Laura looked like she wanted to slap him. "Like that's important?"

"Somebody's still jealous," Chet muttered under his breath, and J.C. cast him a murderous look.

Leo said, "Look, stop arguing. We've gotta stop these murders from happening. Asher and I couldn't think of a connection between him and Robert—well, now Donovan too—except they went to the same school."

Laura's face lit up and she faced Asher. "And that horror movie you all made."

"We thought of that, too, but I can't figure out anyone who might be after us from that."

"Wait a minute." Chet gazed at them all as though he'd just had a revelation. "I just had a crazy thought. What if all the kids on this movie who went to that high school are targets?"

"Oh hell," mumbled J.C.

"You might be right, Chet," Laura said, studying Asher as though for clues. "How many others are there?"

Stunned by Chet's suggestion, Asher took a moment to think. "Uh, well, Cassie, of course. Then there's, um, William and Baxter working with camera and sound. Diego. Kristen. And Jaden. He's a PA."

Laura turned to Leo. "You have to, Leo. We need to know."

Leo nodded. "I'll do it."

"Did you notice that Leo seemed kind of spooked?" Donovan asked Cassie as they organized their notes and tasks for the day.

Cassie's mind was already upstairs where they would be filming. "Huh? Oh, Leo? He's always a little out there."

"He's not 'out there', Cass. He's a nice guy. Just super shy." He sounded miffed.

She looked up from her task list. "I'm sorry. My mind was on the shoot. He is a nice guy. I still wanna know how he knew about Robert."

Before Donovan could reply, Leo entered the drawing room and hesitantly approached.

"Speak of the devil," Cassie murmured, but she smiled politely as Leo stopped before her, looking indecisive as always. "Hi, Leo, long time, no see."

Leo offered a smile but kept his gaze averted, as usual. "Do you have a minute, Cassie?"

Surprised, Cassie glanced at Donovan before replying. "Uh, sure. What's up?"

Still averting his gaze, Leo said, "Well, um, I'm trying to get over my shyness and, um, I just wanted to talk to you for a minute where we, you know, make eye contact, so I can practice."

"Sure, I mean, it sounds like a good idea," she replied. "But why me?"

Leo looked embarrassed. "Well, um, I don't want to sound mean, but you're kind of intense, so I figured if I could do this with you, it should be easier with other people."

Cassie flinched at the word "intense," glancing at Donovan, who merely shrugged. She wasn't sure how to respond, so she just said, "Sure."

Leo seemed to draw in a breath and expel it, and Cassie wondered, *Am I that scary?*

Leo looked up and suddenly their eyes met. He winced, as though with pain, but then said, "What do you like most about making movies?"

Taken aback by his facial expression, which looked distressed, she fumbled a moment with her answer but maintained eye contact. "Oh, well, I, uh, I love the process of story to script to film. I really like the shooting process and piecing everything together."

He nodded, but maintained eye contact, clearly forcing himself. "Cool. Well, thanks, Cassie." He averted his gaze and fell silent.

Cassie felt like a weird moment had just ended but forced herself to smile. "That was good, Leo. Did it help?"

He nodded, but looked like he might faint. "It's just…hard. Thanks, Cassie. Later, Donovan." He fled the room as though pursued by a monster.

Cassie noted Donovan staring at her. "What? Am I really that intense?"

He offered his gorgeous smile. "When you're working, yeah."

She cringed but quickly recovered. "I'm just really focused on what I'm doing."

"I know that, but he wouldn't. You almost bit his head off yesterday about the Robert incident."

"I did not." Her instant denial was a reflex. Reflecting on that moment, she *had* come on stronger than was necessary. "You're right. I'll try to be less 'intense' when I'm talking to people."

"That sounds like a plan." He glanced around, and they were momentarily alone, so he leaned in for a quick kiss. Cassie wished it could've lasted longer, but she enjoyed it, nonetheless.

Leo found J.C., Laura, and Chet waiting in the bustling foyer, and the four quickly ducked into the alcove under the stairs.

J.C. blurted, "Well?"

Laura shushed him and leaned in close.

Leo whispered, "Cassie too."

"I was right." Chet didn't sound smug, more resigned to the inevitability.

"Who're you going to try next?" Laura asked.

Leo shrugged. "I think they're filming me and J.C.'s characters exploring the upstairs rooms, so Diego should be free." He eyed J.C. "Know where he is?"

J.C. looked defensive. "How should I know?"

"Chill, J.C.," Laura whispered. "You brought him with you, right?"

"Yeah, but he's not on call right now so he could be anywhere."

Leo gazed at his best friend's stiff posture. J.C. looked like he'd been caught with his hand in the cookie jar. He knew J.C. loved having Diego around, especially because they both enjoyed working on dance routines together. But could there be something more between them that J.C. didn't want to talk about?

Laura must've felt the tension because she said, "Let's keep ourselves on track, you guys. If the crew is upstairs, you can hit up William, Baxter, and Jaden."

Leo nodded, dreading the bloody deaths he expected to see in their eyes. Cassie's death had been like Donovan, throat slit open. In fact, he was sure she and Donovan were propped up beside each other in some horrifically twisted romantic tableau.

"What about Kristen?" Chet asked.

"She's hot but intense," J.C. commented, eyeing Leo. "How's she been at your house, Laura?"

Laura shrugged in that nonchalant way she excelled at. "She's kind of driven, I guess, really focused on making it big. I guess that's why she seems forceful. Does she make you nervous, Leo?"

"I make you nervous, Leo?"

Leo spun around to find himself face-to-face with Kristen, who wore a sly, mocking smile. He took in her perfect features for a moment before looking away. "Uh, hi, Kristen."

J.C. and Chet just stared at her in silence, as though unable to look away.

"Hey, Kristen," Laura said, breaking the awkward silence. "When's your call time?"

"Noon," she replied with a smile. "I get the morning off." She studied Leo again, causing him to squirm. He felt her penetrating gaze but couldn't bring himself to make eye contact. Fortunately, Laura was on the ball.

"Do you have a minute to help us out?" she asked Kristen.

"Sure. What do you need?"

"Well," Laura went on, nudging Leo with one hand, "Leo's trying to overcome his social anxiety and look people in the eye when talking to them. Can he try with you?"

Kristen grinned. "Course. With a face as handsome as his, who wouldn't want to look?"

Leo felt himself turn red, but he said, "Thanks."

"Whenever you're ready, Leo," Kristen went on, adding, "I'll try not to be too forceful."

Oh crap, Leo thought, *she heard us talking about her.*

Taking a deep breath and letting it out, he raised his eyes and locked them onto her vibrant blue ones. Instantly, he saw blood, stab wounds, Kristen hanging lifeless from a tree. It reminded him of a movie he once saw.

"So, uh, what kind of movies do you want to do most?"

Keeping her eyes fixed on his, she answered, "All kinds, really. Horror movies are my fave, but I think actors should stretch themselves by taking on every kind of part, no matter how small. But of course, I hope to be leading lady material."

Leo couldn't believe he maintained eye contact all through her response. "You're sure pretty enough for those parts," he said, cursing himself for sounding so stupid. Then he had to break eye contact because the bloody images were making him queasy.

Kristen clapped slowly and said, "That was very good, Leo. I think you held my gaze for thirty seconds." There was always an undertone of derision in Kristen's voice, so Leo wasn't sure if he was being mocked or not.

J.C. must've thought he was because he looked riled up. "Don't make fun like that. It's hard for him."

Kristen's face and tone softened. "I didn't mean to sound insincere. You should keep practicing, Leo. You have beautiful eyes and people should see them. Later, Laura." She sauntered off toward the back of the house.

"She's uppity," J.C. muttered under his breath, clearly not wanting a confrontation should Kristen overhear him.

"She is kind of brittle," Laura agreed, "but once she lets her guard down, she's not half bad. Too much into her looks for my taste, but whatever." She faced Leo. "Well?"

Still processing what he'd seen, Leo nodded. "Stabbed and hung from a tree."

"Whoa," Chet mumbled, "that's brutal."

"Hey, how's it going?"

Startled, Leo turned to find Diego right behind him, dressed in his costume and grinning. J.C. stepped forward, maybe to ask Diego about Leo talking with him, but it was too late. Leo locked eyes on those of the handsome actor and froze as visions of Diego stabbed and thrown off a balcony assailed his mind. He looked away.

"Hey, Diego," Laura said to distract him. "You ready to shoot?"

"Uh, yeah. You okay, Leo?"

Leo glanced up and offered a forced smile. "Yeah, just, you know, hard to make eye contact."

"That was me in elementary school," Diego said, placing a supportive hand on Leo's shoulder. "Acting really helped me get over it. Let me know if I can help."

Leo felt a rush of good will for Diego—really for all these young people whom he'd gotten to know this week. He had to stop what was going to happen.

"Thanks, Diego."

Diego noted J.C.'s pained expression. "You all right, J.C.?"

J.C. forced himself to relax. "Yeah. Just thinking about our dance routine."

"We'll work on it more tonight. I've gotta find Diana for some makeup. See you later."

He gazed a long moment at J.C. and then vanished toward the back of the house.

The second he was gone, J.C. grabbed Leo by the arm. "What happens to him?"

"Stabbed and thrown off a balcony."

J.C.'s mouth dropped open, but he didn't say anything.

"He *did* go to that school, J.C.," Chet commented.

"Yeah," J.C. replied.

"Let's go find the crew guys," Laura said, calm and casual.

Leo marveled at her ability to take everything in stride. "Okay."

CHAPTER NINE

I CAN'T TELL YOU HERE

LEO LED THE WAY UP the creaky wooden stairs to the second floor, leaning against the banister to avoid crew personnel carrying lights up or down. Mr. K stood chatting with his assembled crew members. William and Baxter were examining the camera and sound equipment respectively and no one was paying them any attention. It was now or never. Leo left the others to wander around, as though checking out all the equipment, and pressed forward to stop in front of the two young men.

William looked up first, brushing his thick bangs off his face to gaze quizzically at Leo. "Hi, Leo, what's up?"

Baxter, munching on chips, was bent over the sound recorder. He stood at the sound of William's voice and noted Leo standing in front of them. "'Sup."

Leo said, "Hi, guys. I'm just wandering, talking with everyone. How's it going?"

William and Baxter exchanged a glance, like they didn't understand why Leo was talking with them. Baxter reached into the fanny pack wrapped around his pudgy waist and grabbed more chips, shoving them into his mouth.

"We're good," he mumbled around the mouthful.

Leo tried for a casual smile and decided to focus on William while his eyes were visible. "Donovan tells me you wanna be a DP in the business. I'm curious to know what you like about that job."

William grinned. "I get to be behind the camera."

Leo returned the grin. "I get that part." He made eye contact. William had soft, soulful green eyes that revealed his bloody death in no uncertain terms.

"I like being an important part of how the movie looks," William went on excitedly. "There's nothing better."

"Except sound," Baxter jumped in, and Leo pulled his gaze from William and locked onto Baxter, hoping his face wasn't giving away how horrified he felt. Since neither guy noticed, Leo began to think maybe he could be an actor after all.

"Sound is the trickiest part to get right, Leo," Baxter went on, his boyish voice filled with joy. "What good is a movie if you can't make out the dialogue, right?"

Leo nodded, having seen enough blood and stab wounds to Baxter's plump body for a lifetime. He smiled and broke eye contact, flicking his gaze between the two crew members. "I can see why Mr. Ketchum hired you both. You really love your work."

William's face clouded over. "Do you think your mom likes us? We're hoping she might hire us for other movies and, you know, help us get into the unions."

Leo smiled. They were genuinely good guys. "I'll put in a good word for you."

Baxter's eyes magnified behind his wire-rimmed glasses to the size of golf balls. "That'd be awesome, Leo."

The shyer of the two, William let his hair fall back in front of his face but offered a little smile. "Yeah. Thanks, man."

Leo nodded. "No prob. See you around." He turned to retrace his route along the second floor to where the others awaited him, but then turned back. "Any idea where Jaden is? I hear he might be even more shy than me."

Baxter nodded vigorously. "Oh yeah. Shy's his middle name. Creepy sometimes too. He's a PA, so he could be anywhere."

"Thanks." Leo hurried back to J.C. and the others and reported what he'd seen in the eyes of the two young men.

"So I was right," Chet said, looking thoughtful. "Someone is after all the kids from that school."

"There's still one more," J.C. said. "The one with the cool cornrows."

"Did they know where to find him?" Laura asked Leo.

He shook his head. "We'll have to wander around till we see him."

"Can we go downstairs now?" J.C. asked, glancing about nervously. "This floor gives me the creeps."

"He might be in one of these rooms setting stuff up," Leo replied, "so we gotta check first."

J.C. looked pasty in the face. "I was afraid you'd say that."

"C'mon, J.C., it won't take long," Laura said and took J.C. by the arm, leading him down the hall to the first open door.

Leo found Chet staring at the lone door leading up to the third-floor attic room and placed a hand on his shoulder. "You don't have to go up there, Chet."

Chet faced him, looking grim but determined. "Yeah, I do."

"Let's check it out, then." Leo led the way to the door at the end of the hall and pulled it open. He waited for Chet to ascend the stairs inside. The taller boy stood stiffly, looking up those stairs a long moment before taking them two at a time. Leo followed.

The attic room, with light filtering in though the ragged, threadbare curtains, looked much more harmless during the day than it had that night. Chet stared at the lone wooden chair in the center of the room, his face impassive. Leo figured Chet was recalling the time he was tied to that chair by his older brother and left all night in the old, creepy house. Chet had been eight.

"You okay?"

Chet nodded. "Yeah. Doesn't look so bad now, does it?"

"I was thinking the same thing."

Chet stood rigid for a moment longer. "Well, no Jaden, so let's blow this place."

Leo led the way down the stairs and Chet closed the door behind them.

They met up with J.C. and Laura in the upstairs hallway and descended the stairs to the first floor in search of the elusive Jaden.

"He's a PA, so maybe Stuart knows where he is," J.C. said, pointing out the tall young man who'd always been so helpful.

Without hesitating, Leo crossed the bustling foyer to where Stuart chatted with Diana, the super nice makeup artist. Both smiled at him as he approached, but it was Diana who spoke first.

"Well, here's the most handsome boy in the place. No offense, Stuart."

Stuart laughed. "No worries."

"You must pose for me, Leo," Diana said, looking excited at the prospect. "You need to see how handsome you really are. I won't take no for an answer."

Leo felt his cheeks redden. "Well, um…"

Laura gave him a slight shove. "Go for it, Leo."

Leo felt trapped; he gave in to move things along faster. "Sure, Diana. We can do that."

She beamed, the crow's feet around her green eyes stretching joyfully. "Trust me, you'll be happy you did. I'm an excellent photographer, if I do say so myself."

Stuart laughed. "You need anything, Leo?" he asked, his voice upbeat and his smile infectious. "We PA's aim to please."

"Uh, actually, I was looking for Jaden. Have you seen him?"

Stuart shrugged. "He might be outside helping to bring in equipment."

Diana eyed him, but Leo kept his gaze lowered, examining their exposed wrists. Both wore short-sleeve shirts, and neither had a tattoo of Chucky on the wrist.

"That one's even shyer than you, Leo," Diana commented. "I think it's cute."

Leo offered a tight smile. "It's hard too. See you both later."

He waved the others toward the front door.

"He might be outside," Leo whispered. "And don't act so suspicious." Leo glanced across at Stuart and Diana, who were watching him, and smiled. Then he was out into the bright sunshine, the others around him.

"I checked their wrists, by the way," Leo said, eyeing his surroundings for any sign of Jaden. "No tats."

"I wouldn't even have suspected them," Chet commented.

"We trust no one," Laura intoned with a solemnity that chilled Leo's heart.

A figure came around one of the big equipment trucks heading for the house.

Jaden.

"There he is." Leo strode quickly forward, hoping to intercept Jaden before one of the other crew members might request his help. "Hey, Jaden, wait up." He glanced back to see J.C. following but waved him back. He didn't want to spook Jaden by having all of them approach at once.

The teen glanced over at Leo and, to Leo's surprise, smiled as he drew nearer.

"Hi, Leo." In a gesture Leo knew all too well, Jaden quickly glanced down at the ground, allowing Leo to note the perfect cornrows weaving their way around his head with not a hair out of place.

"Hey, Jaden," Leo began, suddenly unsure how to begin. "How's it going?"

Jaden glanced up but avoided direct eye contact. The little smile was still there, however. "I'm good. How's it with you?"

"Well, I, uh, I was wondering."

"Yeah?"

"I know you and me are a lot alike, being super shy and all."

"Yeah. Kinda sucks, don't it?"

Leo studied him, but Jaden still refused to make eye contact.

"Yeah, it does. That's why I wanna practice making eye contact with people when I talk to them and, well, I thought you might be a good guy to practice with since you, you know, understand how hard it is."

Jaden looked up at Leo's nose, his face bright and expectant. "That's a great idea. We could really help each other."

Leo nodded. "On three, we make eye contact, okay? Then we see how long we can talk before we gotta look away."

Jaden bit his lower lip, shuffling nervously. He glanced around at other crew members heading for the house, then nodded.

Stealing himself for more blood and death, Leo raised his head and locked eyes with the other boy. He froze, shocked by what he saw. No blood. No death. Just Jaden as an old man lying in what looked like a hospital bed. His eyes were closed, his breathing raspy. He was near death. A second elderly man, also African American, sat beside the bed, tears rolling down his cheeks as he held one of Jaden's hands.

"So, uh, what do we talk about?"

Jaden's voice cut off the vision, and Leo, feeling more relaxed than he had all morning, shrugged. "Dunno. Do you like working on movies?"

Jaden considered his answer a moment. "Yeah. I like the work and I think being around so many people might help with my anxiety."

"Cool."

"So, I seen you the other day in that tank top and you're, like, really ripped." He eyed Leo's forearms and pointed. "And you got veins on top of veins. What's your secret?"

Leo smiled, not feeling so embarrassed as he normally did. "Gymnastics and aikido. Been doing both since I was little. Got me a cool gym at home. You like to work out?"

Jaden nodded. "Got some weights at my house. Plus, pushups, pullups, stuff like that. Helps me stay calm."

"I know, right? My mom, well, she drives me crazy sometimes, so the workouts really help."

Jaden pulled a sour face. "I bet your mom's got nothing on my dad. I can't wait to move out. I'm saving up everything I'm making on this movie to do that. Me and Diego been talking about maybe getting a place together. His dad's worse than mine."

Not for the first time, Leo felt a twinge of guilt for being so wealthy that he'd probably never have to worry about such things, unless his mother cut him off or something.

"I hope it works out for you guys. I never knew my dad, but my mom is trippy enough."

During all their conversation, neither boy broke eye contact, and Leo felt as relaxed around Jaden as he did around his friends, including Asher. As with Asher, he felt like he'd always known Jaden, and he hoped to spend more time with him.

"You should come over and check out my gym sometime."

Jaden grinned. "I never did any gymnastics, but maybe you could teach me some moves."

"Sounds like a plan," Leo said, sticking out his hand.

Jaden shook and they finally broke eye contact. Jaden glanced down, the grin still plastered across his face. "That's the longest I ever talked to anyone eye to eye."

Leo smiled. "It's up there for me too. We need to chill more often. Good for both of us."

Jaden looked up and their eyes met again. "That's a deal."

"Hey, Jaden, we need your help!"

Jaden turned to see two crewmen standing by one of the equipment trucks. "Okay, be right there." He faced Leo. "I gotta jet. Later, Leo. And… thanks."

Leo offered up his best smile and Jaden trotted over to help the men unload some equipment. Leo returned to J.C., Laura, and Chet, who'd stood in the front yard of the old house watching the exchange.

"Well?" Chet looked anxious.

Leo shook his head. "He dies of old age, I think."

The others reacted with surprise.

"You sure?" Laura asked.

"Looked like it. He was super old, lying in bed real calm, but not awake. Another old guy was holding his hand, I think just waiting for him to go."

"Another guy?" J.C. looked surprised. "You mean he's gay?"

Leo studied his best friend. He'd been so wrapped up in the ease of conversing with Jaden that he hadn't considered what his vision meant. "He might be, I guess."

"So, what next?" Chet asked, pulling his gaze from J.C. and fixing it onto Leo.

Leo stared up at the haunted house, considering options.

"Do we tell them?" J.C. sounded anxious, and Leo figured he was mostly worried about Diego.

Leo turned to face his friends, knowing he had no choice. "Yes. I'll have them come to my house tonight. We wrap at eight thirty, so we can all meet up at nine. My mom will be locked in her office for the night."

Laura furrowed her brows. "You're going to tell them everything? About you, I mean?"

Leo shrugged. "Got no choice. Their lives are more important, right?"

Especially Asher, but he didn't say that.

"How will you convince them to show up?" Chet eyed him with concern.

"Cassie will come, and she'll get the others to go along."

Cassie couldn't get Leo's odd behavior out of her mind, even while making sure everyone was where they were needed *when* they were needed.

Donovan noticed her distracted state, but since she didn't make any errors, he clearly decided not to mention it.

The filming upstairs was routine stuff and posed no challenges to cast or crew. Asher and Diego performed their parts flawlessly with almost no need for retakes. Mr. K tried a few different camera angles to capture the action of the boys creeping around, checking out the rooms for any possible threat. These scenes were shot day-for-night since the old house was shadowy anyway, and as far as Cassie was concerned viewing the monitor, they looked great.

They managed to bring enough equipment up to the attic room to capture a heart-to-heart between Asher and Diego's character. That room had threadbare drapes, so black paper was placed beneath the curtains to block out the sun. Once more, Cassie marveled at the acting by both of her friends. Sure, the two of them had known each other all through high school, but they had never been buddies. Yet in the film, they portrayed best friends, and watching them go through their paces, she truly believed they loved each other as only best friends can.

The lunch break came at one o'clock and Cassie was ready for some time off. She wanted to talk with Donovan about the way Leo reacted when he looked at them both that morning. Oddly enough, she hadn't seen Leo or his friends since their initial encounter. None of them had come upstairs to watch the filming, which was probably best given the tight confines of their shooting areas. The upstairs hall was narrow and the attic room tiny.

Once again, lunch was offered beneath large tents down by the beach. The hot food was less inviting—given the high eighties temperature outside—than the salads and desserts, so Cassie made herself a green salad with sides of potato and pasta salad, while Donovan loaded his plate with baked chicken and fries. It amazed her how much he could eat and stay slim, but then she'd noticed that most guys seemed capable of pulling that off more than she ever could.

They found an empty table and sat down. Fatigue suddenly overcame her, and she realized that she'd been on her feet since eight that morning.

"Feels good to sit," Donovan said as he took a swig from his water bottle.

She smiled. "Exactly what I was thinking."

He grinned and dug into his chicken with gusto.

Cassie worked on her salad, realizing that she was famished. She got so focused on her job that even snacking never entered her mind. "I can't stop thinking about that deer-in-the-headlights look Leo had when he bumped into you this morning."

Donovan set down his stripped chicken leg and wiped his fingers on a paper napkin. "Give him a break, Cass. The guy has social anxiety. I startled him."

"Maybe. But he looked the same when I made eye contact with him."

"That's because you're scary. He said so." He grinned and popped a fry into his mouth.

Cassie still smarted at the idea that she was scary. "He didn't say scary. He said intense."

Donovan shrugged and snagged another fry off his plate. "You *are* intense when you're working, but that's not a bad thing."

She frowned. "I still think there's more to it than that."

"Ask him yourself. Here he comes." He indicated the area behind her.

Cassie turned to find Leo, J.C., Laura, and Chet sauntering up to their table. They carried no food, so she figured they wouldn't sit down.

Striving to be less "intense," she smiled and offered her most inviting expression. "Hey. We missed you during the filming this morning."

"Yeah," chimed in Donovan. "You should've seen Asher and Diego. They knocked it out of the park, especially when Diego apologized to Asher for pulling a gun on him."

J.C. lowered his head, clearly embarrassed, and Leo tried to cover for him. "Yeah, they're great. Can't wait to see the footage." He suddenly looked tongue-tied.

Cassie eyed Donovan a moment and then said, "You wanna join us? We can pull up another table."

Laura offered a smile. "No thanks. Leo wants to ask you something." When Leo continued to look at the pavement beside his feet, Laura nudged him with her elbow.

"Uh, yeah," Leo said, forcing himself to look at them.

He didn't make clean eye contact as he had that morning, but at least Cassie felt he was focused on their faces.

"I, uh, I wanna…invite you both to my house tonight after we finish. It's an early night and I live close by. I wanna invite the others, too, the ones from your school, like Asher—well, he'll already be with me. But, you know, Diego, Robert, Kristen, Jaden, William, and…" He trailed off a moment, as though recalling. "Oh yeah, the guy with the chips."

"Baxter," Donovan said.

"Yeah, Baxter."

Cassie exchanged a look with Donovan. He seemed as puzzled as her. "Tomorrow is another long day, Leo," she began, trying to understand the urgent tone in his voice. "We'd probably all like to get some sleep tonight."

Leo lost the hesitant look. A grave expression overtook his features, and it chilled her. "It's important, Cassie. More important than this movie."

She felt another shiver run through her. Images of the guy in the mask, of Robert's accident, of the incident in the fog filled her mind, and she almost trembled. "This has something to do with what happened to Robert, doesn't it?"

Leo didn't look surprised, as though he'd known she would guess. "Yes. I'm going to tell you the truth about how I knew what was going to happen to him. And what's going to happen to all of you."

Cassie started, and Donovan let out a small gasp of surprise.

"What do you mean, what's going to happen to us?" She fixed her most forceful stare on him.

Leo glanced around nervously at other cast and crew members coming and going and leaned in closer. "I can't tell you here. Come to my house after the shoot. Here's the address. Please give it to the others." He unfolded his left hand, and in it sat a scrap of paper.

Cassie took the paper and glanced at it. There was a phone number and address scrawled in black ink.

Donovan leaned forward across the table and whispered, "You can't say anything more? I mean, you're scaring me, man."

Leo shook his head. "Tonight." Without another word, he hurried out of the tent, J.C. and Chet trailing after.

Laura met Cassie's gaze, but her eyes gave away nothing. She offered a nod and followed the others.

Cassie realized she was leaning so far forward as to almost be out of her chair. She sat back slowly and gazed at Donovan. His face was a mask of worry and confusion. "What do you think that's all about?"

Donovan shook his head. But his stiff body posture indicated his level of unease. "It sounded like a scene from a horror movie and I'm…well, I'm kinda scared. Leo doesn't seem like the practical joke type."

"No, he doesn't." She paused a moment to consider what might be so terrible that Leo couldn't share it in front of other people, but came up empty. "How many more hours till we're off?"

Donovan slipped out his phone. "About seven."

She nodded, eyeing the food before her. Suddenly, she didn't have much of an appetite.

CHAPTER TEN

I VOLUNTEER TO GO FIRST

Leo had lost his jitters about telling the others the truth shortly after leaving Cassie and Donovan at lunch. It was now almost nine. He and Asher had returned to his house twenty minutes prior and awaited the arrival of everyone else. Leo felt Asher's eyes on him and glanced across the dining room table.

"You ready?" Asher's calm voice further soothed Leo's nerves.

"Yeah. I mean, it makes me sick to see what I see in your, well, yours and everyone else's eyes, but I'm ready to move forward and stop it all from happening."

Asher bit his lip, obviously triggered by the mention, however oblique, of his impending murder. "I'm no fighter, but I don't let anyone push me around and I'm right with you on this."

Leo nodded.

They'd chosen the dining room to wait because both boys had eaten a snack upon returning to the house and Leo wanted to make sure he was close to the front door. His mother had returned before him and was ensconced in her office, no doubt hammering out future deals beyond this current film. Leo had told the others to knock when they arrived so his mom wouldn't hear any doorbell and come out to check.

As though his mind made it happen, there came a soft tapping at the front door. Leo and Asher exchanged a look. It was time. They rose and Leo led the way out of the dining room into the foyer. Pulling open the heavy wood front door, he stepped back as J.C. marched in, followed by

Diego, Laura, Kristen, Chet, Robert, William, Baxter, Jaden, and finally, Cassie and Donovan. Leo put a finger to his lips.

"My mom is working down the hall," he whispered. "Follow me."

He led the way across the foyer to the wooden staircase ascending to the second floor. He tiptoed up the carpeted stairs and the entourage followed just as quietly. Leo opened the wooden door leading into his room. Everyone slipped inside and he eased the door shut.

Purposely avoiding eye contact with anyone, he waved his arm around the room. "You can sit on the bed or at my desk or just crash on the floor. I'm gonna stand." He pointed behind him at an open door. "Oh, bathroom's there, if anyone needs it."

No one did, and he waited until everyone sat on his king-sized bed, in his chairs, or on the floor. He was grateful that J.C., Laura, and Chet all remained by his side, probably standing in anticipation of having to defend him. Asher chose the beanbag chair close to Leo and offered a nod to assure his support.

Leo scanned the curious faces before him. They were young, beautiful, expectant faces and he was about to announce their impending deaths. He breathed deeply and began. "I know you all have been wondering how I was ready to save Robert from falling through that hole."

They nodded.

Leo knew he should be terrified, especially with Cassie and Kristen boring into him with their penetrating stares, but he was past that. Now was the time for action, and he had to lead.

"I spend most weekends helping out at downtown homeless shelters. Last April, I met a man I'd never seen before who said he'd been watching me."

"Whoa," Robert interjected, "you mean, like stalking you?"

Leo shook his head. "Sizing me up, he said."

"For what?" Cassie gazed at him with furrowed brows.

Leo let out another breath but maintained decent eye contact with the group. "He gave me the power to see when people will die."

Everyone but Asher erupted in surprise, exchanging looks of disbelief and exclaiming variations on "the hell?", "huh?", or "no way."

Leo held up his hand and they settled down. "He said he'd had the gift, or curse—he wasn't sure which it was—for a long time, and when he took my hand and looked in my eyes, he passed it on to me. Then he died."

"He died?" blurted Baxter. "Just like that?"

"Just like that. Anyway, that's how I knew J.C. would be killed. I messed everything up trying to stop it, but we got lucky anyway."

J.C. stepped boldly forward. "Like hell you messed it up. We're here, aren't we?" He glanced at Chet for support.

Chet closed the gap between him and J.C. "Hell yeah. Somehow, even with everything that seemed to go wrong, it ended up happening the way it was supposed to so we could all be saved."

J.C. gazed at Chet in amazement. "Hamilton and I will probably never be, like, you know, close friends," he said, facing the rest of the group again. "Never like me and Leo. But everything he said was true. Leo too. All he has to do is look in someone's eyes and he can see their death."

Leo felt a rush of gratitude that his friends stood up for him so staunchly.

Cassie's face took on a look of understanding. "That explains a lot." Then she frowned. "But why did you make a point to look into all of our eyes today?"

This was the moment of truth. "Because all of you except one will be murdered next Wednesday."

Jaden squinted but remained stoic. Cassie gasped. Baxter made a choking sound, while Kristen stared aghast, her mouth hanging open.

"That's crazy," Robert blurted, looking around at his former schoolmates. "Why would someone wanna kill us?"

Laura joined Leo and said, "That's what we hope to figure out tonight."

"You said everybody except one," Donovan said, his shocked face drained of color. "Who's the one?"

Leo fixed his gaze on Jaden, who did not look away. "Jaden."

Kristen threw her arms up in exasperation. "Of course. It has to be Jaden. Again. You hate us that much?"

Jaden leaped to his feet, fists clenched. "Back off, Kristen! I never killed anyone during that shoot, and you know it. You were more of a suspect than me."

Donovan stood between them. "Calm down, you two." He looked

long and hard at Kristen. "Don't jump to conclusions, Kristen. You're too smart for that."

To Leo's surprise, Kristen backed down, giving him the instant impression that Donovan might be the only one of her schoolmates she respected.

Donovan faced Leo straight on. "You're sure about this, Leo?"

Leo wanted to look away but didn't. He shoved both hands into his pants pockets. "Yeah."

Now Cassie and Robert stood, leaving only the shell-shocked Baxter and William still sitting cross-legged on the carpet.

"Are you saying that accident I had wasn't an accident?" Robert glared at Leo like being targeted for murder was somehow his fault.

"Yes. I saw it when you looked at me the other day."

"So, you decided to check out all of us?" Cassie asked.

"Yeah. See, uh, I accidently looked into Asher's eyes when he tapped me on the shoulder and surprised me. When I saw..." He glanced at Asher, who remained sitting beside him. "Well, him being killed, I got to wondering about the rest of you, since Robert and him went to the same school."

"That's the connection, isn't it?" Cassie suddenly looked more excited than afraid. "The killer is targeting all of us on this shoot who went to Performing Arts High."

"That's what we think," Laura agreed.

"Whoa." Robert looked floored, arms folded across his chest, features scrunched with disbelief. "Who could hate us so much?"

Kristen offered a nervous guffaw. "If anyone has enemies, it's you, Robert, the way you messed with so many girls at school. The number of dads who probably want you dead is higher than I can count."

To his credit, Robert flushed with embarrassment but didn't deny the allegation.

"Uh, can I say something, please?" Leo studied their faces as they turned from each other. "Thank you. I didn't call you over here so you could jump all over each other. I promised Asher I would stop what's going to happen, and I'm making the same promise to you all. I'm pretty sure that's why I have this gift. Or curse. But I need your help."

Cassie looked impressed, as though he'd just risen significantly in her eyes. "So, what do you propose?"

Leo glanced at Laura, who held up a notepad and a pen. Leo faced the attentive group once more. "I only saw a flash of what was going to happen to each of you because I looked away quickly. Now I want to stare into your eyes for as long as I can and describe everything I see. Laura will take notes and even scrawl images that I describe. She's a kickass artist. Then, we compare all the visions and look for clues to the killer's identity."

Donovan gazed out from beneath his fedora. "That's a great idea."

"I agree," Cassie echoed, eyeing the others. "Anyone not wanna go along?"

No one spoke up except Jaden, who questioned Leo. "Since you didn't see nothing in my eyes, how come I'm here?"

Leo forced himself to look resolute. "You won't be murdered, no, but I thought you might be helpful once we have all the clues on paper, so I invited you."

Jaden nodded. "Fair enough." He paused. "But you saw me die, didn't you?"

Leo nodded. "We can talk about that later."

Jaden fell silent.

"Let's get started," Robert announced, looking fierce and resolute, "so we can figure out how to take down this scumbag."

"I agree," Cassie said. "I volunteer to go first."

Donovan raised his eyebrows, but she just squeezed his hand and fixed her gaze on Leo.

Leo was impressed by her boldness. He glanced back at Laura. "You ready?"

She nodded, taking a seat at his desk, facing the group.

Leo felt his palms sweating and wiped them on his short pants. His heartrate had risen at the prospect of describing such horrific murders. But he had to do it. Asher's life—all their lives—depended on him. Forcing his social anxiety deep down into his butterfly-filled stomach, he stepped toward the patiently waiting Cassie. He stared at the bridge of her freckled nose, not having previously noticed just how many freckles she had. Shoving aside his nervousness, he raised his eyes and locked them onto hers.

She was in a house. He began talking in a muted monotone, describing in detail what he saw. It was dark. There was almost no light. She seemed to be in a living room, but the vision was hazy. Large hands grabbed her from behind. The Chucky tattoo came into view: the leering doll's face, goofy overalls, and one hand holding out a dripping knife. A real knife flashed before his eyes and flew up and around to Cassie's throat, digging into her flesh and slicing her neck from ear to ear.

Leo fought to hold onto the vision. What other details could he make out? The killer wore a short-sleeve shirt, but none of his face was visible. Cassie was dropped onto a couch of indistinct color, her nearly severed head lolling on the back of the couch. Her eyes bulged wide with shock and her freckled face looked pale and ghastly.

Just when Leo was about to break eye contact, something off to one side flashed slightly, like a reflection in a window or mirror. He couldn't be sure, but was there a vague human outline in that haze? He focused a moment longer, but then smelled the fresh, coppery blood pouring from Cassie's throat and closed his eyes, sucking in a few long breaths to calm his frazzled nerves.

When he opened his eyes, everyone was staring at him with deep revulsion etched into their young faces, Cassie most of all. Leo glanced over at Laura, seated at his desk. "Did you get all that?"

She nodded, clearly disturbed by his recitation.

Cassie's mouth hung open and Donovan wrapped both arms around her from the side, comforting her trembling body.

"Holy shit," murmured Robert, shaking his head in disgust.

Leo eyed Cassie, who looked more rattled than he'd ever seen her. Every bit of composure and self-assurance was gone, and she looked ready to crumple tearfully to the floor.

"I'm sorry, Cassie." He wasn't sure why he said it. *He* wasn't planning to kill her.

She fought to regain her cool demeanor, waving a hand before her. "No, I needed to know."

Donovan eased her over to the bed and helped her sit. Then, looking more resolute than usual, he stepped boldly forward. "I'll go next."

Leo nodded as Donovan approached and stood before him. The taller boy had his fists clenched and his brows furrowed. He tilted back his fedora and pushed aside his thick hair. He trembled but bravely stood his ground to await the inevitable.

Leo made eye contact.

Donovan's eyes were filled with fear. And blood. Much like Cassie, his throat was viciously slashed and crimson blood spilled forth to soak his shirt and cover the Chucky tattoo on the killer's wrist. Leo noticed that Donovan was seated on what looked like the same couch as Cassie, his head lolling to one side, his glassy brown eyes wide with horror at the way he'd died.

Then, as before, Leo saw a flicker of something, as though someone else lurked in the background. But then it was gone. He described in detail everything he was seeing before feeling an intense need to disengage.

Breaking eye contact, he glanced at Donovan's face. All the blood had drained away, and for a split second he looked like the corpse he'd just been. Maybe because he'd been expecting it, Donovan didn't overreact. He looked stunned but kept his composure and silently sat beside Cassie on the bed, pulling her in close.

Leo glanced around at the others. The silence in the room felt thick and oppressive. Having been through this with J.C., he sort of understood the sense of betrayal these kids felt, like life itself had turned against them at an early age. Leo made eye contact with J.C., who looked shaken by what he'd heard. But the look in his eyes clearly said, "I've got your back." Leo appreciated his best friend at that moment perhaps more than ever before.

Robert, his face set like flint, lurched forward as though he would take on the murderer right then and there. "Nobody's cutting my throat, I can tell you that," he announced to the room at large. "I'm ready, Leo."

Leo steeled himself against the bloody images he knew were imminent. He'd never liked horror movies because of the gore, and here he was immersed in one. The muscular Robert stood rigid as a totem and gazed straight at Leo as if to say, "Bring it on."

Leo made eye contact.

"You're outside somewhere," he began, focusing on the hazy images reflected back at him. "There's a house…you're up against a wall and it's dark." He gasped as a large shadowy figure leaped into his field of vision and plunged a long kitchen knife through Robert's chest, pinning him to the side of the house. "You're struggling, trying to fight him off but he… Oh God, he has more knives. He stabs you again in your right shoulder and leaves it in, stuck to the house behind you. There's blood, so much blood. You're still fighting with your right arm, but he stabs you through that shoulder and pins it to the wall."

He paused, almost unable to continue reciting such brutality. "You're screaming at him, but then he shoves another huge knife into your stomach and blood pours out of your mouth. The killer steps back and you're dead, pinned to the house."

Then Leo noticed that reflection again, mixed in with Robert's corpse, but as before it remained vague and indistinct. Not seeing any details that might be helpful, Leo broke eye contact and the horror movie ended.

The same thick silence hung over the room like a blanket of fog. When Leo looked up at Robert, he didn't see horror or fear. He saw determination.

"No way is that gonna happen to me," he swore quietly, his face rock solid with resolve. "Now that I know, I'm gonna stop it."

"Exactly," Leo agreed, focusing on calming his pounding heart. "That's why we're going through this now."

Chet stepped up beside Leo and touched his arm. "You need a break, Leo? You look, well, you look…" He trailed off, clearly at a loss for words.

"Thanks, but I…need to get through this."

Chet nodded and stepped back. J.C. eyed him with surprise, as though he never suspected Chet really cared what happened to anyone.

Before Leo could say more, Asher stood up from the beanbag, tight-lipped, but with a steely look in his eyes. "Now me."

Leo hesitated. He still didn't understand his feelings for Asher, the connection he felt to the young man, but he knew more than any of the others, he didn't want to watch Asher being murdered. Could he do this without breaking? He glanced at J.C. He'd done the same with him, at Laura's urging, to glean more clues that might help catch the killer. And it had devastated him. If he could make it through with his oldest friend, he could with his newest.

"Okay." He stared intently at Asher's perfect features, recalling that headshot photo and how it had so captured the essence of the young man, especially those kaleidoscope eyes. Forcing calm into his body, Leo raised his head and locked his brown eyes onto those hazel ones.

A hand rising and falling, plunging a shiny blade into a prone body over and over again. Leo almost lost his breath with the brutality of the attack. The knife seemed to stick in the flesh with each plunge and pop out with a sucking sound that nauseated him. Asher's bloody face came into view as his head lolled to one side on the grass. No longer beautiful, it had been sliced to ribbons.

Leo felt as if that knife was plunging into him. He lost count how many times that bare arm rose and slammed downward, but at least Asher no longer felt any pain. The knife finally stopped descending. Two arms grabbed Asher by his bloody shirt, and Leo saw that it was the black hoodie he wore in the film. The hands slammed Asher's corpse up against a tombstone. That's when Leo realized they were in a graveyard. He could just make out some of the name carved into the stone: "yers." The rest was blocked by Asher's slumped, blood-soaked body. The hands pulled back, but not before Leo caught a glimpse of the Chucky tattoo. Always Chucky. But then a flash farther out in the cemetery caught his eye. No, not a flash, a glimmer. The mirror thing again! What did it mean?

Finally unable to take any more, Leo clamped his eyes shut and dropped his head to his chest. He knew he'd been describing the vision in detail and wondered just how his voice sounded detailing such barbarity. Maybe it was like those guys on the news who reported horrific events in a weird kind of monotone.

His body burned as if with a fever and sweat dripped from his forehead onto the plush carpet beneath his feet. He hadn't realized he was perspiring so much. Suddenly his throat was parched. "J.C., my water, please."

Head still bowed, he felt his friend brush past him and moments later, a cool plastic water bottle was thrust into his clammy hand. Leo unscrewed the cap and downed the entire bottle without stopping. His insides cooled, but his heart still hammered away in his chest more intensely than after any gymnastics workout. He wasn't cut out to watch people being murdered, especially people he liked.

"Leo, you okay?"

Asher's calm voice was laced with worry, despite what Leo had just told him, and a feeling of warmth spread throughout his body at Asher's concern.

"Let him chill a minute," J.C. said, his voice also filled with loving support.

Leo realized that despite being the odd kid out his entire life, he really did have some good friends. Great ones, even. Including Asher, whom he'd barely gotten to know. He stood rigid in place, head bowed, breathing in and out with the calm, measured control practiced most of his life through aikido. He felt nauseated, yes, but anger also bubbled up within him like lava, and he needed to remain in control right then. He looked up at everyone.

"I'm ready now."

For a moment, no one moved or spoke.

Then Diego detached himself from the group as though ripping the band aid off a wound. "I'll go next."

Leo studied Diego's brooding face, already picturing it covered in blood as it had been in the brief glimpse he'd gotten the first time he looked in the other's eyes. Diego looked scared but also resigned, as though somehow, he'd always expected to be murdered one day. Leo lifted his eyes and locked onto Diego's brown ones.

Sweat coated his face. Diego looked around in desperation, but Leo couldn't make out any details. Then, as if a haze had lifted, he realized Diego was on the balcony of an unfamiliar house. Only the white railing and an open glass door behind him were visible.

"You're on a balcony," Leo said as though narrating a movie for someone blind. "You're scared. There's an open door behind you and…I think you're trapped. You turn to face the door. You see something. Or someone. Now you're…" Leo focused on the vision. It was chaotic now, like Diego was fighting with someone. "You're fighting him, I think. I see the knife. And the tattoo. The knife swings and stabs you in the back. Again and again. There's blood flying everywhere." Leo realized his voice had gotten higher, the pace faster, but he had to keep going. "You're slumped against the railing, trying to stand. Then… I see his foot. He's wearing a boot, like an army boot. He kicks you. The railing breaks and you…you fall."

He was about to break the connection when a new image appeared. Diego on the ground, his body twisted, like maybe his back was broken. He lifted his head. "You're on the ground, I think after the fall. You're alive. You lift your face, and it's scraped and bloody. You're badly hurt, but you're trying to move away. Then… Oh no, those boots are near your head. It's him! I see him squatting, but only his legs. Then the knife plunges down and—" Leo clamped both hands over his mouth to keep from screaming and closed his eyes, breaking the connection.

Diego's desperate hands were on him, clutching his shoulders. "And what. Leo? What happened?"

Leo lowered his hands from his mouth, his heart pounding so loudly he knew they must all hear it. "He, uh, he…he drove the knife down through your head so hard it stuck in the ground."

"My God," mumbled Diego, lowering his arms to his sides and trembling with either fear or anger. Leo didn't know which.

Jaden stepped forward and took Diego by the arm, leading him over to the bed where he sat, looking shellshocked. Leo glanced at Jaden, who met his gaze with a steady calmness.

Kristen placed a hand of support on Diego's shoulder, but her usual smug, "I've got this" expression had long since fled her face, replaced by a look of incredulity, as though she'd never imagined life could throw her such a curveball.

Leo glanced down at William and Baxter, who sat cross legged beside each other, staring with deep concentration at the carpet beneath them. They looked like petrified trees. He didn't have the heart to ask which of them would go next. His problem was solved when Kristen stepped up to him, her resolve set in stone.

"My turn."

Leo studied her firm expression. She was ready for the worst, and he suspected she might take the news better than some of the boys. He met her gaze head on and stifled a gasp. He could barely describe how the knife slashed and sliced at her body and face while she kicked and struggled to crawl away. His throat was so dry his voice came out raspy. Blood flew everywhere. Kristen's clothes—what was she wearing? It looked like one of her costumes for the film.

Leo was grateful his "power" didn't offer sound along with the images. He couldn't have taken her anguished cries and curses at the maniac who sliced her to pieces. Finally, she stopped thrashing and the knife plunged into her inert body no more. There seemed to be a break, almost like a fade to black in the movies. Then he saw her hanging by the neck from a tree in a cemetery. Her face was shredded, her dangling body not much better off. Her feet partially covered one of the headstones. There must not have been any wind because she wasn't moving at all. The name on the gravestone was murky, but he made out part of the last name: "albot." Then he had to break free. He could almost smell her fresh blood dripping down her legs and onto the dirt of the grave beneath. And then, slightly to the left and behind her bloody corpse, was that persistent reflection that never coalesced into anything he could make out. Needing to end this bloodbath, Leo closed his eyes and stepped back, almost afraid to open them for fear her expression might be one of rage for telling her all that.

But when he did look, she stood like a statue, her jaw clenched, her hands opening and closing spasmodically at her sides. She nodded at him but said nothing. Turning back to the bed, she found Diego standing with an arm outstretched. She allowed him to engulf her in a hug of support.

Leo glanced behind him at Laura, who sat at his desk, wide brown eyes swimming with horror, pen poised in her hand as though she'd been turned to stone. "You getting all this, Laura?"

She nodded slowly but didn't respond. For something to freak out Laura, that something had to be bad, and what Leo was witnessing for each of these young people was worse than bad could ever be. This was evil of the highest degree, and it sickened him. Suddenly desperate to end this part of the nightmare, he turned to face William and Baxter.

"Let's get this over with, guys," he said, compassion filling him. He wasn't seeing his death, but theirs, and he couldn't imagine how that must feel.

For the first time, both young men looked up at Leo. Their faces were ashen, and Baxter had tears in his eyes. They exchanged a long look and then rose together to stand before Leo, arms around each other's shoulders.

"We've been best friends since first grade," William croaked, his voice strained. "We're gonna support each other now like always. I'll go first."

Leo glanced at J.C., standing resolutely by his side. He knew that kind of friendship. Facing William, he reached out and gently brushed the long, wavy bangs off William's face, revealing his potent green eyes. He looked into those eyes and flinched.

William lay in the graveyard, on the thick grass. The killer's hand plunged down again and again with a jagged hunting knife. It ripped and rended William's flesh. Blood flew everywhere, but William had stopped breathing; the butchery of his body continued. Leo counted at least thirty thrusts, as though the killer were tenderizing meat for a barbecue. Repulsed, he focused on the gravestone just behind William's head, hoping for a clue. The name was hazy, so he willed it to become clear. "Bateman." That was the last name, but the first remained unclear. Then a flicker distracted him, and there was that reflection yet again! He fixed on it, struggling for clarity, but it was too vague and indistinct. There seemed to be a shadowy human silhouette. Was there a gun in its hand?

William closed his eyes, probably unable to take any more, and Leo lost the afterimage. He gazed at the trembling young man before him, long bangs once more hiding an attractive face but introverted personality, and wanted to hug him, to comfort him, to apologize for describing such a horrific death. But he couldn't. He was becoming numb to the butchery of this killer, and he needed to finish with Baxter before he lost all ability to feel anything.

"Ready, Baxter?"

Baxter shook his head but brushed his own scraggly bangs off his forehead in preparation for what was to come. "Try not to, you know… describe everything. Please."

Leo nodded. At this point, the brutality wasn't providing any clues. He would focus only on surrounding details that might indicate the location of the murders. He made eye contact.

Baxter was running into one of the houses. Leo felt his palpable fear and sensed the killer closing in. But he focused on the house. It looked like two stories, but the haze didn't reveal paint color. Baxter ran up several steps and threw open a single front door with a beveled glass oval in the center.

The scene seemed to switch to Baxter in a modern kitchen, yanking open drawers and pulling out cooking utensils. There were spoons and whisks and spatulas, but the terrified Baxter was clearly looking for something more lethal. Desperate, he snatched an extra-large fork from one drawer and spun around. The killer was on him, but Baxter managed one hard thrust of the fork before a thick hand gripped his wrist like a vice and snapped the bone. Baxter's twisted expression made Leo glad he couldn't hear the scream of anguish.

The fork fell to the floor and the knife rose. Chucky's grin looked even more ominous in the meager light as the knife rose above Baxter's head and plunged down into his skull. Baxter froze, then twitched before dropping to the tiled floor. Leo struggled to make out the color of the tile, but the murk of his vision was too thick. The killer knelt and the knife hand rose again, only to plunge straight through Baxter's throat and embed itself into the tiled floor beneath.

The fact that it stuck told Leo, somewhere in the back of his mind, that the tile couldn't be real tile, but maybe the fake stuff. As blood gurgled forth from Baxter's throat, Leo looked away and closed his eyes.

He only described Baxter being killed in the kitchen but had given no details except the fake tile floor. He supposed had he kept looking, he'd have seen the same reflection that always seemed to appear. What could that mean? Was there something even worse awaiting them out there?

CHAPTER ELEVEN

I WANT THE POLICE ON OUR SIDE

LEO SAT IN HIS BEANBAG chair, drained from having absorbed so much brutality and death. He needed time for his nerves to stop jangling, his heart to slow, and life to return to his soul.

Fortunately, Laura had taken charge once he finished with Baxter. She read through the clues, omitting the graphic details, and challenged the shellshocked group before her to come up with anything that might help narrow down the killer or the location.

Leo studied their silent faces as everyone digested her words and seemed unable to speak, let alone offer suggestions.

"If I can say something."

Leo turned to Chet, who'd hovered in the background the entire time. All eyes landed on him.

"My mom's police chief here in Costa and I've lived here my whole life. The houses didn't sound like any in town, but we do have a graveyard. I think, as a cop might think, the biggest question would be why all of you and not Jaden?"

Now everyone looked at the silent Jaden, including Leo. Kristen's eyes narrowed with suspicion.

"Yeah, why not Jaden? Are you the killer?"

Diego beside her looked horrified. "Whoa, Kristen. You really think he could do…what Leo described?"

She didn't look at him, but her threatening glare softened slightly. "Then why isn't he on the hit list?"

Leo decided to defend his new friend before this got ugly. “So, Jaden, any ideas? I know it’s not you ’cause, well, I looked in your eyes too.”

“So what?” That was Robert. “You said he died a natural death. Doesn’t mean he couldn’t be a psycho killer. You didn’t see him on set with that skull mask he wore. He loved playing the killer.”

Still Jaden didn’t defend himself, but Leo thought he knew why. The shyness and social anxiety made it hard to be challenged, to fight back *when* challenged.

“Look,” Leo went on, pushing himself up from the beanbag and deciding to take charge, “he’s like me. Super shy. Social anxiety. Hiding his face behind a mask, well, I get that. It’s what we do if we can. Doesn’t make him, or me, a psycho.”

Jaden gazed at him with wide grateful eyes. “Thanks, Leo.”

Leo nodded. “Is there someone who knows all of you but not Jaden? Someone who might want revenge for something you all did? Maybe something to do with that movie you were making?”

“Yeah,” Chet jumped in. “I read about that online. Maybe there’s still somebody out there who was part of that?”

Donovan nudged Cassie.

“Uh, no,” she said haltingly, as though still adjusting to her newfound status as a potential murder victim. “My dad’s a cop and his girlfriend, well, she was the detective on that case. They said it’s wrapped up. No outstanding suspects.”

Chet gave her a hard look. “Maybe you should have ’em reopen the case, especially with what we know now.”

“He’s right, Cass,” Donovan said, clutching her hand like he’d never let go.

Cassie brushed wild reddish curls off her face and studied the group, mainly Leo. “And what will I tell him about how we know all this?”

Chet flinched, then eyed Leo beside him. “Oh, yeah. Didn’t think of that. Sorry, man.”

Leo remained silent. He knew what telling the cops meant—his secret would be out. His mother would probably find out. Maybe everyone would find out. And would the cops even believe him in the first place?

Robert interrupted the heavy silence. “Your dad’s a cool guy, Cass. If you tell him to keep Leo’s secret, he will, right?”

Cassie looked thoughtful. She released Donovan's hand and stood, clearly considering her answer. "He'd have to tell Marisol. She's his detective girlfriend. But I guess no one else needs to know."

"Good," J.C. said, his tone almost threatening. "'Cause all of you know about Leo already and that's too many for me. He's the best guy I know, and I don't want anyone thinking he's some kind of freak."

Leo placed a hand on J.C.'s shoulder to draw his attention. "I am a freak, J.C. Nothing anyone says will change that."

Now Asher stepped forward, brows scrunched with anger. "Don't call yourself a freak. You're special, that's all."

Leo felt warm inside at the affirmation from his friends. "Thanks, guys."

"What do you think, Leo?" Laura asked, finally entering the conversation. "About involving the police?"

Leo considered a moment. "First of all, no one is going to kill any of you if I can stop it. Second, we have the high ground here. The sadistic bitch who's planning all this doesn't know we're onto him. We might not be able to figure out who he is or where he plans to do these things, but we can make sure you're all armed and ready."

"What do you mean armed?" Robert said. "Like with guns?"

"No." Leo paused to collect his thoughts. He'd been mulling over options ever since he foresaw Asher's death. "From what I saw, all of you actors are wearing your movie costumes, which tells me that somehow the killer gets to you on Wednesday before you change back. That means he'll have to be on the set."

"So, what do we do?" Cassie studied him overtly, but this time Leo wasn't fazed.

"Since none of our sets look like what I saw, the killer has to lure you or capture you and bring you to the new location, right?"

Everyone nodded, clearly seeing Leo's logic.

"For sure he'll take any phones you have on you, but since he doesn't know you know about him, he won't think to look for weapons or things that can be used as weapons."

"Like what," Kristen sneered, "a hair comb? Some people call them hair forks."

Leo nodded. "Exactly like that. My mom has some that are made of metal and they're sharp. Even the boys with longer hair can have one hidden up against the back of their heads."

Kristen looked shocked, but then nodded appreciatively. "I like the way you think."

"Depending on their shoe styles, we could stash tiny knives inside the heel," Chet chimed in excitedly. "I've seen that done in movies."

"Exactly," Leo agreed. "That's the way to think. All of you, consider belts and belt buckles, any item of clothing or anything small you could keep in a pocket."

"Pretty smart, Leo," Laura said.

"Yeah," Asher chimed in. "I never suspected you were so devious."

Leo shrugged. "My mom makes movies. Mostly that rom-com stuff I hate, but sometimes spy films."

William looked up and spoke from behind his bangs. "What about Cassie's dad? I want the police on our side."

Leo felt William's fear as well as Baxter's beside him. These two weren't fighters. They were too mellow, too gentle.

Leo turned to Cassie. "Tell him, Cassie. But please ask him and the detective not to tell anyone else about me."

Cassie nodded. "No worries. My dad's the best."

"I agree," Asher added. "He helped me out a lot this year. He's a good guy."

"Then it's settled," Leo said, casting his gaze around the room in case anyone else had a comment. "Tomorrow, me and the crew"—he indicated J.C., Laura, and Chet—"will check out the local cemetery for those names on the gravestones I saw, but I'm pretty sure the places in my visions aren't here in town."

"The rest of you, think about what Leo said," Laura put in. "Think about how you can arm yourself without it looking like you're packing."

"And if anyone thinks of someone or something they forgot that might be connected," Chet said, "send a group text. We can set that up now."

"I'll do that," Laura said. "Everyone give me your number."

The assembled youth gathered around Laura, except William and Baxter, who remained on the floor.

J.C. hung close to Leo, whispering, "You okay after all that?"

Leo made eye contact with his best friend. Having already changed

J.C.'s timeline by saving him last spring, he no longer saw how and when his friend would die, which meant he didn't have to worry about eye contact. He felt pretty certain it worked that way for everyone. "I'm kind of drained."

"If you need me, I'm always here."

Leo cracked a weak smile. "Thanks, man."

Chet indicated William and Baxter still seated on the floor, heads bowed. "I don't think these guys can make it home tonight. Not after all that."

Leo studied the two young men on the floor, and then the others exchanging phone numbers with Laura. They all lived in the Valley, which was a drive, and every one of them looked washed out. He wasn't sure any could make it home.

"I think you're right," he answered Chet. "Not sure any of 'em should try."

He watched as Laura squatted down to William and Baxter. When she stood, he cleared his throat. Everyone looked his way.

"Um, after all the stuff I told you, I feel like I got run down by a bus, so I figure you must be pretty shook up too. You're welcome to stay overnight here, or if Laura, J.C., and Chet agree, we could split you up in our houses. That way you don't have to make that long drive to the valley tonight."

Laura's face lit up. "That's a great idea, Leo. How about it? Cassie, you could stay at my place."

Cassie eyed Donovan. Both still looked perturbed.

"I think it's a good idea, Cass," Donovan said, eyeing the others. "We can call our folks and let them know we're staying over with friends tonight."

Kristen didn't look thrilled as she eyed Cassie, but she nodded. The boys all agreed.

"Uh, great," Leo said, noting how deflated William and Baxter seemed. He kind of understood how they felt, even though he wasn't a target. "I got a couple more rooms, so maybe Donovan and Jaden? You guys wanna crash here?"

"Sure," Donovan replied at once, as though he'd been hoping Leo would ask him. "That work for you, Jaden?"

"Absolutely." The boy eyed Leo without his usual shyness.

Chet and J.C. exchanged a look. "I guess that leaves us," Chet said. "So, who wants to stay with Robert and me?"

William and Baxter glanced at each other and shrugged. "I'll stay with you," Baxter said, his voice without energy or enthusiasm.

"So then, William comes with me and Diego," J.C. said, not looking especially pleased about the arrangement but trying to appear as though he was.

"Okay," Leo said. "So, we'll see you all in the morning." He flicked his gaze to Cassie. "When will you tell your dad?"

She considered a moment. "I think it's better to tell him in person, so tomorrow night when I get home."

Leo nodded.

He didn't really want more people knowing about his freak status, but on the other hand he didn't know if he could save all these people by himself.

Once the others had left, Leo took Asher, Donovan, and Jaden into the kitchen for something to eat before bed. As before, Leo felt at ease with all three guys and his social anxiety was all but forgotten.

He showed them the two extra rooms, both of which sported queen-sized beds, but they looked hesitant, and Leo thought he knew why. Asher articulated what was going on better than Leo could have.

"I think we all wanna stay together, Leo. I mean, nothing's gonna happen till Wednesday, but, well, after everything we heard about… Anyway, is it okay if we crash in your room?"

Leo was about to protest that even his king-sized bed couldn't accommodate all four of them when Donovan said, "We can sleep on the floor. It's okay. But Asher's right, I don't wanna be alone."

Jaden shrugged. "I'm not even on the killer's list, but I still wanna stick with my friends. That cool?"

"Sure," Leo answered. "C'mon, we'll grab blankets and pillows for you guys."

Soon, Leo lay atop his bed, while Asher, Donovan, and Jaden lay wrapped in blankets on the floor nearby.

Leo sat up to turn out the light, but before he did, he studied the three young men beside his bed. Donovan and Asher stared at the ceiling wearing grim expressions, and Leo suspected they were reliving the details of their impending deaths. Jaden was gazing up at Leo as if to say, "Is there anything we can do to help them not stress?"

Leo decided to distract them before exhaustion finally set in. "So, Donovan, when did you know that Cassie was, well, the one you loved?" He didn't mean to, but found his eyes drifting to Asher's beautiful face. As though in sync, Asher looked up at him, and Leo blushed.

Donovan lost the grim look and smiled. "Cassie and I have been best friends since first grade. I guess it wasn't till high school that I realized I liked her more than that, but I wasn't sure how she felt. It's funny. She and Kristen don't like each other, but they're not so different. Both are focused on their careers before everything else. It wasn't till we got hired on this film that Cassie let on how she felt about me, but I think, deep down, I always knew. I was never into any girls 'cept her."

Asher was listening intently, but Leo kept eyeing him all through Donovan's story. Why did he feel such a kinship with Asher?

"That's cool," he said to Donovan.

"Yeah," Jaden echoed. "The perfect couple. I hope I find someone like that."

Without thinking, Leo said, "You will." His mind had gone back to what he'd witnessed of Jaden's death.

As though reading his mind, Jaden said, "You were gonna tell me how I die, Leo. I'd like to know."

Leo was surprised by the request. "In front of these guys?"

Jaden offered a rare smile. "They're my friends."

Leo understood. No secrets between friends. "You were really old and lying in bed. I'm not sure where you were, but you looked calm and peaceful. There was another man with you. He was old too and sat by the bed holding your hand and crying. You just sort of drifted away, I think. Like I said, you looked peaceful."

Jaden smiled. "I wonder who the other dude was."

"Sounds like you found your guy," Asher said, looking happier than he had all night. "That's awesome, man."

There was a moment of silence while they all processed Jaden's peaceful end many decades in the future.

Jaden looked up at Leo. "Thanks for telling me."

"Uh, sure." Leo's insides squirmed, but he maintained a cool outward demeanor. "So, when did you, you know, understand you were gay and all?"

Jaden looked embarrassed but didn't turn away. "Dunno, really. I always been so shy I never checked out anybody, girl or boy, until maybe last year." His dark face reddened as he glanced at Donovan. "That's when I, well, crushed on Donovan, if you wanna know the truth. I mean, who wouldn't, right?"

Now it was Donovan's turn to redden, bowing his head to avoid making eye contact with anyone. "I never thought of people being, you know, into me, so I was kinda shocked when I found out." He lifted his head and gazed at Jaden beside him. "I still think you're crazy though."

Jaden grinned. "No way. Diego will confirm. You're hotter than hot."

Donovan chuckled and pretended to burn his finger on his arm, making a sizzling sound with his tongue.

Everyone laughed at that, which filled Leo with a momentary sense of calm. These were all great guys. They knew their futures and, other than Jaden, they would change their fate. And he would help.

After that, they lay down and Leo turned out the light. It wasn't long before he heard gentle snoring coming from the floor beside his bed and he was happy the others had drifted off. He considered Jaden's words about growing up and realized how similar their childhoods were, at least in the arena of not looking at other people. Except for J.C., Laura, and Chet, Leo never gave anyone more than a passing glance. Could that be why he was so drawn to Asher, because he could look at Asher and commune with him without stressing? It was with these thoughts that sleep finally took him.

After Laura showed Cassie how to find the kitchen and bathrooms, she'd said goodnight and padded down the upstairs hall to her bedroom. Cassie looked around the room she'd be sharing with Kristen. It was nicely apportioned and reasonably large, with a main bed and an extra daybed against one wall that would be hers. She'd tried brushing her hair when she took care of her teeth, but the frizz factor seemed worse than usual, and she finally gave up.

If she could get her mind off her impending death, and those of the others, she'd have recognized that she would prefer not to share a room with Kristen, not because Kristen hadn't gotten less snarky over the past few months, but because, if she were honest, she was a little jealous of the other girl's natural beauty and poise.

Cassie had to admit these Costa kids were incredibly kind and accommodating. She'd never heard of this town before last spring when the attack on J.C. and other kids made the news, but she felt like she might be making friendships that would stand the test of time, which she hadn't expected on a film shoot.

"I can help you control your hair, if you want."

Lost in her thoughts, Cassie whirled to find Kristen sitting on the other bed and gazing at her with smug amusement, a look Cassie didn't appreciate. Still, she kept her calm. "Oh, that's okay. I should just cut it one of these days."

Kristen clambered off the bed and crossed the room to her. "No, you shouldn't. The color is eye-catching, and the length suits you. But you need to tame it."

Cassie immediately became defensive. "Why does it matter?"

Kristen had been reaching out toward her mop of hair, but quickly pulled her hands back. They stared at each other a long moment. "My mother drummed into my head that a girl has to be beautiful at all times," Kristen said, almost to herself. "I guess that's why I get so full of myself. But..." She trailed off before making eye contact with Cassie. "I've always kind of envied you."

"Me? Why?"

"Because you never cared about that stuff, and you always seemed happy and relaxed. I know we have different career paths in this industry, and for mine, I have to look gorgeous or I'm replaced by someone younger and prettier. But I wouldn't mind not having to stress over it all the time."

Cassie was taken aback by Kristen revealing so much of her inner self. "You don't have to."

Kristen smiled wryly. "Yeah, I do. It's built in now. But I'm good at what I do. So are you. And one of the things I can do is to help you. Not that Donovan cares. He's such a babe and totally into you. I just, well, I just want to do something nice for you. So can I help you tame your hair?"

Cassie studied her a long moment in case a "gotcha" moment was forthcoming, but Kristen looked sincere—without acting this time. "Sure. That'd be cool. Wait'll you see it tomorrow after I shower."

"I've got just the thing for that." She hurried to her travel bag in the corner by her bed and rummaged inside. Then she returned with shampoo and conditioner. "Use these in the shower and leave the conditioner in for five minutes. After that, I've got something that'll really smooth it out. You'll look amazing."

"Thanks." Cassie wanted to ask why Kristen was doing all this but didn't want to spoil the other girl's positive mood.

Kristen nodded, then studied Cassie a long moment. "You know, Donovan was probably the hottest guy in our high school."

Cassie tilted her head at the change in topic. "Course he was."

"A lot of girls were circling the water, hoping he'd get tired of waiting for you."

"Seriously?" Cassie was stunned. Then she chuckled wryly. "I guess I *was* pretty focused on my work. You and I are alike that way. But now that we have our first gig, I knew it was time to move forward with him."

Kristen smiled. "I've noticed. I guess I'll have to get around to a social life one day before I'm old and wrinkled."

A thought struck Cassie and she articulated it. "Have you noticed that Robert has changed for real? Everyone knows how much I hated him for hitting on me in high school, but he's different now. I haven't seen him flirt with any girl in the cast. Have you?"

Kristen shifted her position on the bed, thinking. "Now that you mention it, no. He is different."

"And good-looking."

Kristen eyed her suspiciously. "You trying to play matchmaker, Cass?"

"No way. It's just a thought."

Kristen offered a sly smile. "Yeah, it is."

CHAPTER TWELVE

I DON'T WANNA LOSE YOU

LEO ENJOYED HAVING SO MUCH company for breakfast, and Sylvia loved cooking for them. After hearty helpings of scrambled eggs, bacon, and toast, everyone showered and made ready to report to the set.

Leo's mother popped into the dining room while the boys scarfed their food and marveled at "so much male beauty on display," which Leo thought was creepy, but the boys took it in stride. He supposed, being in the business, they were accustomed to such fawning comments. Leo haltingly explained that they'd all been up late talking, so he invited them to stay rather than drive home. His mom gave him a look but merely reminded them not to miss their call times.

After everyone was dropped off at the filming site, Leo, Laura, J.C., and Chet set off in Leo's Prius to the local cemetery. Leo was already certain it was not the one he'd seen in his vision, but he wanted to check off that box before Cassie's dad got involved.

Since La Costa was built before the first world war, some of the graves and mausoleums were ancient, while other graves displayed the more modern in-the-ground-style memorial plate. Stone angels and crosses rose all around them as the four—each armed with a copy of the partial names Leo had seen—split up and wandered among the graves, checking the names on headstones. Since the ones Leo had seen were the aboveground tombstones like they'd find in a Halloween store, everyone avoided the inground or mausoleum types.

Simply looking around told Leo this was not the setting of his visions. There were no houses abutting the cemetery, and the arrangement of gravestones didn't look at all the same. After examining his tenth headstone, he decided this was a fruitless task. When he turned to find the others, he nearly jumped in surprise to find Laura right behind him.

"This isn't the place, is it?"

He shook his head. "We should go back to the school and tell the others. Where are J.C. and Chet?"

Laura indicated the far side of the cemetery where the two boys moved from headstone to headstone, comparing names to the papers in their hands.

"Can I ask you something, Leo?"

He gazed at her in surprise. "We're friends. You can ask me anything."

"Are you attracted to Asher?"

Leo felt his face burn and he looked down at the freshly trimmed grass beneath his feet. "Is it obvious?"

"Kind of."

He looked at her, uncertainty flooding through him. "Laura, I've never checked out guys before. But there's just something about him, a connection I feel."

Her understanding face calmed his fears. "I dated boys before I met Tara, but none of them did it for me. When I kissed them, I didn't feel a connection. Not until Tara kissed me. Then I knew."

"What's your point?"

"Maybe your social anxiety has made you suppress connections to everyone except J.C., and maybe now me and Chet, so you might not know who you're into."

Leo wanted to disappear through the grass. "You're like my mom. You want me to be gay." As soon as he said it, he wished he hadn't.

Surprisingly, she didn't look hurt. "I just want you to be happy. Your mom, well, she's out there. No doubt. But maybe she sees something in you that you never have. We females can do that sometimes. All I'm saying is don't panic over feeling something for Asher. I can see he feels something for you too. I saw it again this morning when we dropped him off. Just let it be. Don't worry about labels. Hang out with Asher. Spend time getting to know each other. If there's something there, you'll feel it."

Leo felt the stiffness melting away. He was relieved to be talking about this with someone who cared about him. J.C. would never understand, he was sure, but Laura did.

As though reading his mind, Laura offered a tight smile. "And don't worry about J.C. Haven't you noticed him and Diego?"

Surprised, Leo opened his mouth to reply but heard, "This is a waste of time, Leo."

He looked to his right to find J.C. and Chet trotting toward him between graves.

He glanced back at Laura, who shrugged and said, "You're right, J.C. This isn't the place. Let's head back to school."

As they strode across the quiet, empty cemetery toward Leo's parked Prius, J.C. grumbled, "Like we don't get enough of that sorry-ass school already."

Cassie found her focus wandering several times during the day's shoot, and Mr. K expressed both alarm and concern. Mortified, she apologized and promised it wouldn't happen again. But it did. Those horrific images Leo had described of her murder kept disrupting her concentration. She fingered the steel-cut hair comb Kristen had given her that morning. Having never owned a barrette, Cassie wasn't sure how to use it, but Kristen expertly swept a large swath of her now-smooth hair to one side and locked it in place with the shiny, four-pronged hair comb. Cassie had to admit that sweeping her hair to the side in this way was quite fetching.

"Let the crew get used to seeing you wearing that so if the killer is out there, he won't think it strange that you suddenly have one next Wednesday," Kristen suggested. "I'll wear mine whenever I'm not on camera."

She, too, sported a four-pronged comb that pushed up the rear section of her long hair, so it almost looked like a bun.

"Thanks, Kristen," Cassie had said, feeling truly grateful to this girl who seemed to have changed so much under threat of death. Kristen merely nodded in reply.

Cassie was grateful when it came time for their lunch break so she could recalibrate. The whole crew from Performing Arts High was joined by Leo and his friends, who reported no success at the local cemetery. Cassie wasn't surprised, and little was said among them as they mechanically ate their food. She could tell that all of them, especially the morose William and Baxter, were feeling deep despair over what was to come, but Robert reminded them that they had the upper hand and would not be taken down like sheep.

"I agree," Leo added. "And you have us four helping you. Plus Cassie's dad and his girlfriend. Right, Cassie?"

She nodded. "I'll tell them tonight. They'll probably want to talk with you, Leo. Is that okay?"

He nodded but said no more.

Lunch was finished in silence.

The afternoon and evening filming went well, with Cassie back to her focused self, and the remaining scenes set at the high school were completed to Mr. K's satisfaction. The following day, Saturday, would complete the location shooting with scenes in a nearby park that featured an enormous Moreton Bay tree that figured into the action.

Cassie didn't spot any suspicious behavior on the part of any crew members but found herself scrutinizing every action, even Stuart bringing her coffee throughout the day. She gave him such a piercing stare at one point that he looked taken aback.

"Did I do something wrong, Cassie? You look, well, spooked."

She realized her mistake and shrugged it off as the long hours. "I'm sorry, Stuart. You're awesome, really." And since he didn't have a Chucky tattoo on his bare wrists, she felt truthful saying that.

He eyed her with uncertainty before smiling. "Thanks. I try my best." He moved on to hand Mr. K a Styrofoam cup of steaming coffee and then drifted among the crew scattered about the quad area.

Cassie had barely taken time to notice the art deco stylings of the older school buildings that contrasted with the ultra-modern metal and glass cafeteria in which much of their filming had taken place these past few days, but when she had time to take it all in, she found the campus inviting. It wasn't as fancy or Avant Garde as her former high school, but it was a step above most schools that usually resembled prisons.

She'd already texted her dad that she needed to speak with him and Marisol that night when she got home, and he assured her they'd both be there. He wanted to know what it was about, but she sent the message that she was too busy to get into it until they were face-to-face.

She managed to get through the afternoon with no more flubs, somehow compartmentalizing her upcoming murder into a corner of her brain where she could effectively ignore it and focus on the tasks at hand. By the time shooting wrapped at eight thirty that night, she felt depleted, dreading the drive home. Thankfully, Donovan, who'd never left her side all day, volunteered to take over the driving duties.

They spoke little on the forty-five-minute trip other than what they would say to her dad, and some thoughts on items each might carry that could be used as weapons. Donovan kissed her goodnight in front of his house, and she watched him enter before getting behind the wheel and heading for home. He'd offered to be there when she told her dad and Marisol the news, but Cassie waved away the idea.

"You're as tired as me. Get some sleep. Last location day tomorrow, remember?"

Upon entering her single-story Craftsman-style home, she found her dad and Marisol at the small kitchen table sipping coffee. Her dad still looked like he had when he'd been in the military as a young man, his crew cut and neatly clipped sideburns matching old photos he'd shown her. He was a big man with a large chest and an imposing stature, but his engaging smile put everyone at ease. That's why he was everyone's favorite neighborhood cop.

Marisol, on the other hand, looked stately and professional in a pantsuit with her hair pulled back off the face so it dangled about her back and shoulders. Cassie had always admired her beauty and poise, and hoped the detective would one day marry her dad.

"You look bushed, Cass."

"I am." She lowered herself into a third chair and smiled wanly at Marisol. "Hi, Marisol. Thanks for coming."

She offered a welcoming smile. "Edward said you sounded ominous on the phone. Is it that serious?"

She nodded, facing her dad, having made the decision to just blurt out the truth. "Dad, I know this'll sound crazy, but next Wednesday I'm going to be murdered."

His face froze, and then his mouth dropped open in shock.

Leo sat on a bench overlooking a sea of gravestones. He was back at La Costa Memorial Park awaiting the arrival of Cassie's dad and detective girlfriend. He'd seen Cassie that morning when he brought Asher to the shooting location beneath the massive Moreton Bay Fig Tree in Shelby Park. Town residents—mostly older people out for walks—had gathered to watch the filming, and the rest of Leo's friends were already present.

On the drive over, Asher assured him he had no reason to be nervous. "Cassie's dad is the best, Leo. He won't betray your secret."

Leo nodded. "I was thinking about you."

"Me?" Asher's tone displayed pleasure at the notion.

Leo kept his eyes on the road ahead. "Uh, yeah, well, all of you. And what you might have on you to fight off an attack."

"Oh." Disappointment flooded the car.

Leo recalled Laura's words the other day and glanced over, heartrate rising. "I…I know I only just met you, but…I don't wanna lose you."

Asher looked up, flashing that picture-perfect smile that had probably netted him a gazillion modeling jobs. "You don't?"

Leo's cheeks burned. "No. And I won't." He returned his eyes to the road. "We'll stop this guy."

"Yeah, we will." Asher sounded strong and hopeful, more so than when they'd left the house.

When they'd arrived, Asher locked eyes with him for one last moment of solidarity before he headed over to the makeup trailer.

J.C., Laura, and Chet were hanging around while the crew set up the first shot. Just being at this location where a raging J.C. had pointed a loaded handgun at him barely a few months back sent chills up Leo's back, so he was grateful when Cassie approached and spoke to the group in low tones.

"Leo, my dad and Marisol want to meet you somewhere away from the crew."

"Why?" That was J.C., sounding suspicious before Leo could even open his mouth.

Cassie shrugged. Her hair looked different, Leo noticed, pulled back off her face and locked in place with one of those hair combs.

"My dad has a plan of some kind and doesn't want anyone on the crew to see him. Where should I tell him to meet you?"

Leo considered a moment. Probably the quietest spot was the cemetery. "The cemetery. Unless there's a funeral, it's always pretty dead there."

She gave him a funny look and J.C. grunted before Leo realized what he'd said.

"Sorry, I wasn't trying to be funny. It's called the La Costa Memorial Park. His GPS ought to find it easily."

"Got it." She slipped a phone from her jeans pocket and rapidly typed while Leo made eye contact with J.C. His best friend looked worried, but not for himself. Even Chet seemed overly anxious because of Robert's impending murder, Leo supposed.

"We're gonna stop this guy," Leo asserted, forcing more strength into his voice than he felt. Depending on what went down, he might not even be near enough to help his friends. Asher's bloodied face flashed through his mind, and he closed his eyes to shut out the image.

"Dad says one hour, at the cemetery."

Cassie's voice brought him back to the moment and he nodded.

That was how he now found himself seated on a cracked stone bench, watching as a man and woman emerged from a dark blue SUV and strolled nonchalantly in his direction, as though they planned to visit a grave. Both were dressed in casual clothes. Cassie's dad was big and intimidating, while his lady friend was small and attractive.

He stood to greet them, squinting against the bright morning sun, which gave him an excuse not to make eye contact. Cassie's dad stuck out his hand and Leo shook it.

"It's an honor to meet you, Leo," he said, catching Leo off guard. "I'm Edward and this is Marisol."

She smiled warmly. "Nice to meet you, Leo."

"May we sit?" Edward indicated the bench.

Still confused by Edward's opening line, Leo stepped aside awkwardly and said, "Sure."

Marisol seated herself and crossed her legs, while Edward sat beside her.

"Please sit, Leo," Edward said, glancing around at the empty cemetery. "If anyone should show up, I want us to look like we're visiting a loved one."

Leo thought it unlikely anyone would show up, but he sat beside

Edward anyway, feeling dwarfed beside the large man. "Why did you say it was an honor to meet me, sir?"

"First of all, let's lose the 'sir'. I'm Edward and she's Marisol. You'll understand the informality in a moment. As for why I'm honored, it's because so few people have courage these days, especially the courage to put their life on the line for others. I know what you did for your friend last spring. I remember telling Marisol at the time that you had more courage than most men I know."

"It's true, Leo," Marisol confirmed, adding to Leo's discomfort at being put on a pedestal. He hated too much attention, even the positive kind. "And what you're doing now for Cassie and the others confirms your strength of character."

Leo kept his eyes lowered, hoping the shade of the tree beside them hid the blush rising to his cheeks. "I just don't want to see my friends get hurt or…" He trailed off, not wanting to say the word "murdered."

He felt Edward's large hand settle onto his shoulder and glanced up at the man's serious expression.

"Without you, I'd have lost Cassie next week, and Donovan, who's like a son to me. You already have my eternal gratitude, and we still have a long way to go."

"Did she, you know, tell you what I saw?"

His mouth turned downward, and he momentarily looked afraid. "Yes. And showed me the notes your friend Laura took."

"We won't put you through that again, Leo," Marisol interjected, her soft voice soothing his frazzled nerves. "But we are interested in learning more about how you acquired this…ability."

Leo nodded, having expected this question, so he repeated what he'd told Cassie and the others.

Both adults listened intently to his story, but neither face revealed whether they believed him or not. Leo supposed being cops, they'd learned to keep poker faces when listening to stories like his.

Edward and Marisol exchanged a look.

"Makes sense, based on what we know so far," she said.

"I agree." Edward faced Leo again. "I confess that supernatural stuff isn't really my thing, but I guess I've watched enough horror flicks with Cassie over the years to keep an open mind. In any case, what you told us helps explain how you were able to save your friend last March. You knew he was going to be killed."

"Yes, sir. I mean, Edward."

"I think we should move on to the current situation," Marisol said. "How to prevent the murders of Cassie and the others."

Mainly Asher, Leo found himself thinking, but quickly refocused on the conversation.

"Cassie told us what you said, about them having the high ground here, and we agree," Marisol went on, clearly in charge of this case. "Having all the kids armed with self-defense tools was a brilliant idea, Leo. We can help in that arena too."

"We plan to meet with your mother today," Edward said. Leo flinched and started to protest, but Edward raised a hand to reassure him. "Don't worry. We won't even mention you."

Leo relaxed. "How will you manage that?"

"We're going to tell your mother that we have a credible threat against the production," Marisol took up the narrative, "and that Edward and I need to be on set beginning Monday. We'll let her decide how we might best fit into the crew. You'll be filming in a soundstage next week, correct?"

Leo nodded.

"That's good. It's an easier location to keep the kids under surveillance. You're sure the...attacks will happen at night?"

"Yes," Leo replied, shuddering as images of the brutal killings flashed through his mind. "There was definitely a graveyard, and it was dark out."

"There have been some vicious stabbings in Los Angeles over the past few months that appear to be the work of a serial killer," Edward said, causing Leo's blood to run cold. "What you described in your vision seems to fit that MO."

"MO?" Leo didn't know that term.

"Modus operandi," Marisol chimed in. "Unfortunately, we have no leads at present. Only your description of the Chucky tattoo, which we've run through our criminal database. So far, we've turned up nothing. If this guy was arrested before, likely he didn't have the tattoo at that time."

Leo nodded. That made sense. As he saw the image in his mind of that tattoo, its vibrant colors seemed to leap out at him. "The colors were bright. It looked new."

"It should be easy to spot on one of the crew members," Edward commented, almost to himself.

"We checked out everyone on this location shoot," Leo said. "Nobody has it. But location crew and soundstage crew are different. The main people are still there, but the grips, gaffers, PAs, people like that are usually different."

Edward looked mystified. "What are grips, gaffers, and PAs?"

"Grips carry stuff, gaffers work the lights, and PAs are production assistants," Leo explained, realizing that, despite his best efforts not to be part of his mother's business, he understood more than he thought.

"We know nothing about the film business," Marisol commented, sharing a look with Edward. "But we'd better get up to speed fast if we're to look legit. Hopefully, your mother will be cooperative."

"Hopefully," Leo muttered, wondering how his mother would react to this news.

Edward glanced around the rolling hills of the cemetery, but they were still alone. "We'd better let you get back to the shoot, Leo, so people don't wonder where you are. We might speak on the phone, but the next time we meet it will be on the studio backlot. And it will be for the first time." He offered a tight smile.

"We'll mostly communicate through Cassie," Marisol added as she rose to her feet. "The less contact we have with you and the others, the better."

Edward agreed and stood. Leo rose and stood beside them, feeling awkward but not uncomfortable. Asher had been right. There was something about Edward, about his demeanor, that made Leo feel at home with him. He extended a hand and Edward shook it.

"Thanks for helping us out. I mean, Cassie's your daughter and all, but you could've just, I guess, pulled her and Donovan out of the film to protect them."

"And let something happen to the others? No way." Edward wore a hard, resolute expression that Leo liked.

"We'll leave first, Leo," Marisol said, shaking his hand. "Once our car pulls out, you head back to the shoot."

Leo watched as they strolled down the path to their parked SUV, noting that they didn't hold hands. Hadn't Cassie said they were a couple?

In any case, they had a killer to catch.

CHAPTER THIRTEEN

NOBODY'S GONNA HURT MY GIRL

CASSIE WAS HAPPIER TO BE home that night than she had been in the longest time. Sitting in her own kitchen nursing a cup of warm tea with her dad across the kitchen table helped ease the tension that had built up since Leo "saw" her murder. He'd told her that morning about his meeting with her dad and Marisol, and between them they promised to get the word out to the other members of their team.

Team. An interesting word. Sure, she and her former classmates were a team, but now that group had expanded by four with the inclusion of Leo and his friends. She really liked all of them and hoped they could continue their friendship after the film wrapped.

Assuming she survived Wednesday, of course.

"You look wiped, honey. Why not go to bed?"

Her dad's voice pierced her reverie like popping a balloon, and she offered a wan smile. "I was just realizing how tense I've been since Leo told me."

He lowered his coffee mug and nodded. "I can't imagine how stressful it must be. But I'm not going to let anything happen to you. Or the others. You agree with our plan, right?"

Cassie nodded. She and Donovan had sat down with her dad and Marisol the moment they'd arrived home and hashed out a partial plan. Yes, the kids would arm themselves with everything from nail clippers to breath spray—innocuous items that, should the killer get the drop on them, would not likely be taken away. But—and here was the *big* but—if no clues to the killer were unearthed by her dad or Marisol Monday or Tuesday, Cassie and the other targeted victims would not report to the set on Wednesday. Her dad had already made this clear to Leo's mom, who reluctantly agreed to the stipulation, though she did ask for guaranteed updates on the investigation.

"Obviously, we wanna catch this guy," her dad went on. "Like we told you and Donovan, it sounds like it could be the same guy who's already killed several people over the past few months."

"Do you think Marisol might strike gold with that Chucky tattoo?"

He sipped his coffee. "If the perp has ever been arrested with that tattoo, it was photographed. My fear is it's too new and we have no record of it. In that case, we'll be scrutinizing every crew member on Monday. If need be, Leo's mom has tagged Tuesday as favorite tee shirt day for the entire crew to enable us to see everyone's wrists, so hopefully they'll all comply."

She nodded again, fatigue weighing her down. She'd need to crash soon.

"I know tomorrow is a day off for all of you, but I'd like to gather everyone here in our yard so I can teach them some basic self-defense. I've already taught you and Donovan these techniques over the years, but I don't know about the others."

That perked her up and she smiled. "That would be great. Baxter and William are worried because they don't know how to fight."

"Good. I'm off all day, so you set it up whenever the group is available."

"Thanks, Dad."

He reached out and took her hand in his, gently caressing her soft fingers with his calloused ones. "Nobody's gonna hurt my girl. Or her friends."

She nodded, but an overwhelming sense of doom still pervaded her thoughts. She fought to overcome them but did not entirely succeed.

Leo felt glum that Sunday afternoon as he sat around his backyard table surrounded by J.C., Laura, and Chet. The only one talking was Laura, but so far, her musings about what items might make good weapons seemed to fall on deaf ears.

Leo had felt a deep sense of loss when Asher departed the night before, even more because Asher seemed at a loss for words and ended up leaving without much of a goodbye. Of course, they'd see each other Monday on set, but Leo had grown comfortable over the past week having Asher, and even the others, staying at his house. He'd always been a loner except for J.C., but the house had never felt empty until last night. Still, he understood that Asher's house in the Valley was closer to the studio than his in La Costa, so it would save on driving time.

He'd noted the expressions on J.C.'s and Chet's faces when they'd arrived a short while before and suspected they felt the same way. Like him, J.C. was an only child and it had been obvious that he really liked Diego. From what Laura implied in the cemetery, maybe more than liked him. Chet's older brother had been a psycho and Chet no doubt enjoyed a regular guy like Robert to chill with at home. Plus, they both loved weightlifting and had been working out in Chet's home gym all week. But they all lived in the Valley, so, just as with Asher, it would be easier to carpool from their homes.

Laura was the most chipper; maybe she was glad Kristen was gone. Leo could understand that sentiment. And, of course, it was Laura who instinctively knew why the others were so glum.

"Look, I get that you miss them," she said when no one would engage her on any other topic. "I could tell you all really connected with them. Me, I'm an only child and I kinda liked having company, especially Cassie. Kristen's too into herself for my taste, but we still had some good talks. But it isn't like we won't see them again. We'll be with them for weeks to come, and you guys can always hang out after the movie wraps."

"If they're still alive," J.C. mumbled. He pulled his hand away from his mouth, looking self-conscious about biting his nails.

He must be really worried about Diego if he's biting his fingernails again, Leo thought, squeezing a sand-filled ball and watching the prominent veins in his forearm bulge each time.

"Asher texted me this morning that he and the others are gonna learn self-defense from Cassie's dad," Leo said, suppressing a smile as he recalled the rest of Asher's text: "You better watch out, Leo. I might be able to kick your butt soon." He'd included a laughing emoji. And then, the best part: "Miss hanging out with you."

"That sounds like a great idea," Chet said. "I could use some of that too. Hey, Leo. Think you could teach us a few moves, like that one you used to take me down last spring?"

Leo looked across at Chet, who was smiling but looking earnest. "Don't see why not. Been trying to teach this fool for years." He lightly punched J.C. on the shoulder.

J.C. grunted. "Yeah, like I been trying to teach you some dance moves."

Leo chuckled.

"It sounds like a great way to spend the afternoon," Laura said eagerly. "I'm in."

Leo agreed, which was how they all ended up in his workout room with him sharing what he'd learned in aikido, like how to deflect a knife attack and how to quickly disable an attacker. Laura and Chet learned fast. J.C. took longer, but he improved, and the afternoon proved to be engaging and fun.

Leo only thought of Asher a few times.

Cassie was impressed by how quickly everyone took to her dad's self-defense training. She and Donovan assisted him because they'd been taught over the years and only needed a quick refresher, which her dad had given before the others arrived.

Robert and Kristen, no strangers to aggression, soaked up the instruction and learned fast. Cassie almost pitied the man who got too fresh with Kristen. Between elbows to the gut, kicks to the shin, and knees to the groin, these basic techniques should serve all of them in a tight situation.

Asher learned fast too, making Cassie suspect he'd been sparring with Leo over the past week. He seemed a bit distracted, as though he couldn't stop thinking about either the reason for this training or… Once again, she considered the possibility that Asher and Leo were becoming more than just friends.

Diego and Robert were the most athletic of this group, so they picked up on the techniques quickly but needed to work on their speed, since both were into weightlifting, which tended to slow them down.

William and Baxter took the longest. Neither was the least bit athletic. Baxter ran out of steam quickly, no doubt due to his excess weight, but by mid-afternoon even he was able to rebound with relative speed. As always, her dad was patient and encouraging.

When they finally took a much-needed lemonade break, her dad said to the group at large, "I'm impressed by how fast you're all learning these techniques. They're simple, yes, but to be effective they must be initiated with lightning speed. You're all doing that."

Kristen preened and bowed.

"Best workout I've had in a while," Robert commented, stretching his arms and legs.

"Me too," Diego agreed. "I need to do this more often."

"It's not something you learn once and forget about," Edward said after a gulp of lemonade. Beads of perspiration lined his forehead. "You need to regularly practice with a partner to maintain your speed."

"We can do that," William said, glancing at a tired but content-looking Baxter. "This stuff makes me feel like a real guy for a change."

"What does that mean?" Donovan asked, lounging in a lawn chair beside Cassie.

Baxter replied, "We only played, like, one season of YMCA soccer when we were little and always got made fun of by other boys for being klutzy. Course, I was fat shamed all the time too."

He fell silent and William addressed the group. "We were into tech stuff, not physical stuff like the other guys, so they said we weren't real boys. But now…it's weird, but using my body like this, my muscles and everything, I just feel, I don't know, more like a guy, I guess."

"When you two are bringing in the huge paychecks for your tech skills," Donovan said, admiration in his voice, "those kids will be hitting you up for a loan."

William swept his hair away from his eyes to offer Donovan a winning smile.

"Well said, Donovan," Edward said, focusing on William and Baxter, who looked more confident than they had when they'd first arrived. "As a kid, I didn't play sports either. Worse yet, I was a dancer."

Baxter's mouth dropped open in shock and William's eyes bugged.

"You never told me that, Dad," Cassie said, exchanging a look with Donovan.

Edward shrugged. "It never came up." Again, he fixed his gaze on

William and Baxter. "Trust me, boys who dance are punked constantly, and I was no exception. By the time I hit puberty, I had a huge growth spurt and most of the comments died away."

"Why did you decide to become a cop?" Robert gazed at Edward, his eyes wide with curiosity.

"Walking to the dance studio, I'd always meet Officer Rick, who patrolled the area on foot," Edward explained, his expression reflecting joy at the memory. "Nicest guy ever and always ready to help anyone, even if it was just to hold open a door or help an elderly person to their car. He'd seen me looking dejected, I guess, and expressed a desire to help. When I first explained the problem, he just shook his head. 'You know, Ed,' he said, 'I thought the physical training at the academy was tough. But my best friend was a ballet dancer, and when I saw what he went through every day, I didn't think so much of my own abilities. I bet you could wipe the floor with most of those sports boys on sheer strength alone.' His words had a huge impact on me, and so did the positive influence he had on the community. I loved dancing, yes, but I realized as I entered my teens that it only served me, and I wanted to serve others the way I'd seen him do. So here I am."

Cassie felt her heart swell with love once more for this man who'd been her everything in life. "How come you never told me this before?"

Edward shrugged. "You never asked."

The others laughed as Edward swigged more lemonade.

Baxter jumped up from his chair. "Let's practice some more."

William stood beside him. "Works for me." He glanced at Robert and Diego, both wearing tank tops that showed off their muscular arms. "I gotta take on these guys."

Diego laughed good-naturedly, while Robert stood with a grin. "You're on, Camera Boy."

Edward set down his lemonade and rose to his feet. "Okay, let's get to it."

Everyone was quiet on the drive to the studio Monday morning, and Leo wondered if it was because they were tired from his self-defense lessons or they were dwelling on what might happen between then and Wednesday.

Only as his Prius approached the studio main gate did his friends come alive.

"This is pretty cool, actually," Laura said, her head out the window gawking at the tall buildings and soundstages visible beyond the gate.

"It really is," Chet commented, also straining to see everything all at once. "I've never been inside a movie studio before, except for the Universal tour."

"I'm sure this place will look the same," J.C. commented in his usual off-hand tone. "Nothing special."

There was a guard gate just ahead and a wooden arm blocking entry into the studio grounds. Leo pulled up to the gate and stopped. An older man with white hair and a white mustache stepped out of the booth and flashed an excited Stan Lee smile at Leo. Leo eyed him a moment before the memory kicked in, and then he grinned with delight.

"Hey, Larkin, I didn't know you were still here."

Larkin, dressed in an official-looking uniform with the studio logo stitched to the left chest, beamed. "If it isn't my old pal, Leo," he blurted, his wide smile revealing yellowed teeth. "When your mom told me you'd be helping with her new film, I was tickled."

"Thanks, Larkin." He hadn't seen this man since the last time he'd set foot on the studio lot when he was six. By then, he knew his mother would never make time for him, so the nanny stopped bringing him. But Larkin always had a little toy for him, something to play with while on set, and Leo was pretty sure he'd saved all those gifts in his old toy chest back home.

"Look at you, all grown up and driving," Larkin went on, still gushing. "I don't have a toy for you today, but I do have these." He stepped back into the booth and emerged with four large ID cards on lanyards, handing them through the window to Leo. "Yours'll gain you access to anyplace on the studio lot, per your mom. Course, you can take your friends along, too, but they can't go anywhere without you."

Leo gazed in shock at the all-access ID card with his photo on it. "My mom did this?"

"You bet," Larkin affirmed with a nod. "She delivered those to me personally, said she was so excited to have you on the lot and wanted you to get a real feel for the business. I can't say as I've ever seen her so chipper."

If Leo hadn't already been sitting, he'd have needed to. His mom came all the way down here to deliver his badge instead of sending one of her assistants? That was unheard of behavior. Maybe she was finally changing after seventeen years of neglect? Or maybe she felt guilty for those comments about Asher.

"Let me know if you need anything, Leo," Larkin added. "How about a map of the studio?"

Leo knew which soundstage the film was using, but a map might come in handy. "Sure, Larkin. That'd be great."

Larkin vanished into the booth again and then popped back out like a jack-in-the-box, folded map in one gnarled hand. Leo took the map and handed it to J.C. beside him.

"Thanks, Larkin. You're the best." As an afterthought, he added, "I still have all those toys you gave me as a kid. They meant a lot."

Another toothy grin greeted his words. "Well bust my buttons. I'm pleased to hear it. I guess we'll be seeing a lot of each other, so I won't make you late. Good to see you, Leo."

"You, too, Larkin." Leo offered a genuine smile of affection as Larkin stepped back to press a button in the booth. The wooden arm rose straight up into the air, and Larkin waved as Leo drove past the booth and into the studio proper.

The enormity of the backlot had wowed Leo as a young boy, and even now he marveled at the massive soundstages spread out before him, the transport vehicles ferrying crew and actors to various sets, the bustling groups of people hurrying here and there. The high activity level somewhat unnerved him because he so hated crowded venues, but after the location filming and all the cast and crew he'd had to deal with, he felt certain he'd be okay. His friends would be there, after all, and that was most important.

J.C. and Laura ogled the sites, with J.C. constantly pointing out someone he thought was an actor he'd seen on TV. Leo had never been star struck, even as a child, so he focused on the road ahead. The map Larkin had given him was marked with an X next to Soundstage 25, their destination, and Leo soon arrived, unsure where to park his Prius. He spotted a few cars parked beside the gigantic rectangular-shaped soundstage that looked like an airplane hangar. He pulled into an empty space that wasn't marked "Producer" or "Director" and they piled out of the car.

The door into the soundstage stood open and a few crew members carrying electrical cables entered.

"This is so cool, Leo," J.C. gushed, gawking at all the surrounding activity with awe.

"It is kind of amazing," Laura echoed, eying her surroundings with keen interest. "I've never been on a backlot before."

Chet tossed off a grin. "This is the real deal, a lot different than Universal."

Leo sighed. He'd so resented these soundstages and backlots as a kid because they were more important to his mother than he was, but now that he was older, he had to admit that moviemaking was kind of cool.

"Let's go in and find the others."

He led them to the open door, and they stepped inside. J.C. gasped and Chet whistled in surprise. Rising before them was a massive warehouse-like interior with lights blazing down from the rafters. But that wasn't what so amazed Leo and his friends. It was the sets that took their breath away.

One set was an exact replica of the basement of the haunted house back in La Costa. Leo shivered as they made their way past and looked inside. Images flashed through his mind of being knifed to the gut and bleeding out. He wasn't looking forward to reliving those moments when it came time to film them.

There was also a bedroom set that looked remarkably like Leo's own, but the art director had chosen different colors for the bedcover and carpet, which he suspected had to do with what would look best on camera. Other sets included an accurate high-tech kitchen, a hospital room, a classroom, and the most amazing of all was an artificial Moreton Bay fig tree that dominated the center of the soundstage, its branches almost touching the catwalks above, its trunk surrounded by fake grass. Leo's mouth hung open as he stared at the tree. The massive branches looked so real that he expected leaves to fall off. Cassie and Donovan approached.

"Pretty real, isn't it?" Donovan said, indicating the tree.

"It's incredible," Laura muttered, shaking her head. "All of this is."

Cassie grinned. "It is cool, isn't it? This is our first time seeing it too."

"Kind of creepy how they made everything look so real," J.C. muttered, glancing over his shoulder at the basement set. "Especially the basement."

"Sometimes the art directors make up their own thing," Donovan said, clearly noting the edge in J.C.'s voice, "but I guess this time they liked the real location too much. Come on over and I'll show you where we're rehearsing the first scene."

Cassie and Donovan led Leo and the others down a realistic-looking street toward the Moreton Bay tree replica. Leo noticed a large fishing net draped across the upper branches with two crew members making last-minute adjustments. Below the thick, shading branches were the four main actors rehearsing a recreation of an event that would haunt Leo for the rest of his life. But his body tingled with warmth at the sight of Asher chatting with Mr. K, and that moment of joy drove away the dark thoughts.

Asher briefly caught his eye and smiled before the rehearsal resumed. Leo squirmed and eyed J.C., whose gaze was riveted to Diego pointing a handgun at Asher and freaking out because Asher refused to let him shoot Robert. The scene played out almost exactly as it had in real life, and Leo regretted providing so many details to the writers. He felt queasy as he watched the actors reenact that moment, and finally had enough. Ducking around the Moreton Bay tree, he dropped back against the solid, realistic-feeling trunk and closed his eyes, wishing he could close his ears too.

"Leo?"

Leo opened his eyes to find J.C. standing before him, a look of horror on his face. "I guess I thought I knew how it felt for you, but watching it now, I know I didn't. I'm so sorry."

Leo offered a wan smile, placing one hand on his friend's shoulder. "I accepted your apology a long time ago. What say we go grab something to drink. Skip this scene."

J.C. grinned with relief. "I thought you'd never ask."

Leo led the way away from the tree back toward a corner of the soundstage, away from all the sets, where craft services had set up long tables laden with snacks and cold drinks. He snatched up a bottle of water, twisted off the cap, and chugged it in three gulps, while J.C. snagged a Coke and swigged it.

CHAPTER FOURTEEN

LET'S SCOPE OUT THE CREW

LEO AND J.C. FOUND THEMSELVES drawn back to the basement set. J.C. kept glancing at the hole in the ceiling, no doubt recalling the night he almost died. Leo stared at the spot where he'd collapsed to the hard floor, bleeding profusely. The longer he stared, the more he felt he could perhaps file that terrifying moment away in some dark corner of his brain, where it would not rise to the surface anymore.

Maybe this movie will be good for me after all, he thought.

"Hello Leo and Leo's friend."

Leo turned to find Tank standing behind him.

The burly stunt coordinator gazed into the empty basement set. "This is pretty much the only stunt, the actors falling through the hole, but we gotta get it right. The distance from hole to floor is identical to the real place, did you notice?"

Leo nodded. "Yeah."

J.C. faced Tank. "You sure Diego's gonna be okay?"

"Not to worry, son," Tank replied, rubbing his bald head absently. "After that mishap on location, I'll triple check the rigging here. No one's getting hurt on my watch."

Leo thought about Asher climbing down that rope. "I taught Asher how to rope climb at my house, so he should be fine."

J.C. eyed him. "Yeah, but he's gotta fall partway too, remember?"

"No worries, boys," Tank insisted. "I'll be right there, and he'll fall on a nice cushy mat."

"Good." Leo smiled.

"So, I heard you're thinking of producing films one day?"

Leo didn't make eye contact, of course, but he tried to focus on Tank's lower face. "Oh, maybe. Depends on if I can control my social anxiety."

"Leo, it's been my experience we can learn to control anything if we want to," Tank replied. "Take me, for instance. Did you know I used to be afraid of heights?"

J.C. gasped and Leo's mouth dropped open.

"Seriously?" Leo exclaimed. "How'd you get over it?"

Tank grinned. "I wanted to be a stuntman more than I was afraid of heights."

He slapped Leo on one shoulder and then headed toward the Moreton Bay Tree set.

J.C. shrugged. "You heard the man, Leo. If you wanna produce movies, you'll stop being shy. Piece of cake."

"Easy for him to say. Let's scope out the crew for that tattoo."

J.C. nodded and they began wandering from set to set. They found they didn't mind missing the filming. This was the first time they'd hung out, just the two of them, in weeks. Enjoying each other's company prevailed over finding any crew member with a Chucky tattoo on his wrist. When the cast and crew broke for lunch, they searched for Laura and Chet before heading over to the commissary.

On their way, they ran into Cassie and Donovan chatting with Edward and Marisol. Nudging J.C., Leo headed in their direction, reminding himself to not give away that he already knew them. Cassie, he noted, was doing a fantastic acting job filling in the "newcomers" on details about the shoot. Leo would never have known Edward was her dad.

"Hey, Leo, J.C., come meet our newest crew members," Donovan said as he spotted them.

Leo waved J.C. over, happy that he had never met the two detectives. He did, however, know they were plants, and Leo hoped he wouldn't give anything away.

"Leo, J.C., this is Edward and Marisol, our newest production assistants," Donovan said with a smile.

Edward stuck out his hand and Leo shook. "Pleased to meet you, Leo. And you, J.C."

Marisol did the same, neither giving the slightest hint they'd already met Leo.

"I was catching them up to speed on the film shoot," Cassie said cheerfully, then turned to the two adults. "Leo and J.C. are consultants because this film is based on their own experiences last spring with a serial killer."

Edward's eyebrows shot up in surprise. "Do tell. I can't imagine what that was like."

"Me neither," Marisol chimed in, looking shocked. "It's so good of you to relive those memories to help make the film even more realistic."

Leo glanced down. "Well, my mom is the producer and she has a way of getting what she wants."

Edward nodded. "My father was like that. But I'm grateful to your mother for giving us this job, so I can't complain."

"I feel the same way," Marisol added with a smile.

"We're all headed to lunch, Leo," Donovan said with a smile. "You two wanna join us?"

Leo glanced at J.C., who shrugged, and answered, "Sure."

They grabbed their food and found an empty table where crew members ate. Leo noted it was as far as possible from occupied tables, and he figured they wanted to talk quietly. He was right. After chatting about the film, Cassie leaned in close to Edward.

"Have you seen anyone sketchy?"

"No one wearing a short-sleeve shirt has that tattoo."

"I agree," Leo put in, glancing around to make sure no one was approaching. "J.C. and I have been looking for hours."

Marisol leaned in closer on the pretext of grabbing the saltshaker. "We can only hope Cassandra's idea for tomorrow pays off."

"Speak of the devil," Leo mumbled, nodding his head toward the entrance to the food area.

Cassandra Cantrell, heavily made-up and dressed in modest but attractive stylings, stood near the entrance, ringing a bell in her hand. The chattering among the assembled crew quieted down and everyone looked in her direction.

"Good afternoon, my wonderful crew," she began, casting her wide smile around the room. "I want to thank you for making this shoot one of my smoothest, and for not going overtime."

She laughed and Leo cringed, hiding his face in his hands. There was scattered laughter among the crew.

"I thought it might be fun for all of you to wear a favorite tee shirt tomorrow," she went on, still smiling. "Nothing political or offensive, of course, but something you love. A favorite sports team, your favorite anime or superhero, even a favorite movie. Extra points will be given if the movie is one of mine."

She tossed off that artificial laugh Leo had always hated, and he sank farther down into his chair. He knew she was doing this to help his friends, but did she have to sound so arch about the whole thing?

"Just kidding," she added with a wave of her arms. "My goal is for each of you to show something that's you, that *you* love. Many of us have worked together in the past, but others are new, and something like this is a quick, easy way to reveal important information about ourselves."

Tank raised his hand.

"Yes, Tank?"

"Can I wear a picture of a tank?"

The stuntmen at his table laughed.

So did Leo's mom. "I can't think of anything better, unless the tank is jumping off a building onto a thick mattress."

This time, many of the crew laughed and Tank raised his soda to her with a grin.

"I look forward to wandering around tomorrow and checking out all your shirts," Cassandra added. "Enjoy your lunch."

Everyone applauded, some enthusiastically, others with a few pats of their hands. Leo looked up and saw his mother heading in his direction.

Please don't embarrass me, Mom!

"Everyone enjoying their lunch?" She stood where she could look at Leo but addressed the entire table.

"Yes, Ms. Cantrell," Donovan said. "The food's delicious."

"I'm glad you like it…"

"Donovan," he replied, looking slightly embarrassed.

"Of course, Donovan. Your cameo films tomorrow, by the way."

"I remember," Donovan said. "I'm ready."

"Excellent." She eyed Edward and Marisol. "I trust you're both finding your sea legs, as the saying goes?"

"Absolutely," Marisol answered. "Everyone has been helpful in getting us up to speed."

Cassandra smiled. "Wonderful." Then her gaze fell on Leo, who refused to look at her. "Have you used that all-access pass I left for you, Leonardo?"

He looked up, but not all the way. If he met her eyes, what might he see? "No, Mom, I, uh, I've just been here today. But thank you for the pass. I'm looking forward to exploring."

"Be mindful of filming, dear."

He nodded. "'Course."

"I'll see you all later." She sauntered off to another table.

When she was out of earshot, Donovan leaned toward Leo. "She's intense."

"Tell me about it."

J.C. passed Leo his fries and Leo stuffed several into his mouth.

Edward leaned across the table. "Let's not lose our focus. Eyes and ears open at all times."

Leo and J.C. exchanged a knowing look and nodded.

After lunch, J.C. wandered off to find Diego before filming resumed, and Leo found himself wandering alone, thinking about the fate of his new friends and whether he'd be able to help them. Staring into the basement set, he felt awash in memories of that stressful time barely four months before.

"Hey, Leo, I've been looking everywhere for you."

Startled from his reverie, Leo spun around to find a smiling Asher standing behind him. Just seeing the other boy's cheerful demeanor pumped up his mood.

"Hey, Asher, how's it going?"

"Great. This scene is powerful, and I think it's gonna look awesome. How come you haven't been watching?"

Despite feeling comfortable with Asher, Leo glanced down. "I, uh… That scene is hard for me to watch. It's weird seeing it play out, how I must've looked at the time. You're an amazing actor, by the way. But I just couldn't watch."

Asher's face fell. "I'm sorry, Leo, I never even thought about that. I like having you there, but I can only imagine what it felt like in real life."

Leo nodded. "Did you finish that scene?

"No, we're back to it in a few. Don't worry about watching. I'll catch up with you later and we can hang out."

"Thanks for understanding." Leo offered a smile and Asher returned it.

"Well, I gotta get to the set." He looked reluctant to leave, and Leo didn't want him to. "See you, Leo."

Asher turned and hurried away, leaving Leo with an empty feeling that was quickly dispelled by the arrival of J.C., Laura, and Chet.

"You split earlier, Leo," Laura said, "but J.C. told me why, and I get it."

"Thanks." He eyed them both, pointing at his wrist. "Any success?"

Chet shook his head, leaning closer so passing crew members wouldn't overhear. "If someone here has that tattoo, it's covered."

"I counted ten male crew wearing long-sleeve shirts," Laura reported. "What about you guys?" She glanced from J.C. to Leo.

"I wasn't looking for that," J.C. said sheepishly. "Sorry."

"I noticed at least twenty," Leo said. "It is kind of chilly in this soundstage, so I wonder if all the crew will wear a tee like my mom asked."

"We won't know that till tomorrow," Laura said, looking around at passing crew members. "What's the next scene after the park?"

Leo pulled the shooting schedule from his pocket and studied it. "Classroom scenes come next at four."

"I'm not sure I can watch those," J.C. said with a grimace.

"Why not?" Chet asked.

"Reminds me that school starts next week."

Chet groaned. "Oh God, I forgot!"

Laura patted him on the back. "Don't worry, Chet, we got your back."

"Let's keep our ears open," Leo said, glancing around warily. "We don't know if there's more than one killer in on this, so we might hear people whispering something important."

"Good idea," Laura agreed. "You and J.C. hang around the other sets until the park scene is done. Chet and I'll keep our ears open over there."

"Do we have to go back?" Chet's face reeked of humiliation. "I hate watching Asher throw Robert around like he's nothing." He eyed Leo and broke into a grin. "But long as Leo doesn't take me down again, I guess I'll survive."

Leo returned the grin, and the two duos went their separate ways.

Leo and J.C. heard nothing suspicious, and before they knew it, they were hovering around the classroom set watching those scenes unfold. Other than the room reminding them of the impending start of real school, there were no painful reminders because nothing particularly bad occurred in the classroom.

He and J.C. stood just outside the set, watching several scenes being shot that would be scattered throughout the film. Stuart entered and delivered coffees to Mr. K and some of the crew, then stopped beside Leo.

"How's it going, Leo? I haven't seen much of you today."

"J.C. and I were just wandering around before, checking out all the sets. They're really realistic."

"Too realistic," J.C. mumbled, scowling into the classroom.

Stuart grinned. "Yeah, set designers are artists, that's for sure. Anything I can get for you guys?"

Leo glanced at J.C., who shook his head. "We're good, Stuart. Thanks for asking."

Stuart smiled again and drifted away. Leo noticed him stop to chat with Diana, the hair and makeup lady, who happened to glance up and catch Leo's eye. She smiled and waved him over. Inwardly groaning, he knew it was about their deal to photograph him, and as he strolled over to her, he regretted agreeing.

Stuart wandered away and Leo stopped beside the portable makeup vanity. Diana's pleasant round face studied his from beneath her dark hair and long eyelashes.

"How are you, Leonardo?"

"I'm fine, and Leo is good."

"Sorry. I've worked with your mother too long. What do you think of the actors portraying you and your friends?"

Leo found his gaze instantly drawn to Asher, sitting at a desk next to Diego, watching Chet and the two actors playing his friends strut around the room. "I think he's amazing." Catching himself, he quickly added, "I mean, they're all amazing."

Embarrassed, he turned back to her.

"You like him, don't you?"

Leo squirmed with discomfort. "What do you mean?"

She smiled in a motherly way—at least, that's how Leo interpreted her look. He wasn't used to motherly expressions of affection. "He's not only beautiful, he's very sweet. Much like you, seems to me."

Leo's tongue refused to move, and he just stood there, wishing he could disappear.

"When would you like to have our photo shoot? I suspect Asher might like to keep one of them." Her smile never wavered, and it wasn't baiting or coy. She sounded genuine.

Leo pictured the photo he'd gotten of Asher and thought it might be nice to return the favor. But would Asher really want a photo of him? There's no way his photos could anywhere match those of Asher.

"Trust me, you're every bit as photogenic, Leo, and I'm going to prove it to you. How about toward the end of the shoot?"

"I'll be back in school then."

"You'll be here on weekends, won't you?"

"Yeah."

"That's perfect then."

"Thanks, Diana. You're awesome. No wonder my mom always hires you."

She laughed. "I'm good with hair and makeup too."

Leo laughed and returned to J.C.'s side.

"What was that all about?"

Leo shrugged. "Just talking."

J.C. eyed him intensely, then watched the scene unfold.

Is it my imagination, Leo thought, watching J.C., *or is he only focused on Diego?*

He watched J.C. watch Diego and realized he wasn't imagining it. Could both of them be suddenly attracted to males? Considering neither had ever shown interest in other boys before, Leo didn't understand what was happening.

Could Laura be right? Had he hidden from the world for so long that he'd hidden from himself too? Had J.C. done the same?

He studied the actors in the scene, which was a classroom filled with numerous young extras in addition to the main cast. All the guys were handsome and well-built, especially Diego. And Kristen was drop-dead gorgeous, as were most of the female extras. But as he stared at them, he didn't feel turned on, and his heart rate remained stable. It only accelerated when he focused on Asher. He felt a surge of connectedness even stronger than his bond with J.C. The sensation was disquieting, so he did what he always did with disquieting feelings: quashed them. They had a massacre to prevent, after all.

Everything else could sort itself out later.

CHAPTER FIFTEEN

WHAT DO YOU WANT TO CHECK OUT?

CASSIE AND HER DAD SAT at the kitchen table relaxing after another long day. Edward swigged from a can of beer, while Cassie sipped lemonade. Cassie wasn't so much tired as anxious and disheartened. There remained only one day until Wednesday. Every time that reality entered her mind, she flashed back to what Leo had seen in his vision.

"I'll protect you, Cass," her dad said, reading her mind like always. "If we don't spot the perp tomorrow, you and the others will go into hiding. On Thursday, Leo promised to check you all out again to see if the killer changed his plans."

Cassie offered a pallid smile. "I know. It's just, who would want to kill us? We're a bunch of film nerds. We never hurt anyone."

Edward set down his beer and leaned forward in his chair, planting both arms on the table. "Most killers are deranged in some way, so you don't have to have done anything. Why you're being targeted, well, we won't know that until we catch the guy."

She nodded, trying to think of something else to talk about. "On a positive note, I think Asher and Leo like each other."

"You mean like boyfriends?"

She sipped her lemonade. "Seems that way. Kristen thinks so too."

"Now don't go playing matchmaker, honey."

"I'm not. It's just something we noticed."

Edward took another gulp. "Well, Leo's a great kid and so's Asher.

They'll be good for each other if it works out. Donovan with his mom tonight?"

Cassie nodded. "Yeah. She's afraid for him, obviously, and wants him near her."

"Makes sense. But Marisol and I assured her Donovan will be safe too. Course, that doesn't stop a parent from worrying."

He reached across the table and took Cassie's hand in his, squeezing gently.

Leo stood in his dimly lit high-tech kitchen, swigging from a bottle of water. He wore workout shorts and no shirt, glancing at the digital clock on the stove. One thirty a.m. He'd be tired on set that day, but he just couldn't sleep. He kept thinking of Asher and the others and the threat to their lives only one day away, wishing there was something else he could do to keep them safe.

Leo tossed the empty bottle into his recycle bin and turned to switch off the light. He froze at the sight of his mother, still in the same pantsuit she'd been wearing on set, staring at him from the open door.

"Mom. You startled me." He noticed her clothes. "You never went to sleep?"

She entered and crossed to the fridge, taking out some iced tea and pouring herself a glass. "Prep work for my next film."

"Seriously? You're not finished with this one."

She drank her tea and offered a smile. "Such is the life of a producer, Leonardo. It's always about the next project. Keep that in mind if you decide to follow in my footsteps."

He nodded, considering if he could ever do such a job.

"Couldn't sleep?"

"No."

"Thinking about Asher?"

He looked up in surprise, wondering how she seemed to know him so well when she hadn't spent more than a few hours with him over his entire seventeen years.

"Yeah, and the others. Tomorrow is Wednesday." He hoped that would cover for the red in his face at the mention of Asher's name.

She accepted his answer. "Curious, isn't it?"

"What?"

She studied him in a way that made him squirm. "That you're in the center of this impending attack on your friends just like you were with J.C. last March."

Leo froze. Could she know about his power? No way. But she was suspicious, that's for sure. His mother might be many things, but stupid wasn't one of them.

"Weird coincidence, I guess." He focused on the floor, awaiting her response.

"I always wondered how you happened to be in the old house with J.C. and the others. You kids never go there except on Halloween. Anything you'd like to tell me, Leonardo?"

"About what?"

"About you. Even before that incident in March, you seemed different. I recall you were anxious to talk to me about something and I put you off. Perhaps we should have that talk now."

He glanced up at her lower face. What he could see of her facial expression indicated genuine interest. Should he tell her? Would that bring them closer together or push them further apart? She wouldn't let this go; he knew her too well, so he decided to lie.

"It's not important now. I just…I guess I was just feeling like I might be, you know, into boys, not girls." He hated feeding that idea of hers, but it was the first thing he could think of to distract her. And it worked.

"Is that all?" She sounded relieved. "J.C.?"

He shook his head. "No. I just started noticing guys at school a lot and it scared me." He focused on the floor once more, hoping his voice sounded honest.

"It shouldn't. Many of my colleagues in the industry have gay children. In fact, I've already been told by several people on set that you and Asher make a lovely couple."

Now he raised his head. "We're not…we're just friends, Mom."

She smiled knowingly. "I've made enough rom-coms to know the signs, Leonardo. Friends now, lovers later. He seems like a nice young man, and he looks gorgeous on screen. I predict more girls will see this picture than boys just because of him. Of course, if you'd played yourself in the movie, the number of female viewers would triple."

His eyes bulged with shock. "You really think so?"

She chuckled. "Leonardo, when do I ever say something I don't mean?"

"Never."

"Exactly. Now, get some sleep. The two detectives will hide your friends in some secret location on Wednesday and we'll film around them as best we can. Hopefully, the information they obtained about these murders turns out to be false." She paused and stared at him long and hard. "Perhaps you can be of help with that on Thursday."

He gasped. She knew! She knew he had something to do with the foreknowledge!

"I don't see how." He turned to leave, then faced her once again, making eye contact with as much of her face as he could. "Thanks for the talk, Mom."

"You're welcome."

He fled the kitchen before she could say more.

Leo marveled at the variety of tee shirts sported by the film crew, but no one he saw displayed the Chucky tattoo on their wrist. There were sports jerseys, college tees, groups of crew members "battling it out" in Marvel vs. DC, not to mention Star Trek vs. Star Wars, and a wide assortment of anime shirts, *Dragonball Z* and *One Piece* taking top honors there. The crew was in high spirits and enjoyed their work more than usual, but not seeing the tattoo was disheartening. J.C., Laura, and Chet had split up and wandered from set to set, all coming up empty.

The school scenes were completed that morning, and after lunch Leo stood watching the four actors meet in the kitchen set to discuss how they might unearth the would-be killer in the movie. Asher flashed him a warm smile every chance he got, which both pleased and unnerved him, but if he told himself the truth, mostly pleased him. Still, the impending nature of the next day loomed ever closer, and Leo stressed over what to do.

It was getting on toward late afternoon when he thought back on what he'd seen in his visions, focusing on location details. The word "location" rattled around in his brain and suddenly, he had a thought he'd not yet considered. He waved over J.C. and said, "Listen, I'm going to use that pass my mom gave me to explore the backlot."

J.C.'s face lit up. "I'll go with you."

Leo shook his head. "I just want to check something out, but I don't want anyone to realize I'm gone, so if they ask, just say I'm checking out the crew somewhere else."

J.C. looked confused. "What do you want to check out?"

"Just a hunch. I'll text you. Cover for me, 'kay?"

"Sure."

Leo made certain no one was looking his way before slinking off, leaving a puzzled J.C. behind.

Because it had been her idea about the tee shirts, Leo's mom spent more time than usual wandering among the crew, complimenting them on their choices and, Leo decided as he found her near the basement set, looking for that tattoo like they all were. He did notice that she'd ditched her typical clothing choices to sport a tee shirt of her own, a crew shirt from one of her rom-coms.

"Leonardo, how are things going with the school scenes?"

"Smooth as always. Mom, are there any other horror films shooting on the backlot besides ours?"

She pulled an insulted face. "My film is a thriller, not horror, and I wouldn't know about other shoots."

"Who would?"

She eyed him with curiosity. "Larkin at the main gate knows every shoot. Why do you need to know?"

Leo realized that he was making his mother even more suspicious than she'd been during the night, but it couldn't be helped.

"Just curious. Cool shirt, by the way."

He hurried away before she could ask anything more.

It took him longer than he expected to reach the main gate on foot, and with the warm summer sun, he was sweating profusely by the time he arrived. He also noticed that it was already six o'clock, despite the sun high in the sky.

"Hey, Larkin."

Larkin beamed when Leo approached but frowned when he saw the perspiration. "Unless you're trying to lose weight, Leo, which you don't need, next time flag down any studio employee in a cart. They'll take you wherever you want to go. Just flash your badge."

Leo stopped at the booth, his mouth open in surprise. "Seriously?"

"Of course. That badge is all-access. I thought I told you that."

Leo smiled. "You did. I just didn't know it got me free rides."

Larkin chuckled, his laugh lines gathering with glee. "So, what can I do for ya?"

"My mom said you'd know if there are any horror movies being filmed on the backlot."

"Besides hers, you mean?"

"Don't let her hear you say that. She calls it a 'thriller'." His hands formed air quotes on the word "thriller."

Larkin laughed. "I hear you. Let me check my master schedule."

He stepped back into his booth and Leo leaned in while Larkin grabbed a clipboard and flipped through papers.

"Looks like…seven movies; I'd call these horror, anyway."

Leo's heart leaped with hope. "Can you tell me which soundstages?"

"I can do better than that. I'll circle 'em on a map for you."

"Thanks, Larkin, that's perfect."

Larkin grabbed one of the studio maps and a pen, looking from clipboard to map as he made seven circles. Setting down the clipboard, he handed Leo the map. "I also circled the main gate here, so you have a point of reference."

Leo studied the map. Some of the circled soundstages were near his location, but others were way out on the fringes. He decided to start far out and work his way back in.

"Thanks, Larkin, you're the best, as always."

"My pleasure, Leo."

Leo started off walking.

"Uh, Leo?"

Leo turned around.

"If you're planning on visiting those shoots, you'll need a ride."

Leo silently cursed his stupidity. "You're right. So how do I find one?"

Larkin stepped all the way out of the booth and stood inside the barrier arm. "Like this." A young man in a golf cart-type vehicle was racing past. "Yo, Pierre!"

The young man named Pierre swung the cart into a U-turn and stopped in front of Larkin.

"Pierre, this here is Leo Cantrell, Cassandra Cantrell's boy. Show him your pass, Leo."

Leo held up his all-access pass and Pierre whistled in surprise.

"Leo wants to visit some of the soundstages. You got time to take him?"

Pierre glanced at his shiny Apple watch. "I can take him to a few. Hop in, Leo."

Leo grinned at Larkin and clambered up beside Pierre. "Thanks, Pierre."

"No problem," the young man replied. "Later, Larkin."

He glanced at where Leo pointed on the map and sped off in that direction.

"An all-access pass," Pierre said with another whistle. "Don't see that often, especially for a kid like you. Course your mother is a hotshot around here."

Leo studied Pierre's face. He didn't look much older than himself, with dark wavy hair and soft features. He wore a short-sleeve shirt with the studio logo stitched to the front.

"So, what's your job here?"

"Just what I'm doing. I run people and props from one soundstage to another."

"Do you like it?"

"Yeah. Gives me the chance to meet guys like you." Pierre glanced over and smiled.

Leo returned the smile, but Pierre kept his eyes on him longer than Leo would've expected before returning them to the road ahead.

"How old are you?"

"Seventeen," Leo replied, wondering if Pierre was interested in him. He had no idea what the signs might be, but he felt nothing toward the young man at all. "How about you?"

"Nineteen," Pierre replied, turning sharply to the left and passing more activity outside several soundstages. "I got an uncle who works here. He got me the job."

"Cool." Leo looked ahead, watching the action as he passed. Despite it being late in the day, there was still much activity.

"How long you planning to visit this soundstage?" Pierre asked, swinging into a right turn. The path ahead opened out with gardens and fake forests interspersed between the soundstages.

"Not long. I just wanna take a quick look at the sets."

"Planning on being a set designer?"

"No way. I draw okay, but nowhere near what these artists can do. I just wanna see how they look."

"If you're not too long at each one, I can probably hang with you awhile." He offered another smile, and Leo was almost positive it displayed interest.

Leo looked away, gazing ahead. "That'd be great. Thanks."

The golf cart lurched to a stop in front of a soundstage situated beside one of the fake forests. Crew members poured in and out, setting up lights in the forest and carrying other equipment. Leo jumped to the ground.

"Be right back."

"I'll be here," Pierre said, putting the cart into park.

Leo jogged up to the soundstage and stepped inside. A female crew member approached with suspicion.

"You can't be here, kid." Leo held up his all-access pass and she looked surprised. "I guess you can be. Anything I can help you with?"

"No thanks. Just taking a quick look at the sets in here."

"Be my guest. Just don't touch anything."

"I won't."

As he wandered farther into the interior, he heard her mumble, "Give anyone a pass these days."

He ignored the comment and stopped in the center of the soundstage, looking around at the various sets. Before him rose a large, creepy three-story house façade, replete with broken shutters and shattered windows. The weather-beaten front door stood ajar, and Leo shivered. It reminded him of the haunted house back in La Costa.

He turned to survey the other sets. There was a graveyard off to his left, so he hurried in that direction. Members of the art department were putting finishing touches on the headstones and some moss-covered trees. They didn't give Leo a look. He studied the trees and wandered among the headstones. No, they weren't the same. And the house wasn't the same.

This wasn't what he saw in his vision.

He hurried from the graveyard and back outside. Pierre sat in his cart as though he'd wait all day. He lit up when Leo approached.

"So, how was it?"

Leo clambered in. "Not bad. Can we go here next?"

He pointed to the soundstage closest to where they were, and Pierre nodded.

"Wherever you like." He grinned and started the cart.

Since Leo had little understanding of people on a social level, he didn't know if Pierre was like this with everyone or just him. So, he smiled in return and bent to study his map as the cart zoomed off.

Just as they arrived at the second soundstage Larkin had circled, the walkie talkie attached to the dashboard squawked. Pierre snatched it up and pressed the talk button.

"Yeah?"

"You were supposed to be over at Soundstage 2 five minutes ago," came over the walkie in a disgruntled tone.

Pierre glanced guiltily at Leo. "Yeah, sorry, I got sidetracked. Be right there."

He clicked the off button and reattached the walkie to its spot near the large steering wheel.

"Sorry, Leo, I'd rather hang with you, but duty calls."

"No worries, Pierre."

Leo stuck out his hand and Pierre took it.

Pierre said, "Just flag down any of us and we'll drive you."

"Thanks." Leo jumped out of the cart.

"Later." Pierre threw him a broad smile before racing off in the direction they'd come from, back toward the main gate.

Leo eyed the imposing soundstage building. There was no activity and he worried that filming had ended for the day. He shoved the map into his pants pocket and hurried to the door, which stood ajar. Just as he reached out to pull it farther open, the door pushed toward him from inside and a man stepped out.

Surprised, the man exclaimed, "Oh, you startled me!"

"Sorry."

The man was tall and thin, dressed in work clothes with a key-filled chain attached to his belt. "Can I help you?" His gray hair glowed in the setting sun. Leo held up his pass and the older man nodded in approval. "Don't see many of those."

"I was wondering if I could take a quick look at the set inside."

The man frowned. "I was just locking up, son. Filming doesn't start till day after tomorrow, so the set's closed."

Leo felt an odd sensation grip him. "Please? It's really important, and I'll just be a few minutes."

The man hesitated, eyeing Leo's badge once more. "Well, you must be somebody to have that badge. Tell you what, I've gotta get to another location. The door here locks from the inside, so take your looksee and then close it when you leave. Make sure it's locked."

Leo grinned. "Thank you so much, sir. I won't touch a thing, I promise."

"That'd be smart. Have a good one, son."

He waited till Leo took hold of the door before jogging to an empty golf cart, speeding off in the same direction as Pierre.

Leo stepped inside. The interior was dark, so he activated his phone light to locate the power switches. Finding one not far from the door, he flicked it up. Dim fluorescents eased their way to life, not enough light to film by, but enough so he wouldn't trip over anything as he wandered around.

Leo kept his eyes downcast, worried he might fall over something anyway as there were piles of light cables and numerous props, like fake tombstones, tossed to each side of the narrow walkway. He passed the refreshments table, scattered with chip bags and a few water bottles, and then the path opened out and he found himself on what looked like a circular driveway. He followed it around and stopped short in front of a two-story house façade.

Leo gasped, the sound echoing around the soundstage as his body turned to ice. His eyes were riveted to the white wooden balcony extending along the second floor. His mind raced with quick flashes of memory: a body lying in a pool of blood in the driveway below the balcony, a struggle happening on the balcony itself, a quick glimpse of Diego's terrified face as he was pushed over the railing.

Leo looked away, his breathing ragged. This had to be the place! Still, he needed to be sure. He remembered what happened to Asher in that graveyard, so he left the driveway and hurried across the soundstage floor. He lurched to a stop when a second house came into view, and then spun to his right. There it was—the graveyard!

He sped up and entered through the waist-high wrought-iron gate onto real grass. Scattered all around him were gravestones of varying sizes. Leo edged forward, memories slamming into his fevered brain, memories he wanted to forget. He stopped to gaze at a gnarled tree and froze. It was the same one, the one Kristen was hanging from! He took three steps forward and paused next to a chipped and pitted old headstone.

A vision slammed through his mind of Asher, throat slit and spouting blood, slumped against the front of this gravestone. He had to be sure. He'd seen the letters "yers" peeking out from behind Asher's head. What was the rest of the name? He took a deep breath and stepped around the headstone, staring in horror: "Judith Myers."

This was the place! *They must be making some kind of tribute to famous horror films*, he decided, looking around. A gravestone off to one side read "Lawrence Talbot." He remembered that one too!

Filled with resolve, Leo opened messages to text J.C., turning to head back toward the front door.

An enormous man suddenly loomed out of the shadows before him, startling him into momentary shock and knocking the phone from his grasp. Before Leo could make a move, one meaty hand grabbed his throat and the other clamped a damp rag over his mouth.

Leo's nostrils were assaulted by a sickly medicine-like smell, and his head swam with dizziness. His vision went in and out of focus, but one image on the man's wrist slammed into his foggy brain: a brightly colored tattoo of Chucky!

Leo struggled, but it was no use. His vision faded and his mind dulled. Then blackness overtook him.

CHAPTER SIXTEEN

THEY'RE GONE!

FILMING HAD MOSTLY WRAPPED FOR the day, but Cassie wasn't tired. True, she'd been drinking lots of Diet Coke, but mostly her anxiety about the following day kept her body coiled like a spring. As always, Donovan sensed her mood.

"You okay, Cass?"

She glanced around to make sure no one was nearby. "Thinking about tomorrow."

"Me too. But at least we'll all be together." He tried for an upbeat tone. "Pop'll keep us safe."

"I know."

Both reacted at the same moment as a text hit their phones. Pulling them out, they opened their messages.

"It's from J.C. to the text group," Donovan said, suddenly concerned.

Cassie opened the message and read it aloud. "Leo's missing. Something's wrong. Meet over by the snacks table ASAP."

Cassie and Donovan exchanged a worried look.

"That can't be good," Donovan said somberly, slipping his phone back into his pocket. "Let's go."

Most of the crew had already left for the night, so no one paid much attention as Cassie and Donovan hurried to the secluded corner that housed the snacks and refreshment tables. J.C. paced in front of Laura, Chet, Robert, Diego, Kristen, Jaden, William, and Baxter. Asher stood off by himself staring at his phone anxiously. All the actors still wore their character clothes.

Cassie stepped in front of J.C., forcing him to stop pacing. "What happened to Leo?"

J.C.'s face was wrought with fear. "I don't know. He said he wanted to check something out and he'd text me. That was, like, hours ago, Cassie!"

Donovan joined the silent group. "Have any of you heard from him?"

"No," Kristen said, looking genuinely concerned. "We all texted him. Nothing."

Donovan hurried past her to Asher. "Asher?"

Asher's face was carved with fear. "Nothing. Do you think the killer got him?"

Donovan froze and turned to Cassie.

She eyed them with uncertainty. "How would the killer know what Leo did?"

"Maybe he overheard us all talking," Diego suggested, his body looking taut with worry.

"How?" Robert asked. "We've been real careful."

Jaden cleared his throat. "I, uh, I always heard stuff back at school I wasn't supposed to hear. People don't see you when you're invisible."

"The guy could've been hiding behind a flat or something," William said, eyeing Baxter.

"Yeah," Baxter mumbled.

J.C. said, "Cassie, call your dad. We need him."

She nodded and pulled out her phone.

Just then, Stuart rounded the corner and saw them all gathered. He stopped in surprise. "Wow, nobody ready to go home?"

"We're just chilling," Chet said when no one else spoke.

"That's cool," Stuart said, flashing a smile. "I've gotta clean up this stuff." He indicated the snacks and drinks on two long folding tables. "Anybody want anything before I do?"

They shook their heads, but no one answered.

Stuart gazed at them curiously. "You all don't seem too happy. Me, I think this shoot is going great. From what I can see, the movie's got the makings of a big hit."

No one spoke for a moment, then Cassie said, "We hope so. The actors are amazing." She forced a smile in the direction of the actors.

Only Kristen smiled back. "Thanks, Cassie. We have a good crew too. Including you, Stuart. You're the best."

Stuart grinned, looking genuinely pleased. He indicated a large drink dispenser labeled *Fresh Lemonade. Help yourself.* "This lemonade is awesome. I had some earlier. Let's toast to a huge opening weekend before I have to throw it out."

He set about dispensing lemonade into paper cups while Cassie and the others exchanged impatient looks. J.C. opened his mouth to say something, but Cassie shook her head. She needed to contact her dad, but not in front of Stuart, since her dad was supposedly just another PA, but the fastest way to get rid of Stuart was to drink the lemonade and then contact her dad and Marisol.

In moments, Stuart was handing out the cups to the reluctant group, but no one spoke, having caught Cassie's admonition to J.C. Stuart raised his own cup to the group. "Here's to the best crew and most excellent actors I ever worked with."

The others raised their cups, and everyone drained them, including Stuart.

"You were right, Stuart, this is delicious," Cassie exclaimed in surprise. It was honestly the best she'd ever tasted.

"It really is," Donovan echoed.

Stuart grinned again. "Oh, here, throw your cups away." He snatched up a plastic bag and walked among them, collecting their cups. Tossing the bag aside, he added, "Well, I better get all this stuff cleaned up." He turned to the table, and Cassie was about to wave the others away when Stuart turned back. "Where's Leo? I just realized he's not here." He eyed Asher directly.

"He's around somewhere," Asher said, his voice surprisingly calm.

"Tell him I said hi." Stuart started to turn, but then William placed a hand to his head.

"What's wrong, William?" Cassie moved closer as William swooned. She and Donovan grabbed him under the arms.

"I feel weird all of a sudden," William muttered.

"Me too," Baxter said before his eyes fluttered and he collapsed onto the floor.

Diego started to bend down to check on Baxter when he stumbled. He barely looked up at Jaden before falling unconscious beside Baxter.

"What's wrong?" Stuart closed the gap as William sagged to the floor.

Cassie faced Stuart a moment, but then Stuart put a hand to his head and staggered.

Everyone looked ill, and Cassie felt light-headed. Kristen, Jaden, and Robert swooned and buckled, along with Chet, Laura, and J.C.

Something was in the lemonade, Cassie realized as Stuart crumpled to the floor, unconscious. Her last thought before she passed out was, *It's the killer!*

Leo drifted into consciousness, his wrists hurting, his eyes finding only darkness. Once his clouded mind cleared, he tried to move but found it impossible. He struggled but could barely wiggle. And why couldn't he see? Panic flooded through him, fearing he'd gone blind, but then his brain fully awakened and he realized he was wearing a blindfold. Not only that, but his hands were tied behind his back and a gag prevented him from speaking. He moved his feet and found them bound, as well. The floor beneath him felt cold and forbidding. He heard a door open, and his senses hit high alert.

"Awake, huh?" The voice was deep and strong. "I don't know how you found this place, kid, but it made me suspicious, so I grabbed a chain mail undershirt from the costume department, just in case I need extra protection. I love the stalk and kill, which is why your friends were brought to this soundstage, so I can hunt them down like vermin. Unfortunately, I can't touch you. Not allowed. So, just sit tight and enjoy the show. At least, the audio portion."

He laughed and then Leo heard retreating footsteps, followed by the door opening and the closing.

Asher! He had to save Asher. And the others. But how?

He struggled against the bindings, but they were snug. Not even any wiggle room. Whoever this guy was, he knew how to tie knots.

Leo replayed the guy's voice in his head. Had he ever heard it before?

He didn't think so, but then he'd talked to so many new people lately he couldn't be sure. He knew one thing—the most important thing. Since he'd been caught, the killer could be onto their plan. If he didn't escape soon, he might lose Asher forever.

Diego pulled himself awake with great effort, struggling to get his bearings. He found himself lying on a soft bed with a thick coverlet.

Huh?

He sat up quickly, then paused when a wave of dizziness almost overcame him.

What happened?

No lights were on, and the details of his surroundings were unclear. He could make out just enough detail to conclude he was in a bedroom, but how did he get there?

The lemonade! It must've been drugged!

He clambered off the bed, noting that he was still dressed the same as before. Nothing had changed except his location.

Diego recalled the training on Sunday. Cassie's dad told them to always listen first for any movement and determine its direction. So, Diego listened. The silence was so pervasive he couldn't imagine where he might be. Not even any distance traffic noise. In LA? That seemed impossible.

Hearing nothing, Diego slipped cautiously to the edge of the bed and planted his sneakers onto what felt like carpet, trying hard to keep his breathing silent. Still no movement around him. He stood up and looked around, trying to get his bearings in the dark. The last thing he wanted to do was bump into a table or something.

He took a step forward, listening for the floor creaking beneath the carpet. Nothing. His eyes adjusted to the dark and he spotted what looked like drapes straight ahead. To his right was a night table with a lamp sitting on top. He was almost certain nothing stood between him and the drapes. He recalled Leo saying something about a balcony. Could that be on the other side of those drapes?

Diego glanced behind him, studying the darkness. He made out an open door, presumably leading out into a hallway, but nothing moved, and silence still reigned. Barely breathing, he inched his way toward the drapes, sweeping his eyes around him with every step. He reached into his pocket and found his breath spray had not been taken, so he slipped it out and popped off the cap. It wasn't much, but it might distract an attacker long enough for Diego to take him down. He hoped his strength training and the defense training he'd gotten on Sunday would give him an edge, especially since the killer wouldn't know that he was prepared to fight.

He stopped at the center point of the closed drapes and listened again. Still nothing. How could it be so quiet? Where had the killer brought him? Body coiled for action, Diego lifted the tiny breath spray with his right hand and gently clamped the fingers of his left around a drape fold. Steeling himself, he yanked aside the drape and leaped back.

A closed sliding glass door led out to the darkness of a balcony and whatever lay beyond. Diego stepped to the glass and peered through. The balcony looked empty. He listened again for any movement. Hearing nothing, he grasped the door handle and tugged. It was unlocked, so he eased it ever so slowly open, wide enough for him to step through.

The balcony beneath his feet didn't creak, which surprised Diego as he glanced side to side to make sure he was alone.

He was.

Then why did he have the unnerving feeling he was being watched?

His eyes roamed the darkness, but nothing moved. There wasn't even the slightest breeze. Where was he?

He took two steps closer to the balcony railing and stopped again, listening. There was nothing to hear, but he still felt those eyes on him. Glancing back at the open sliding door, no one was visible. He decided to try an experiment. He lifted one foot to step forward and brought it down to within an inch of the floor but did not plant it. Behind him, almost inaudible, came the slightest creak.

He was right! Someone was back there, masking their steps with his.

Heart pounding, Diego clutched the breath spray, his body taut and ready to spring as he completed his step and took another, then whirled around.

A huge man stood before him, a man wearing a skull mask that looked disturbingly like the one used in the student film he'd worked on that spring. The man wore overalls and wielded a large knife.

Diego didn't hesitate, or panic. He threw his hand up with the breath spray and discharged it into the open eyes of the mask. The attacker screamed in pain and staggered back, free hand to his masked face.

"You little shit!"

The man blindly lunged at him, but Diego dodged the knife blade, feeling a slight breeze as it whizzed past his face. He elbowed his attacker in the side, just as Edward had taught him. The man grunted but did not go down. Instead, he turned and grabbed Diego's wrist in a vise-like grip, bending it backward. Diego groaned with pain but kicked out at his attacker's shin. The man grunted with pain but maintained his grip.

"Let him go, asshole!"

Diego saw movement near the open sliding door, but he didn't have to see to know that voice.

Kristen!

The masked attacker turned toward the door as a dark blur closed in and kicked him in the groin. The man released Diego and doubled over in pain. Kristen swung her leg out and kicked him hard in his chest. The man stumbled back against the railing. A loud crack of wood filled the air as the railing gave way and the man fell backward, the knife flying from his grasp. Flailing, the attacker clamped one desperate hand around Diego's leg as he toppled, pulling Diego down with him.

"Diego!" cried Kristen, leaping forward.

Diego thrashed his arms in the air, grasping for anything to break his fall, terror coursing through him.

I can't let this guy win!

His left hand touched wood and he grabbed on, at the same time kicking down with his free leg and striking his dangling attacker. He heard a grunt and then his leg was free. Moments later, he heard a thud, followed by silence.

Diego's heart hammered in his chest as he dangled precariously, only one hand holding onto the broken balcony railing. Kristen dropped to her knees and reached out to him.

"Take my hand!" she hissed.

It was too dark for Diego to make out her facial expression, but the urgency in her voice was clear evidence of her fear. He reached up with his free hand and felt the tips of her fingers graze his before he swung away out of reach. Grateful that his strength training had given him a strong grip, he clutched even tighter at the wood of the railing and began swinging his body back and forth.

"You're almost here," Kristen whispered. "A little more."

Diego's swaying had become more pronounced, and he knew this would be his only chance. He swung back toward where he thought Kristen's hand would be, reaching out with his right arm as far as he could. He felt her fingers close within his and pull. Using the momentum of his swing, Diego flung upward with his right leg and found the floor of the balcony through the hole in the railing.

Kristen pulled harder than Diego thought possible, and in moments, he was sprawled out on the balcony floor, panting, with her squatting before him. She lowered her face close enough for him to see and he smiled to let her know he was okay. She released her breath, clearly relieved.

"Remind me not to get you mad," Diego whispered, and he heard her chuckle above him.

"Hey, we got him."

"You got him," he said, sitting up and checking his left hand. It was scraped and bleeding and his shoulder hurt, but otherwise he was okay. "We better get down there and tie him up or something."

"Good idea."

He felt her hand in his and then he was tugged to his feet. They stepped back to the damaged railing and looked down. Kristen gasped.

"Oh shit," Diego murmured.

The driveway below was empty. Their attacker was gone.

"I hate to sound like a horror movie," Kristen said, "but maybe he is the boogeyman."

"C'mon, let's find the others."

He took her hand, and they rushed back into the bedroom.

Laura couldn't breathe. A strong hand across her mouth and nose was cutting off her air. Lungs screaming for breath, she struggled and fought but couldn't break free. As she felt herself fading away, she suddenly sat up with a start, gasping loudly. Her mind felt clouded, and she shook her head, noticing the hand was gone as she glanced at her surroundings.

A dream. That's what she'd experienced.

Wait, am I on the floor?

Then she remembered.

Clambering to her feet, she looked around with frantic worry. Chet, J.C., and Jaden moaned as they came to, but the others…were gone! Donovan's fedora lay upside down on the floor near the table.

Oh no…

She ran to J.C. and lightly slapped his face. "Wake up, J.C." She did the same to Chet. Jaden's alert eyes were already open, and he was looking around in confusion.

Chet scrambled to his feet and noticed the absence of the others. "They're gone!"

"Stuart too," Jaden said, jumping up.

J.C. came around and Laura helped him stand.

"What's going on?" J.C. still looked drugged.

"The others are gone," Laura announced, her tone one of disgust. "We blew it."

"Where's Stuart?" J.C. asked, noting his absence.

"He must've gone to the same high school."

"We never thought to check on that about other people," Chet said.

Just then, Edward and Marisol rounded the corner at a run. Laura hurried to them.

"They're gone," she said. "The lemonade was drugged."

"They took Stuart too," Chet added. "We think he might've gone to the same school."

Edward's face collapsed with despair. "Cassie," he murmured, his tone rife with guilt.

"We'll find them," Marisol said firmly, then faced Laura. "What time did you drink the lemonade?"

Laura pulled out her phone. "It's nine o'clock now. Less than an hour ago."

"Why did you all come back here?" Edward asked, his tone reproachful. "It's too secluded."

J.C. shuffled his feet. "I called everyone 'cause Leo was missing. Cassie was about to call you when we got knocked out."

"What happened to Leo?" Marisol asked.

J.C. explained about Leo leaving. "I tried calling and texting but got nothing."

Marisol turned to Edward. "Try Cassie and Donovan. Maybe we can track their phones, if nothing else."

Edward pulled out his phone and dialed a number. The *Halloween* movie theme song began playing from somewhere on the refreshments table.

"That's her ringtone," Edward said and hurried to the table, the others gathering around.

There was a large plastic bowl filled with granola bars at the far end of the table. The music came from there. Edward replaced his phone in his pocket, cutting off the music, then upended the bowl. Amid the bars tumbled out nine cell phones. Edward snatched up two.

"These are Cassie's and Donovan's."

"Then we can presume the rest belong to the others," Marisol commented with disappointment. "So much for tracking them."

Just then, Leo's mom hurried around the corner and joined them, reacting with surprise at seeing Laura and the others. "You found them, Edward," she said as she glanced around.

"Some of them," Marisol said, sounding miffed at being ignored.

"But I had several PAs check back here," Leo's mom said, confused.

"We were knocked out," Laura explained, pointing to the floor behind the tables. "I guess they didn't see us."

J.C. lurched forward. "Ms. Cantrell, have you heard from Leo?"

"Not for hours, why?"

"He's missing," J.C. said, his voice trembling with worry. "We gotta find him."

Furrowing her brows, Leo's mom faced the two cops. "I don't understand."

"Laura told us the others were here with them," Marisol explained, indicating the lemonade dispenser. "Apparently, this lemonade was drugged. When these four woke up, the others were gone. Including Stuart, your PA."

"Why Stuart?"

"We don't know," Marisol explained, "but we think he might have attended the same high school as the others. That seems to be the only link between them."

Leo's mom eyed Edward. "So Cassie's been taken then?"

He nodded.

"Leo, too, we think," added Marisol.

Now Leo's mom seemed to understand. "Why would the killer take Leonardo?"

"We don't know. J.C.?"

J.C. eyed Leo's intimidating mother without fear, which impressed Laura. "He told me he wanted to check something out and he'd text me. That was hours ago, and he hasn't called or texted."

Leo's mother paused, her face frozen in thought. "Now that you mention it, Leonardo came to me earlier to ask about horror movies."

"Horror movies?" Edward gazed at her with renewed hope.

"Yes. He wanted to know if there were horror films being shot here at the studio. I told him to check at the main gate."

"Why there?" Marisol asked.

"Whoever's running that gate has the list of every film being shot here and their locations."

Laura suddenly had an idea but couldn't say it in front of Leo's mother. "Marisol, can I talk to you for a minute?"

"Excuse me," Marisol said to Ms. Cantrell and followed Laura to a spot out of earshot of the others. "What is it, Laura?"

Laura leaned closer, noting Ms. Cantrell eyeing her. "Leo saw a graveyard in his vision, and today he asked his mom about horror movies."

Marisol's face lit up with understanding. "A movie set?"

"That's what I think."

"That would mean everyone is still here on the lot." She paused a moment. "That fits with the timeline, but I'll still have Leo's mother check with all the gates for any vehicles leaving in the past hour."

They hurried back to the group and Marisol said to Ms. Cantrell, "We suspect the killer took the kids to another soundstage here on the lot. We need to speak to whoever's at the main gate."

Ms. Cantrell turned away from Marisol to focus her intense gaze on Laura, who felt intimidated but refused to show it.

"I just tried tracking my son's phone," Ms. Cantrell announced casually. "It's either off or inside a soundstage."

"Why do you say that?" Edward asked.

"Because our soundstages have been modified to prevent cellular or wi-fi signals from going in or out. Avoids interference with our equipment."

"Then Marisol's right," blurted J.C. "We gotta check the other soundstages."

"Very well," Ms. Cantrell said. "Let's go."

CHAPTER SEVENTEEN

I THINK HE'S GONE

When Asher woke up, he found himself on what felt like a paved street. Robert stood beside him staring out into the darkness. Asher looked up, expecting to see stars or the moon, but there was only blackness. He sat up quickly, then caught himself as his head swam in circles.

Robert squatted down and whispered, "Go slow. Whatever was in that lemonade packs a punch."

Asher focused on breathing, and his head stopped spinning. "Where are we?"

Robert's pale face floated before him. "Where the killer took us, I guess."

He reached down and Asher felt his hand. Gripping it, Asher was pulled to his feet.

"Anything still in your pockets we can use as a weapon?" Robert whispered. "My phone is gone, but the guy left this." He held up a fingernail clipper. "It's not much, but if I get close, I could shove it in his eye."

Asher felt around in his thick, bushy hair, locating the sharp metal comb he'd hidden in there after shooting ended. "Kristen gave me this. It's pretty sharp."

He held it out and Robert's hand gripped his to examine the comb with his fingers. "Sweet."

Asher didn't respond.

"I heard something just before you woke up," Robert whispered. "It sounded like Diego and Kristen, but I couldn't tell where their voices came from."

Asher heard a slight scraping sound and clutched Robert's arm. "You hear that?"

"Yeah."

They both listened. Asher heard it again, something like scraping, and it was closer this time. He waved Robert in the opposite direction and, still holding him by the arm, inched away from the approaching noise. Their feet made no sound as they moved, but the scraping continued to pursue them. Asher tried to make sense of it, like maybe someone was dragging an injured foot?

Asher was so focused on listening that he didn't see the wooden wall until his face banged into it, making a small but audible *thump*.

He turned to face Robert when a whizzing sound cut through the air.

Thunk!

A large knife stuck out of the wooden wall inches from Asher's face!

"Shit!" muttered Robert, dragging Asher along the wall as silently as he could. Without warning, the wall gave way to empty air, causing Robert to almost stumble and fall.

Asher caught him and felt with one hand at the wall. It had clearly ended.

Thunk!

Another knife struck the wall, but nearer to where they were before.

Asher pulled Robert with him behind the wall, almost tripping over a support beam holding it up against the ground.

Where the hell were they?

The boys inched along the wall, mindful of the supports spaced out every few feet. Asher halted and squeezed Robert's arm to stop him. He pressed his ear against the back of the wall and listened.

Nothing. No more knives and no scraping sound. Had the killer gone away?

Asher placed his lips right up to Robert's ear. "We never thought about him throwing knives," he whispered. "What now?"

Asher felt Robert shrug, obviously unsure what to do. Their plan had been to lie in wait and attack the killer before he could attack them. The knife-throwing completely changed that plan. If the killer could see in this darkness, all of them were doomed.

They took two golf carts out to the main entrance, and J.C. kept checking his phone every few seconds, even though he believed Leo's mom about cell phones not working inside soundstages. He just couldn't stop checking.

Laura, Chet, and the silent Jaden rode in his cart, while the others were up ahead in the other one. It seemed to take forever, but J.C. knew it had only been a few minutes before they arrived at the massive main gate.

He jumped out of the cart as soon as it stopped and hurried up to the main booth where Leo's mom was talking to the night guard; J.C. recognized him but didn't know his name.

"What can I do for you, Ms. Cantrell?" the young man asked deferentially.

"I need to know on which soundstages horror films are being shot."

The young man looked surprised, but quickly snatched up a clipboard and skimmed through the pages. "I have them. Would you like a map?"

"Naturally."

Edward looked more stressed than usual as they waited for the young man to finish, and J.C. understood. If the killer succeeded this night, he'd lose both Cassie and Donovan.

And I'll lose Diego, J.C. thought. *And Leo.*

He couldn't live with either possibility, so he squelched those thoughts.

"Here you are, ma'am," the young man said, handing the map to Ms. Cantrell, who gave him an icy look before the two cops crowded in to look. J.C. and the others did the same.

"We're here." Ms. Cantrell pointed to the gate. "These circles represent the seven soundstages in question."

"We need backup," Edward said to Marisol.

"Call it in," she responded, and Edward stepped away from the others to make the call. Marisol faced Ms. Cantrell. "Some of these are far from here. Leo gave you no clue what he was looking for?"

"No."

"Is there a night guard who can get us into all of them?"

"Yes."

"Call them, please. We'll begin with the closest and work our way outward."

Ms. Cantrell leaned into the booth once more. "Call the night man and have him report here."

"Yes, ma'am."

She looked irked. "Yes, *Ms. Cantrell*, will do nicely, thank you."

"Sorry, Ms. Cantrell." The chastised young man picked up a phone receiver and pressed a button.

Asher stood rigidly beside Robert, their bodies touching, neither moving nor hardly breathing as they listened, ears pressed against the back of the wall.

"I think he's gone," Robert whispered.

"And if he isn't?"

"We need those knives, bro," Robert replied, pulling away from the wall. "I'm going to get them."

He let go of Asher and felt his way back along the wall. Asher followed. Robert stopped and peered around the open side. Asher strained to hear any sound, but there was nothing. Robert scooted around the edge of the wall and Asher followed, wondering for the first time why there'd be a wall sitting in the street. Then it hit him.

"Robert!"

He kept his voice at a hiss, but Robert turned and waited for Asher to catch up.

"This is a soundstage. That's why there's no stars."

He heard Robert expel a small breath of surprise. "You're right, which means we're still at the studio."

"Yeah." Asher found himself picturing Leo and wondering where he could be. Was he here somewhere, in the darkness of this soundstage?

Robert tiptoed along the wall and Asher followed. They made no more sounds and heard none around them. Robert stopped again and Asher waited while he wiggled loose the first knife, handing it back to him. Then Robert stepped another foot forward and freed the other knife, gripping it solidly in one large hand.

Asher grasped his own knife. He'd never used one before except for cutting meat, and he'd certainly never thrown one, but he felt more secure with the weapon in his hand. "Let's find the others."

"Right."

They left the relative safety of the wall and slunk out into the darkness.

Leo wriggled and squirmed, but the bindings on his wrists and ankles barely loosened. He thought he'd heard the sound of wood breaking a short while back, which made him struggle all the harder. Asher was out there, not to mention his other friends. He paused to gaze into the darkness surrounding him. His eyes had adjusted by now and he spotted a long table against the opposite wall. Maybe he could use it to help him stand up.

He rolled over and over until he bumped a table leg, then sat up again. He had strong legs and arms from gymnastics and felt confident he could muscle his way upward. Pressing his back against the table leg, he pressed downward with his feet and pushed, inching his way up the solid leg. The table rattled, but stayed put because it was against a wall. The muscles in his quads burned like fire and his wrists rubbed painfully against the wooden leg, but he continued to rise.

Sweat broke out all over his body as he exerted himself like he never had before. His knees were at a ninety-degree angle now. Just a little farther! His thighs screamed with pain, and he gritted his teeth, working through the throbbing to focus on his goal. He saw Asher's face in his vision, bloody and dead, and pushed all the harder, inch by inch.

Almost there…

With a final grunt, Leo surged the rest of the way up and stood on his feet at last! He leaned back against the tabletop to get his ragged breathing under control and allow his wobbly legs a moment to rest.

Feeling stronger, he turned slowly around to face the table and its contents. He spotted some fake tombstones and electrical cords, but they were of no use. Then he noticed a few tools at the far end of the table, and what looked like a large stage light, so he inched his way in that direction, cursing his slowness. Anything could be happening to Asher right now, but he couldn't risk falling to the ground again.

Regaining control of his momentary panic, he stopped to gaze at the tools lying neatly together. Mostly pliers and screwdrivers—nothing he could use. But then he studied the heavy-looking studio lamp. It was thick, with a metal shield over the lens with flaps that opened out to allow more or less light to emerge. The lamp was right near the edge of the table, its back side pressed against the wall.

Leo turned around and began rubbing the rope binding his wrists against one flap protruding from the lamp. The flap was metal and its edges somewhat sharp. He focused on moving his wrists up and down, mindful of cutting himself. After what seemed an eternity, one piece of the rope loosened enough to slip his hand out. He yanked the rope off the other hand and then bent to untie his ankles.

The knot was too tight, so he stood up and snatched one of the screwdrivers, stooping again to work the screwdriver into the knot. He moved and twisted the screwdriver, finally loosening the knot enough that he could get his fingers inside it. Tugging and pulling, he tore the rope away and tossed it aside.

He had no idea how long it had taken to free himself or how long he'd been in that room, but he knew his friends needed help.

All his machinations to free himself spoiled his sense of direction and he had to walk like a zombie with his hands outstretched until he located the door.

Please don't be locked!

He grasped the knob and turned.

It opened!

Leo eased the door open with caution, having no idea where the killer might be. Beyond was more darkness, and he hadn't felt any flashlights in this room, so he inched forward with extreme care. If he had to guess, he'd say the killer was out among the sets stalking his friends, but he couldn't be sure.

And what did the killer mean when he said Leo was off-limits?

He crept forward, hands out like a blind man, hating that he had to move so slowly when anything could be happening to the others. He felt a smidgen of relief that he hadn't heard any cries of pain or anguish, which might mean his friends were avoiding the killer as planned.

Leo's foot bumped something hard, and he stopped. Fumbling in front of him, he found what felt like the railing for a flight of stairs. Then he remembered his talks with crew members on his mom's film. He'd asked how the lights were put in place high above the sets, and one chatty young guy showed him the stairs leading up to catwalks above. The gaffers used those catwalks to set and adjust the lights.

Leo's heart raced as he considered his options. Sure, he could stumble around in the dark and hopefully bump into his friends, or he could climb up to the catwalks and look down from above. Yes, it would be dark, but he'd have the best vantage point to spot his friends and the killer. He might even be able to drop something on the killer from above. Resolve filled his heart, and he took the stairs one at a time.

Edward felt himself sweating as the two golf carts arrived at the first soundstage on the map and stopped outside. The night watchman arrived in his own cart and clambered out, dangling a large ring full of keys.

"Backup is on its way," Marisol told the group.

Edward saw that J.C. and the others were as anxious as he to find their friends. "Detective, let's check this one while we're waiting."

Marisol eyed him with sympathy. "I'd rather have the backup."

"As far as we know, there's only one perp," Edward insisted, glancing at J.C. standing nearby. J.C. nodded.

"We don't know that for sure."

"I can go too," Laura said boldly, stepping forward. "I can handle a gun. My dad takes me to the range all the time."

Marisol seemed impressed with Laura's bravado but shook her head. "I can't deputize a teenager, Laura. I'm sorry."

"My son could be in trouble, Detective," Cassandra told Marisol. "This is my home turf and I say we enter now."

Edward eyed her a moment before facing Marisol once again. "We'd just go in and turn on the lights. We can call out. If any of the kids are there, they should answer."

Marisol gazed long and hard at him. Edward knew she loved Cassie and would do anything to save her. "Very well. I'll lead, Cassandra second, Edward third. You kids remain outside with the night watchman."

"But—" J.C. blurted, but Marisol cut him off with an icy stare.

"This is police business, J.C. Stay put." She turned to the night watchman. "Please unlock the door."

"Yes, ma'am."

The middle-aged man wearing a studio uniform hurried to the door and fished through his keys before finding the right one and inserting it in the lock. Edward noted the red light just above the door that resembled the flashing light on his patrol car. The watchman stepped aside, and Marisol closed the gap, gun out and ready.

"Where's the light switch?"

"Just to your right as you enter," the watchman replied, eyeing the gun nervously.

Marisol glanced back to make sure the others were ready, then pulled open the door. Edward wanted to run inside and call out Cassie's name, but he'd been a cop long enough to know not to allow emotion to dictate his actions.

Fearlessly, Cassandra followed Marisol inside and Edward joined them. It was pitch black for a moment until Marisol flicked a switch to his right. Fluorescent lights glowed to life, but they were moderate in brightness, just enough illumination to move around safely.

Marisol stepped forward, body taut and on the alert. Edward held his own gun firmly, ready to fire at a moment's notice. They rounded a corner, and the main portion of the soundstage came into view.

The set was impressive. There were faux woods along one side and a large mansion on the other. The mansion looked like something out of *The Addams Family*, the old show Edward watched as a kid. His eyes roved the landscape. No graveyard.

"Cassie, Donovan," called out Marisol. "Is anyone in here?"

Silence greeted her question. Edward sagged with relief. Wrong soundstage.

"There's no cemetery set, Marisol," Edward said tightly. "We need to move on."

Cassandra turned to him, one eyebrow raised curiously. "What does a cemetery have to do with this matter?"

Edward realized he'd said more than he should have. Leo hadn't told his mother what he'd seen. Fortunately, Marisol came to his rescue.

"That was part of the information we received, that some of the kids would die in a cemetery," she said smoothly, as though this was the complete truth.

Cassandra gazed at her without expression, but Edward saw it in her eyes—she knew Marisol was lying.

Marisol slipped her gun back into its holster and Edward did the same. “Let’s move on,” she said, and started back toward the door.

Cassandra turned to Edward, but he refused to meet her gaze. Instead, he ushered her forward with a wave of his hand. She hesitated, as though about to speak, and then followed Marisol. Edward sighed with relief as he brought up the rear.

CHAPTER EIGHTEEN

LET'S GET OUT OF HERE

William crouched beside a large tree, peering out into the oppressive darkness. Baxter hunkered beside him, scanning the opposite direction. They'd both awakened to find themselves in a graveyard. Baxter trembled with fright, while William fought to control his breathing. Taking down his friends in combat training was one thing. That was fun. But taking down a deadly killer when he couldn't even see three feet in front of him, that was something else.

His phone was, of course, gone, but he still had one of Kristen's metal combs. His hair was long enough for it to seem natural, and the killer hadn't taken it. But he would have to be right in the killer's face to use it.

Baxter still had a packet of gum, inside of which he'd slipped a razor blade, but again, sneaking up on a killer who likely knew the terrain would be tough, if not impossible.

William felt the bark of the tree with one hand. It was rough but felt more like plastic than wood. Shadowy gravestones were vaguely visible around him. He glanced over at Baxter, who sat huddled against the tree trunk staring out into the darkness, and then crawled as quietly as he could toward the closest headstone.

The ground beneath his hands felt like grass, with something harder underneath. Wood maybe? A suspicion of their location crept into his mind as he reached the headstone and gripped it. The headstone wobbled.

I knew it!

He squeezed the sides and his fingers made tiny indentations. Styrofoam. Or something close.

They were inside another soundstage!

William glanced back but could no longer see Baxter in the darkness. He gripped the headstone and wiggled it back and forth, finally yanking it free from whatever anchored it. He tried to read the name, but it was too dark.

He heard a barely noticeable sound behind him. Spinning, he was startled by a big man wearing a white skull mask looming over him. The man swung his arm downward, and William countered with the tombstone to block the blow. A large knife blade tore through the Styrofoam, snapping the headstone in half and whizzing past William's shoulder as he scooted to one side.

Leaping to his feet, William lurched backward as the man came for him. He wanted to snatch the comb from his hair but worried the killer would lunge at him if he did.

Without warning, Baxter leaped onto the killer's back and drove his razor blade into the man's neck. The killer roared with rage and flung Baxter to one side. He collided with a headstone and broke it as the killer spun around and threw his knife. Baxter grunted in pain as the knife sank into his upper chest, and he lay on the ground, unmoving.

"Baxter!"

As the killer pressed one hand against his bleeding throat, an enraged William slipped out the comb and plunged it toward the back of the killer's neck, but the killer turned and backhanded William with his free hand.

William stumbled and went down, stunned by the killer's strength. He spotted Baxter's unmoving form and desperately wanted to assist his friend, but he knew he needed help. He leaped to his feet and took off running, hoping to exit the cemetery and find the others. He also wanted to draw the killer away from Baxter, praying his best friend still lived. His ploy worked. The killer pelted after him, large shoes pounding on the thick grass, so William increased his speed.

He glanced back and slammed hard into a fence encircling the cemetery, banging his knee hard and crying out in pain. Heart pounding, he fumbled along the fence until he came to an open space. A hand grasped at his collar just as he bolted through the gate. William swung back with the comb and connected with the arm grabbing him. The killer cursed in pain and let go. William darted out into the darkness.

After a moment, the running footsteps followed.

Leo walked stealthily along the catwalks high above the sets below. He could make out shapes of the buildings, especially a rooftop close enough that he could jump onto it if he wanted. So far, he'd not seen anyone on the ground, but he heard an unfamiliar voice cry out in pain and curse in anger. The killer? It had to be, and his anger must be directed at someone who scored an attack on him.

Leo hurried as fast as he could, fear ramping him up. Could Asher have been the one who attacked the killer? Could Asher have been hurt in the struggle? He stopped and stared down into the darkness. No movement or sounds were detectable. He hurried on.

Cassie found herself with Donovan and Stuart in the living room of a house. At least, that's what it felt like in the near-total darkness. She'd awakened on a couch next to Donovan, and Stuart woke up shortly after in a nearby chair. She'd immediately recalled Leo's vision of her and Donovan being killed on a couch, and her heart began to hammer.

Once her head cleared from the drug she'd ingested, Cassie forced herself to remain calm, like her dad had always taught her, and she studied the location for clues to her whereabouts, not to mention items that could be used as weapons.

She and Donovan had each grabbed a table lamp by the time Stuart shook off his lethargy. Cassie was surprised Stuart was even there. She noted, because it was obvious in its absence, that Donovan's fedora was gone as he peered around him for potential threats. She felt her way to Stuart and helped him to his feet.

"Where are we?" he asked, "And why is it so dark?"

"I don't know," Cassie replied more calmly than she'd have imagined. "But I need to know what high school you went to."

Even in the darkness, she heard the confusion in his voice. "Performing Arts High in the Valley. Why?"

"I knew it." She searched for Donovan in the dark and found him right behind her. "Donovan, we never thought to check other crew members."

"No. Maybe your dad did?"

"It doesn't matter now."

"What are you talking about?" Stuart asked, then noted the lamps they carried. "And why do you have those lamps?"

"For protection," Donovan said, his voice breathy and fearful. "You better grab something too."

"Someone plans to kill us all tonight and we need to fight back, maybe even catch him off guard." Cassie stared at the surprised look on his face, forcing her own fear to one side.

"How do you know this?"

"It doesn't matter," Cassie said dismissively, "we just do. Now grab something so we can find the others. We made a plan to meet outside in the open. Less chance of someone catching us by surprise."

She was amazed that she could think so clearly. She'd been racked with fear leading up to this moment, but now that their fight to survive had arrived, she felt calm.

Clearly mystified by her words, Stuart felt around the room for something to use. He stopped at the coffee table and grabbed something.

"What'd you find?" she asked.

"It's a paperweight of some kind," Stuart said. "Heavy, too."

"Okay." Cassie eyed Donovan and Stuart. "Let's find a way out of here."

Somewhere in the house came the sound of a door opening and closing quietly, as though the person didn't want to be heard.

"Looks like we fight here," Donovan whispered, tightly gripping the lamp in his right hand. "This feels like metal, so it should do some damage."

"Could you tell which direction the sound came from?" Cassie eyed both young men, fighting to control her accelerating heart rate.

"I think it came from that way," Donovan whispered, pointing off to their right. "I'll lead. Stuart, you bring up the rear."

"Got it."

Donovan stepped in front of Cassie and led the way across the room, all of them taking baby steps to avoid giving away their location. Cassie felt a strong urge to take Donovan's hand but resisted because each of them had to be ready to attack at a moment's notice.

She listened intently for any further sounds, but there was nothing. With carpet beneath their feet, their footfalls were silent. Donovan suddenly stopped and Cassie nearly bumped into him.

"What?" she whispered.

"There's an open door here," Donovan whispered back, his breathing ragged. "I can't see what's on the other side."

She reached out and found his free hand in dark, giving it a quick squeeze. "Be careful."

He didn't reply but inched forward. As Cassie followed, she felt the jam of an open door with her free hand and glanced back to make sure Stuart was there. He was, his facial expression obscured by the darkness.

She followed Donovan out into what might have been an entry hall of some sort, but she couldn't make out enough details. She stopped suddenly and listened. "Do you hear that, Donovan?" she whispered.

He turned to her, his face close enough for them to kiss. "What?"

"I hear breathing," she whispered back, looking from side to side. "Raspy breathing."

They both paused to listen and then Donovan jerked his head up. "I hear it too." He pointed in front of them. "Over there."

Donovan pressed forward, lamp raised high. Cassie and Stuart followed, flanking him on both sides, their own weapons ready to attack.

"It's me, William," wafted out of the blackness, so low that Cassie thought she'd made a mistake.

"William?" Donovan whispered.

Cassie still couldn't see anyone up ahead.

"It's Donovan and Cassie," Donovan whispered. "And Stuart."

Cassie heard a deep sigh of relief, then William's sweat-streaked face floated out of the darkness. "The killer, he's after me."

Before Donovan could reply, Cassie heard a door open somewhere behind them, and froze with fear.

"He's here!" hissed William, his voice rife with fear. "Quick, come in this room."

He reached out a pale hand and Donovan grabbed it. William pulled

Donovan away into the blackness, Cassie and Stuart tiptoeing after them. Cassie found herself in another room, smaller than the one with the couch, with what looked like floor to ceiling bookcases.

She eased the door closed and grabbed Donovan to huddle behind it. Donovan pulled William with him, and Stuart crowded in as well. The door opened inward, so they'd be hidden should the killer decide to check this room. They might even be able to get the jump on him.

Cassie held her breath. Her heart hammered loudly, giving her the foolish impression that the killer might actually hear it. She listened harder than ever in her life.

Why doesn't the floor creak in this house?

She'd never been in any house that didn't make some sounds. Whoever built this one did an incredible job.

She felt, rather than heard, the door opening and someone entering the room, so she gripped her lamp all the harder, raising it to strike. Donovan and Stuart did the same. William stayed behind them.

Suddenly, the door was shoved backward, slamming all four of them hard against the wall. William grunted in pain and Stuart's paperweight crashed to the floor, but Cassie and Donovan held onto their lamps. A large dark figure materialized before them. Cassie didn't hesitate. She swung out with her lamp and struck the figure. The lamp broke, and pain ripped through her hand, which began dripping blood.

Donovan swung his lamp with both hands, striking the figure hard enough to send the man staggering.

Knowing they were out of weapons, Cassie hissed, "Let's get out of here!"

She grabbed Donovan with the hand that wasn't bleeding and shoved him forward, around the open door into the entry hall.

William darted in front. "Follow me. I know the way out."

He led the way through the darkness to their right and hurried through an open door. Cassie and Donovan followed, Stuart bringing up the rear.

Cassie realized at once that she was outside the house because she felt the openness around her. Looking up, she saw no stars, no moon. But slight movement above caught her eye, and she stared a moment. When the movement didn't recur, she followed William down steps that led to what felt like a driveway or road.

"Hurry," William whispered. "Baxter's hurt! He might be dead."

"What happened to Baxter?" asked a male voice from the darkness.

Cassie spun to her right in fear, relaxing when Kristen and Diego appeared out of the gloom, close enough to be recognizable. Diego hurried to William. "Did that guy get him?"

"He threw a knife," William rasped, his breaths hitching in his chest. "It hit Baxter and he went down. The guy came after me, so I ran."

"Where?" Donovan asked.

"Graveyard," William gasped. He pointed out into the blackness. "Over that way, I think."

"Everyone okay?"

Cassie recognized Robert's voice, then saw him hurrying through the darkness to join them. She was pretty sure she saw Asher with him. They appeared to be unhurt, as far as she could tell, which helped to relieve her mind.

"I heard you say Baxter's hurt?" Asher focused on William, who nodded.

Robert said, "The guy can throw knives really well. We hid behind a wall until he left." He held up a sharp knife. "But we got the knives he threw."

Asher held up a knife of his own, noticing Stuart at the same time. "What're you doing here, Stuart?"

Stuart, who'd been staring back at the house they'd just left, turned. "From what Cassie said, I went to the wrong high school."

Startled, Asher turned to Cassie, who nodded.

"The killer is inside that house back there," Donovan said, pointing at the large structure behind them. "We hurt him, but he's still moving. This is our chance to take him down."

"Donovan's right," Cassie affirmed. "We're all together now, and we have weapons." She indicated Robert and Asher.

"So, what's the plan?" Stuart asked. "Do we go back inside?"

The others exchanged looks.

"I think we're safer out here," Robert suggested. "We should surround the front door, and when he comes out, we get him."

The others nodded.

"Sounds like our best option," Cassie agreed.

"What about Baxter?" William moaned. "We have to save him."

Asher placed a comforting hand on William's shoulder. "We will, soon as we take down the killer."

William looked like he might say something more, then threw his arms around Asher, crying. "He's my best friend, Asher, and I couldn't help him."

"We'll save him," Asher said, his voice soothing as he patted William on the back.

The group turned to face the house, prepared to re-enter, when from somewhere above, the lights came on.

CHAPTER NINETEEN

WE DIDN'T KILL HER

LEO HAD SPOTTED HIS FRIENDS running out of a large structure far below but couldn't make out specific faces. He heard their voices, just barely, and got the impression the killer was somewhere nearby. If that was the case, he didn't want to be spotted just yet. But he did want to help his friends, so he examined the klieg lights clamped onto the railing at different locations, pointing downward toward various parts of the set.

He spotted one that seemed to illuminate the very spot his friends had congregated, but now he had to locate the on switch. He knew that most of these lights could be turned on and off remotely so that crew members didn't have to be in the rafters all day. His worry was that this light wouldn't turn on because it may be part of an overall grid that was currently powered down.

Fumbling in the dark, he felt around until he found a switch. Not sure what it would do, he pressed it and hoped for the best. Soft light sprang forth and struck the ground below, illuminating his friends and a large house behind them. He ducked down to prevent them from seeing him.

Cassie covered her eyes as light seemed to explode around her. Peeking out, she saw the others doing the same. What they didn't see, but she did, was the hulking form of the skull-masked killer lurching toward them.

"Look out!" she cried, pointing toward the house.

The others turned, still blinking against the sudden intrusion of light. Then William grabbed the knife Asher held and ran toward the big man.

The killer was clearly injured. He bled from several places and limped. But he raised one hand, revealing a long knife.

"William, look out!" shouted Donovan.

"You asshole!" William shouted, raising the knife and throwing it at the man.

Cassie stared open-mouthed as the knife spun in the air and struck the man point first, embedding itself in his chest. The killer staggered backward but threw his own knife as he did. William dove for the ground, the knife whizzing over his prone body and vanishing into the darkness.

Robert took off at a run, knife raised to attack, and bore down on the staggering killer. He swung downward with the knife just as the man raised a thick, meaty arm for protection. Robert's knife buried itself in the man's arm, blood erupting in Robert's face.

Kristen lunged forward holding a sharp hair comb and sunk it deep into the killer's shoulder. More blood shot forth as the others surrounded the killer, kicking, punching, even shooting breath spray into his eyes.

A gunshot echoed around them. Cassie turned in shock to find Stuart holding a handgun, aimed straight at her.

"Leave him alone," Stuart said, his voice cold and detached, "or I kill my former director here."

Cassie's mouth fell open in stunned surprise. The others left the battered, groaning killer on the ground and turned to face Stuart, equally shocked.

"The hell are you doing, Stuart?" Donovan stepped forward.

"Not another step," Stuart warned, "or she dies."

Donovan stopped, glancing from Stuart to Cassie and back as the others crowded around him.

"Why are you helping this creep?" Robert demanded, pointing at the wounded man on the ground.

Stuart eyed Robert coldly. "Because I'm the one who hired him."

J.C. stood beside Laura and Chet next to one of the golf carts, waiting for Edward and Marisol to exit the soundstage. This was their fourth stop.

More cops had arrived. Some were inside while others milled around outside. The longer they went without finding Leo, the more worried J.C. became. He checked his phone again, knowing he'd not see any texts from his friend.

The young guy driving their cart walked over beside him. "Waiting for an important call?"

J.C. glanced at the guy. He didn't look much older than him, good-looking, seemed nice enough.

"I keep hoping I'll get a text from my friend who's missing," J.C. replied, slipping his phone back into his pocket.

The guy nodded, then stuck out a hand. "I'm Pierre."

J.C. shook it. "J.C." He gazed morosely at the open door into the soundstage and the cops standing guard out front.

"I'm sorry about your friend," Pierre said, his voice gentle and filled with real concern. "When did he or she go missing?"

"He," J.C. replied, his body sagging with fatigue. "This afternoon. Somewhere in this studio."

"Really? That's crazy."

"Leo's too smart to get lost, which means somebody's got him."

Pierre flinched with surprise. "Leo? That's who you're all looking for?"

"Yeah, why?"

Pierre became animated. "Is he young like us, buff, really good-looking?"

J.C. puffed up with energy. "Yeah, that's him."

"I drove him around today," Pierre explained.

By this time, Laura and Chet had joined them.

"Where did you take him?" Laura asked.

"Some soundstages on the other side of the lot," Pierre replied. "I got called away and had to leave him. I told him to call when he needed another ride, but he didn't." He sounded disappointed.

J.C. grabbed both of Pierre's arms. "Can you take us there?"

"Sure."

J.C. released Pierre and bolted toward the open door. "Edward! Marisol!"

Hunkered down out of sight, Leo watched the scene below him unfold, his astonishment nearly overwhelming him. Stuart? The nicest guy on the whole film crew? He was behind this nightmare? And he had a gun, which meant Asher could die any second. Leo ignored his pounding heart and examined the lights everywhere about him. One was suspended directly above Stuart's head. If he could just loosen the clamp…

Thunderstruck, Cassie's mouth hung open, and her body trembled with fear. Her friends gaped at Stuart, who pointed his gun at them with the clear intention of using it.

"You…hired him?" Cassie managed to say, pointing at the seemingly unconscious man behind Stuart. "Why?"

"To kill you all, of course." Stuart didn't sound smug or gleeful, but more like killing them was an inevitability.

"What'd we do to you?" Donovan asked, inching closer to Cassie.

"Yeah, we just met you on this movie," Kristen put in, her anger evident in her tone. But she made no move that might further antagonize Stuart.

"You all killed my sister."

Stunned, the group exchanged looks of astonishment.

"The hell you talking about, Stuart?" Robert demanded, clenching his fists. "We don't even know your sister."

He made a move as though to rush Stuart, but the production assistant swung the gun to face Robert dead on, forcing him to stop.

"Watch your mouth, Robert," Stuart said coldly. "You were my main target, but the first two attempts to kill you failed."

Robert's face twisted with realization, clearly remembering those attempts, but his eyes revealed confusion about Stuart's motivation.

"Honestly, Cassie, it's pathetic how little you remember," Stuart said, focusing on her once more. "I know I was only an expendable extra, and even though I did go out of my way to look different this time, I *was* in your film last April."

Cassie lurched with surprise, glancing at Donovan for help, but he just shrugged, clearly mystified.

Stuart stared, his face twisting with annoyance. "You probably don't remember me with no goatee, no blond hair, oh, and without a spear shoved through my throat."

Donovan gasped, and Cassie flinched.

"Grant?" Cassie's body felt numb with shock.

"In the flesh," he replied smoothly, looking like he might take a bow.

Cassie couldn't believe it, glancing in horror at Donovan and the others.

William got to his feet, slowly. "Then your sister was…"

"Yes, the girl you and your dead pal out in the graveyard loved to antagonize on set," Grant spat, glowering with unchecked contempt at William.

"Hey, wait a minute, she treated us like crap," William blurted, bolder than Cassie had ever heard him.

"A bullet is too good for you. All of you."

"Now hold on, Stu—I mean Grant," Donovan said, inching still closer to Cassie. "We didn't kill her."

"You wrote the script," Grant shot back, "and you and Cassie were directing. If you weren't making a horror film, there wouldn't have been any murders to copycat."

Donovan's face fell with guilt. "Don't you think we feel guilty about that?"

"But we didn't kill her or the others," Cassie jumped in, worried that Donovan might break down when they needed to stay focused.

"You all treated her like shit," Grant said, fixing his glaring eyes on each of them in turn. He settled on Kristen. "Especially you."

"Excuse me? That bitch was trying to take away the guy I was dating, and you expect me to like her?"

"Your sister was the real bully," Robert said boldly, eyeing Kristen with support, "so how would you expect us to act toward her?"

"You used her," Grant spat in fury at Robert. "Flirted, won her over, got what you wanted, then just let her die."

"She flirted with me first," Robert insisted. "She flirted with every guy in school, even guys like Asher who weren't interested."

Grant gazed at Asher coldly. "She really liked you, Asher, but now that I've seen you with Leo, I get why you turned her down."

Asher's face reddened, but he didn't respond.

"Speaking of Leo," Grant continued, glancing slightly upward, "it's time to come down, Leo, before I blow Asher's head off."

Realization blanching his face, Asher looked up toward the catwalks above. "Don't do it, Leo, he's gonna kill me anyway!"

Leo had just loosened the clamp enough to push the heavy light off its mount when he heard Grant call his name. He'd been listening and understood what was being said because Asher had previously told him about their film shoot in April. But when Grant threatened to blow off Asher's head, Leo knew he had to act.

Asher's voice sounded brave when he called out, but there was no way he'd let Asher be killed. Except now that Grant was focused on the catwalks above, he'd easily see the light falling and jump clear.

Now what do I do?

He peered through the catwalk at Asher and froze. Asher's eyes were fixed on his from far below. How? It didn't matter because Asher nodded slightly, as though he'd gotten a message from Leo. Before Leo could react, Asher took a step toward Grant.

Grant looked down at once, fixing his gun on Asher's moving form. "Not another step."

"Why not? You're gonna kill me anyway, even though I tried to be nice to your sister."

Grant was momentarily distracted, his face softening slightly. "That's true, actually. The only two she liked were you and Donovan."

"Me?" Donovan looked surprised.

Good job, everyone, keep him talking, Leo thought, as he eased the heavy light off its bar. He scooted behind the light, which was twice as large as his head, and gave it a shove.

"She liked you most of all, Donovan, though she detested Cassie."

"I never mistreated her," Cassie insisted, understanding that the game was to distract Grant from Leo up above. She made the connection at once when Grant said Leo's name. Who else could've turned on the lights? "I can't help it if she was jealous."

Grant guffawed with disgust.

That's when Cassie heard a slight whizzing sound, like something falling. Unfortunately, Grant heard it too and glanced up.

The heavy klieg light soared downward straight at him. He leaped back and the light slammed into the fake road with a deafening crash. Its lens shattered, sending shards of glass flying everywhere.

William lunged forward, stunning everyone, determined to catch Grant off guard, but Grant quickly regained his balance and fired the gun. The bullet struck William and he staggered, blood seeping from a hole near the abdomen.

"William!" Cassie started forward as William toppled but halted when Grant called out, "Nobody move!"

She stopped, only then realizing that Donovan was right beside her, ready to die for her if necessary. She took his hand and squeezed.

"Nice try, Leo," Grant called out, fury in his voice this time. "Now get your ass down here or Asher dies!"

Leo leaped to his feet and looked over the railing. "Okay, I'm coming!"

He grabbed a thick extension cord lying on the catwalk and tied one end to the railing. Then he tossed the rest of the cord over the railing. Robert and Asher jumped apart as the plug end of the cord struck the floor between them. Without hesitation, Leo climbed over the rail and started down the extension cord.

It felt slippery, but Leo's grip was rock solid, so he didn't even use his legs as he shimmied down to the floor below. All he could think about was saving Asher. And the others. He'd watched William go down, terrified that William might already be dead. Leo had told them all he'd stop the killer, and now he had to make good on his words.

His feet touched the floor, and he released his hold on the dangling cord, finding himself right next to Asher, who leaned close and whispered, "Why did you come down?"

"To save you," Leo whispered back. Facing Grant head on, he said, "I only know you as Stuart, so that's what I'll call you. Asher told me about that film you all worked on and how your sister died. None of them did anything wrong."

"They didn't save her!" Grant snapped, his tone icy, yet his eyes were curious. "But you…you're responsible for this whole snafu. I don't know how, but you warned them what was going to happen. That's why they were ready to fight back. And you found this place. I had everything planned for tomorrow night, but thanks to you I had to move it up."

Leo flinched. "I don't know what you mean. How could I know anything? I was just exploring soundstages and found this one."

Grant gazed at him with certainty, not the least bit swayed by Leo's denial, keeping his gun hand steady. "I don't know how you knew these things, but you did. Just like you knew that Robert would die in that fall in the old house. How do you do it? Tell me and maybe I won't kill you."

Leo's mind flashed back to the killer's voice when he was tied to the chair.

I can't touch you, not allowed.

He blurted, "I don't think you're allowed to kill me."

Asher gasped and Diego muttered, "The hell?"

Now Grant's mouth dropped open in surprise. "How did you know…? Now, see, you've gotta have ESP to know that. But trust me, Leo, after all you did to ruin my revenge, I wanna kill you more than any of these others."

Leo tightened his body, forcing himself to look straight across the open space at Grant. "Do it. Just leave them alone."

Grant laughed for the first time. "You'll get yours, and I'll be there to watch. But now, thanks to the stupid idiot behind me who couldn't do what he bragged, I've gotta kill you all with this." He waved the gun. "Much less bloody. He wanted to stalk you because, well, that's his thing, which is why you were all brought here." He nodded back toward the prone man wearing the skull mask. "But the only thing that big oaf did right was scare you with the mask a couple of times."

Cassie flinched. "So, it was him at the beach."

Grant grinned. "Yeah, but he was too excited. Almost killed you both then. I made him wait and this is what I get for my trouble. Complete failure. Oh well. If you want something done right, as they say, you do it yourself." He took aim at Cassie.

Leo was so fixated on Grant's twisted expression of glee that, at first, he didn't notice movement behind the young man. Asher touched his hand, and that's when Leo spotted the killer, bruised and bloody, sitting up, still wearing that creepy skull mask. Leo forced himself to focus on Grant, but from the corner if his eye he saw the big man slide William's knife from his chest and stand with more ease than Leo thought possible, given his injuries.

Grant must've sensed something because he started to turn. He was too late. The towering killer slammed the blade into Grant's side as he turned, pulled it out, and plunged it home again.

Grant grunted with startled surprise, dropped his gun, and collapsed into an unmoving heap on the ground.

"Nobody calls me stupid," the big man spat angrily, his breathing coarse and unsteady.

Leo watched in abject horror as the man took a few steps forward. Kristen tensed up and Robert raised his fists, but the others became statues.

"I gotta hand it to you kids," the killer grumbled, his voice raspy, like maybe one of his lungs was punctured.

How is he even standing?

"You put up a good fight, but it's over." He opened one side of his long trench coat, revealing numerous knives sewn into the lining. "I got one for each of you."

He reached in to grab for a knife and Leo broke into a sprint, closing the gap in seconds. He gripped the big man's bloody wrist, but the bodily fluid made his grip precarious. Surprised, the man wheezed as he reached for Leo with his free hand.

But Cassie and Kristen got there first, followed by the others. As a group, they grabbed the killer's arm and pulled it down, away from Leo, who struggled with everything he had to keep the hand he held away from those knives.

How could he still be this strong? Leo wondered, as he used all his aikido skills to bend the man's wrist into a painful angle. He knew Robert and

Asher were strong, but between them and the others, they could barely hold the killer back. Leo feared they would lose.

"Everyone drop to the ground!"

The voice came from behind him, but Leo recognized it at once.

Edward!

He saw Cassie react with joyful surprise and release her grip. She dropped to the ground as instructed and scuttled away, followed by the others. As soon as they broke free, the big man swung his fist toward Leo, who released his grip and dropped to the ground, the fist just missing his face.

"Freeze!" came Edward's voice a second time, followed by Marisol adding, "Don't move!"

The killer reached into his coat for a knife.

Gunshots exploded around them, and Leo clamped both hands over his ears. The masked killer staggered backward under the barrage of bullets and collapsed beside Grant's dead body.

Blood splattered Leo and he scrabbled backward like a crab, meeting up with the others who did the same. He bumped into Asher and turned to face his friend. Filled with joy that they'd survived, he gave Asher a quick hug.

"Looks like we saved each other," Asher said as they separated and stood up.

Leo nodded, taking in the others as the cops surrounded them. Cassie's dad was bent over the killer, so Leo called to Marisol.

"Marisol, William's hurt. And Baxter's in the graveyard. They need help."

Marisol eyed him with admiration. "Paramedics are coming in now."

More lights suddenly came on, illuminating the whole of the soundstage, as four paramedics in uniform raced into the room while others followed with a couple of stretchers. Marisol directed two of them toward the cemetery that Leo now saw wasn't much more than twenty feet away. In the dark, everything had seemed so far apart.

He and Asher stood, the others doing the same. Edward swept Cassie and Donovan into a tight embrace, which they didn't resist. Edward gazed intently at Leo and mouthed, "Thank you."

Leo offered a little smile in return, realizing that the place was suddenly swarming with cops. Entering behind them was J.C., Laura, Chet, Jaden, and…his mother?

The others waited while Leo's mom closed the gap. Even Asher stepped back to give them space. Leo gazed at his mom and she at him, her expression turning to one of horror. Leo glanced down at the blood all over him and smiled.

"Don't worry, Mom, it's not mine this time."

His mother said nothing, looking stoic as always. Then she did something that almost knocked him over with astonishment. She stepped forward and, despite his bloody shirt, pulled him into the tightest hug he could ever remember getting from her.

Not sure what to do, he returned the hug, almost feeling like he was hugging a stranger. "I'm fine, Mom, really. No stab wounds."

She released him, awkwardly wiping a tear from her eye with one well-manicured finger. "You never cease to amaze me, Leonardo."

Uncertain how to respond, he shrugged.

By then, J.C., Laura, and Chet had rushed in, and his mom stepped aside so they could hug Leo and gush over what a fool he was for not telling them his plan.

Happier than he could imagine at seeing his friends again, he asked, "How did you find me?"

"Pierre remembered you and brought us here," J.C. blurted excitedly.

Leo's eyes widened in surprise. "Pierre? That's so cool."

"Yeah," Laura said with a wink, "I think he's got a crush on you already."

Leo's mouth dropped open, and she gave him a shove.

"You get all the hot ones, Leo," Chet said with a grin, also shoving Leo.

Leo turned to look for Asher, finding him with the others watching two paramedics work on William.

"Let's check on William," he told his friends, and started in that direction. The others followed.

Leo stood beside Asher and watched as the paramedics gently lifted William onto a stretcher, then pressed a button so it rose into the air on wheels.

"They said he's lost a lot of blood," Asher said, his voice choking.

"He's tougher than he seems," Leo said, not sure what else to say.

Asher nodded. "You shoulda seen him and Baxter the other day when Cassie's dad taught us self-defense. They were animals."

Leo found a smile creeping onto his face, but then lost it as other paramedics rolled a second gurney with Baxter's inert form past them toward the exit. Edward appeared at Leo's side, watching the retreating gurney, while Marisol barked orders in the background.

"Is he gonna…?" Asher asked, unable to finish his question.

Edward looked grave, the worry lines around his eyes crinkling with concern. "They don't know."

He faced them, all of them who'd come under attack. Donovan had one arm wrapped tightly around Cassie and, to Leo's surprise, Robert had his arm around Kristen. Diego stood beside them, J.C. right behind.

"Are you all okay?" Edward asked.

Kristen snorted. "You taught us too well, coach. Those guys didn't stand a chance."

Everyone gazed at her a moment in shock, then laughed, releasing their pent-up anxiety.

"Seriously," she went on, her voice sounding sincere for a change, "we all worked together to stay alive. It was pretty epic."

"And don't forget our ace in the hole," Donovan added, pointing to Leo, who felt a rush of embarrassment.

"It's true, Leo," Cassie insisted. "More of us would've been seriously hurt or…if you hadn't been here to help."

"And if you hadn't warned us in the first place," Diego said in a hushed voice.

Leo glanced over at his mother to make sure she wasn't eavesdropping. She was chatting with Pierre and another guy Leo didn't know. He faced his friends once more. "Like I told you all before, we make a good team."

"I agree," Edward said, throwing one arm around Leo, who welcomed the supportive gesture.

As Marisol arranged for the young people to be removed from the crime scene and checked for injuries outside, Leo excused himself from the group and approached Pierre, still chatting with his mom.

Pierre lit up, his face displaying relief and excitement at Leo's approach.

Leo said to his mom, "Can I talk to Pierre a minute?"

"Of course, Leonardo," she replied smoothly, swiping back some errant strands of auburn hair before approaching Marisol, who stood giving instructions to various police officers.

"I'm so glad you're okay," Pierre said. "I got scared when they said you went missing."

Leo offered a smile but didn't make eye contact. "I heard I have you to thank for saving me. Not sure how much longer we could've held out against that guy. He was like a bear."

Pierre nodded. "Yeah. I kind of snuck over when they took off the mask to see if I knew him."

That caught Leo's attention. "Did you?"

"Yeah. He was one of the studio's head carpenters. Built this whole set. Always seemed cool to me. Just goes to show, huh?"

Leo was floored by this news. A serial killer who worked for the studio?

"Yeah, I guess it does. Anyway, thanks for remembering me."

"I couldn't forget you." Pierre grinned, then looked awkwardly down. "I mean, you had that all-access pass and everything."

Leo nodded and pointed back at his ever-growing group of friends. "We're gonna all do something fun when our movie wraps, like hang out at the beach or something. You can come too, if you want."

Pierre raised his brows. "Only with the group?"

Now Leo felt awkward, fixing his gaze on Asher, who was chatting with Laura. When he looked back, he noticed Pierre watching Asher too.

"I understand," Pierre said, a tad disappointed. "Sure, I'd love to hang out with all of you."

Leo realized that Laura's joke may not have been a joke, but he liked Pierre and didn't see the harm in having the young man join them wherever they chose to gather.

"Cool. Can I get your number so I can contact you when we're all meeting?"

"Course."

Leo realized suddenly that his phone wasn't in his pocket and looked sheepish. "I don't have my phone. I must have dropped it in the graveyard when the killer knocked me out."

Pierre shrugged. "No worries. Your mom's a bigshot around here and you're Mr. All-Access Pass, so I can find you, no problem."

Leo smiled and stuck out his hand. Pierre shook it. "Thanks again, Pierre."

Pierre nodded and Leo rejoined his friends, standing beside Laura and Asher to make sure they weren't talking about him. They weren't at that moment, but probably had been, if he knew Laura.

CHAPTER TWENTY

THIS SCENE IS ALMOST FINISHED

The following day, the film shoot shut down to allow the victims time with their families. Cassie was relieved that Baxter and William would survive, but saddened they would likely miss the final weeks of shooting after all they'd gone through.

She woke up that morning feeling drained, like a wet noodle, her emotions thrashed, and sat for some time in the kitchen nursing a cup of coffee. Her dad had been up late the night before helping Marisol with the crime scene, so he didn't saunter into the kitchen until almost noon. He wore casual clothes because the department had given him the day off to spend with her. He poured a mug of coffee and sat across the table.

"Did you have trouble sleeping?"

"Yeah," she said, sipping her lukewarm coffee. "I kept seeing William shot and Leo rushing the killer. And the blood. I almost can't believe it's over."

"It is." He sipped from his mug. "Near as we can figure, Stuart, or Grant, met the killer at the studio, probably working on the same film. How they worked out their plans, we'll never know." He reached across the table and squeezed her hand with his. "I've never been so scared in my life."

Cassie smiled at the love in his eyes. "Me either. But we're still together. That's not gonna change."

He released her hand with a smile and picked up his mug, staring over it at her. "I'm sorry it took so long for me to get there, but I'm proud of you for fighting back. If not for Grant being there, you and the others would've knocked that guy senseless."

Cassie chuckled. "We just did what you taught us. And Leo helped a lot. He's amazing."

Her dad nodded. "He really is."

Cassie tensed up, fear curling itself around her heart. "How did you explain to the higher-ups that you knew something was going on without, you know, giving away his secret?"

"I left that up to Marisol," he replied after a sip of coffee. "That's why she's a detective and I'm not."

"I just don't want anything bad to happen to him."

"Neither do I, and nothing will. I owe that boy big time and I won't let him forget it. So, anything special you want to do today?"

She sighed. "I'm thrashed, actually. How 'bout we just stream stuff all day?"

He grinned. "Works for me."

Leo woke up thinking about William and Baxter, figuring he'd call Edward sometime that day to find out their condition. Maybe he'd visit them too, if that was allowed. He also wanted to talk to Asher but didn't want to interrupt his time with his mom. He dressed in shorts and a tee shirt and decided to make something for breakfast, unless Sylvia already had food ready, which she usually did.

As Leo entered the kitchen, he froze in place. His mother was standing at the stove cooking something.

"Mom? Are you all right?"

She turned with a smile. Dressed casually, she asked, "Never better. I forgot how you like your eggs. Actually, I never knew. So?"

Leo's tongue unfroze. "Uh, scrambled, please."

"Perfect," she replied. "My favorite too. Would you mind setting the table?"

Leo thought he must be dreaming. "Uh, sure." He walked stiffly to the drawers and pulled out silverware. "Where's Sylvia?"

"I gave her the day off," his mother replied as she worked on scrambling the eggs. "Since we're not working today, I thought we'd spend it together."

Leo shook his head in amazement as he exited the kitchen into the dining room and set two places. This was not the mother he'd grown up with. For a split second, he thought of sci-fi movies where someone got replaced by a duplicate. A Stepford Mom maybe?

Trembling with uncertainty, he re-entered the kitchen and stared at her cooking. In a separate skillet were sausages and bacon, and she even had out small bowls of strawberries and a bottle of orange juice.

"Anything else you need me to do?"

She glanced over her shoulder. "Grab some plates and glasses and put them on the counter. We'll serve ourselves here and eat in the dining room."

Almost feeling like the wind had been knocked out of him, he did as instructed.

No more was said until they'd served themselves and sat across from one another at the rectangular wooden dining table. Leo gazed at the food on his plate. It looked and smelled delicious, so he dug in. He sensed his mother watching him as he took the first bites, which were surprisingly good.

"How is it, Leonardo?"

"It's, uh, it's really good." He couldn't keep the note of surprise from his voice. "I thought you, you know, hated cooking and stuff like that?"

She offered an unusually self-deprecating smile. "I watched some YouTube videos."

Leo laughed at that and gobbled up the rest of his plate, returning to the kitchen for seconds. Once he felt full, he noticed that she had already finished.

"Thanks, Mom. That was awesome."

"You're welcome." She paused, looking like she was gathering her thoughts, and Leo expected the other shoe to drop. She was being too nice to him. "When the police first told me of the plot against my cast and crew, I recall feeling relief that you weren't a target. Yes, selfish is my middle name and I proudly acknowledge that. But when you disappeared yesterday, I flashed back to that time in the hospital last March when you almost died. I was afraid, Leonardo."

Leo listened, his body rigid with astonishment. "I'm okay, Mom. Not a scratch this time."

She nodded. "I know, and I'm grateful. Of late, I've come to realize that it's just you and me. I told you before I wasn't cut out to be a mother and that's still true. But family is important, and I want you to know I think you're important." She sighed and shook her head in annoyance. "I can recognize a brilliant script, but this kind of talk eludes me."

Leo soaked up every awkward word and absorbed the emotions his mother was trying to project. He'd grown up thinking she didn't like him, but she'd admitted that time in the hospital that she didn't really know him. Maybe now was the time.

"Mom, there's something I wanna tell you. About me."

For once, she didn't say anything. She leaned forward, arms on the table, listening.

"Did you wonder how I knew J.C. was in danger last March, or how the cops knew that Cassie and the others might die today? Or even how I was able to save Robert?"

"Yes, Leonardo. I noticed the anomalies in all those situations."

"I tried to tell you last March, but…"

Her face lit up with a memory, then she frowned. "But I blew you off because I was busy. I remember. This isn't about you liking boys, is it?"

"No, I made that up." He paused. "You know I like helping out at the homeless shelters, right? Well, I met this man who made me look in his eyes, which you know I hate to do. And he gave me the power to know when people will die."

She gasped but recomposed herself at once.

Leo explained about Mr. Franklin, Kyle—the kid from the coffee place—and how he'd found out that J.C. would be murdered. He filled in the gaps he hadn't shared with the police on that case, and how he'd figured out that Robert and others in her cast and crew were going to die. When he finished, his underarms were drenched, his body rigid with anxiety.

She sat back in her chair, silent while she thought about what he'd said. "You know I have no use for the supernatural, Leonardo, which is why this is the first film I've made to even touch on that subject. But what you just told me fits all the facts, so I believe you."

Leo sagged in his chair, deflated with relief. "Please don't tell anyone, Mom."

"Of course not. I'm honored that you told me. I assume Laura and Chet know? And Cassie and her group?"

Leo nodded.

"I seem to recall you sounded scared when you approached me last March. Do you still feel that way?"

"No, because I've been able to save all my friends, so that makes it okay. And now, for everyone I saved, I can look into their eyes and see nothing. I think changing the timeline erases their future to me. Which is cool because finally, I can look people in the eye when I talk to them. It's still hard, but, you know, I'm working on it."

"I noticed that on set. I suspect your severe shyness is partly my fault for being so dismissive of you, but that's all changing. That's why I gave you the all-access studio pass. I want you to know I trust you."

Leo couldn't believe this conversation was happening. Joy filled his being, and he smiled. "Thanks, Mom, for breakfast and, well, this." He waved his hands between her and himself.

"Why don't you invite J.C. and the others over. You can go to the beach or something."

"What're you gonna do?"

"I thought I'd just relax and watch something, a movie, perhaps."

"Can I watch with you?"

Now her face brightened with joy. "I'd like that very much."

The next few days on set were a bit tense, especially for Cassie and Donovan and the actors. Cassie had fended off the media peppering her with questions when she'd arrived that first morning, and all the others had done the same.

Of course, the entire crew knew what happened, and many of them were friends with the deceased killer. The news that a co-worker was a serial murderer devastated those closest to him.

Cassie learned that the police figured out he was the same man who'd murdered those three women in LA in the months leading up to the attack at the studio.

She did her best to focus on her work, as did Donovan and the others. Replacements had been brought in to fill William and Baxter's roles, which saddened Cassie even more, but she vowed to visit both her friends as soon as that was allowed.

She thought it amusing that Kristen had taken her advice about Robert. The two were together whenever they weren't on camera. They were a great-looking couple, destined for Hollywood stardom, in her opinion. She also hoped they'd be good for each other, the way Donovan was for her.

Leo and his friends entered the soundstage just as the first shot was about to roll. Leo looked happier than Cassie could ever recall seeing him, and his smile filled up his face even more when Asher hurried up and gave him a quick hug. She had a few minutes before shooting began, so she rushed over to him.

"Morning, Cassie," Leo said when she joined his group.

She gazed at his face, which looked relaxed, not tense like usual. "You seem different today, calmer."

He nodded, making eye contact. "Yeah. I had the best day ever with my mom. I found out she doesn't hate me. She actually likes me."

Based on her experience with her own parents, who loved her deeply, Cassie was shocked by his admission, but she smiled for his sake. "That's awesome."

Leo leaned in closer and said in a soft voice, "I also told her about my…power."

She and Asher reacted with surprise, but Laura, J.C., and Chet did not, so Cassie figured he'd already told them.

"How did she take it?" Asher asked.

"Great," asserted Leo. "She was happy I told her."

Joy filled Cassie's heart, such a wonderful feeling after all the doom and gloom. "We're about to start shooting. I just wanted to, well, thank you, Leo, for saving me…for saving all of us." She impulsively threw her arms around him and hugged tightly. Startled, he returned the hug with affection.

"Hey, Cass," came Mr. K's voice across the soundstage, "we're ready to roll!"

Cassie released Leo. "Gotta go."

She hurried back to her post.

Unfortunately for Leo, the media knew about him being attacked by the killer and how he helped save the others, so once again he went under a microscope. For the next several shooting days, media was camped out near the main studio entrance, hoping for a soundbite. But unlike before, Leo was no longer afraid. He answered their questions without stressing and allowed his photo to be taken (he couldn't control that) and then went on his way.

That talk with his mom had opened him up in ways he hadn't even known were closed. He felt more relaxed, more free, more confident. He continued to watch the filming but also explored the studio, sometimes by himself, other times with J.C., Laura, and Chet. He learned a lot about studio life and came to a better understanding of his mother and, perhaps, what shaped some of her aloofness.

That Sunday, he and the others went to the hospital where William and Baxter were recovering. The boys had been placed in the same room, so everyone crowded in for their visit.

"Getting shot is a lot different than it looks in the movies," William remarked, touching his abdomen and wincing. "More painful too."

"Talk about pain," Baxter chimed in, "having a blade sticking out of you isn't exactly fun."

He pulled up his shirt to display a large bandage taped to the upper right side of his torso.

"You'll have a cool scar to show off," Robert said with a shrug.

"Funny," Baxter retorted with a fake scowl.

"We want to go back to work," William said, "but the doctors won't let us do anything strenuous for who knows how long."

"We still have at least another month of shooting, right, Cass?" Donovan said, sounding upbeat.

"Yep." Cassie eyed the boys with genuine affection. "Hopefully, you'll be back for the final week or two."

"That's something, I guess," Baxter grumbled.

Leo watched this scene play out as he stood beside Asher, feeling grateful that no one had died.

The next day—Monday—he, Laura, J.C., and Chet had to return to high school. Senior year was supposed to be fun, but Leo dreaded it.

As expected, his heroics in the media made him a short-term celebrity once again. He was mobbed by students, especially girls, the moment he set foot on campus that Monday. All these kids used to mock him and call him Shy Boy, or even Queer Boy because he hung out with J.C., who they didn't like, and now Chet.

He politely refused their invitations to hang out at lunch and, instead, sat at his usual table with J.C., Laura, and Chet. He'd learned already that popularity is fake, but real friends aren't.

School proved more of a drag than ever before. Leo missed being on the set, and so did the others. Every chance he got, he checked his phone for texts from Asher, of which there were many. J.C., he noticed, spent much of lunch texting Diego.

"Uh, J.C.," Laura said one day, "how about visiting with us so we can all complain about school together?"

J.C. looked up at that and laughed. He did participate more as the days went by. After school, they'd all pile into Leo's or J.C.'s car and head to the studio, where Larkin always greeted them with a big smile.

Leo was able to spend some time with Asher on those visits, but most of the time his friend was working. Still, just being on set felt natural to him. School didn't.

And so passed the next month until there was only one week left of shooting. Leo needed to talk with Asher about, well, what would happen after the film wrapped. He was happy to see William and Baxter return to work that Saturday before the final week. They received a hearty round of applause from the entire cast and crew. Even shy William seemed to bask in the positive attention.

The last week would be mostly taken up with filming the basement scenes and, for once, Leo was grateful that school would force him to miss most of it. On this Saturday, the hospital scenes were being filmed, and Leo didn't mind those so much. It was more fun seeing Asher in a hospital bed than himself, and Diego was a riot with the big ankle cast and crutches.

Diana, the sweet makeup lady, hung around the set, in case anyone needed touchups. That way, no one needed to "leave the hospital" to find her at the makeup station. Leo noticed her watching him before she approached and stood by his side.

"How are you, Leo? You look well."

"I'm good, Diana. Thanks for asking."

"Your mother told me you had a chance to talk together recently."

Alarm bells went off in Leo's mind. *You didn't tell her, did you, Mom?* "Yeah. We been talking more lately. She really likes showing me how stuff works around here."

Diana offered a kind smile. "No one better to learn from than her." She paused and they watched another take being filmed. J.C. was on the other side of the set stifling a laugh as Diego kept tripping over his crutches.

"Remember our agreement, Leo?"

Diana's words interrupted his enjoyment of the scene and caught him off guard. *Agreement? Oh no...*

"Uh, yeah. You wanted to take pictures of me. You really don't have to, Diana."

"Now, now, I insist," she said, her voice soft but firm. "Not only do I want to show you my talents, but I want you to see yourself as others do. Your mother agrees with me. You've improved, I can see that, but your self-esteem could still use a boost."

Leo saw in her eyes and heard in the tone of her voice that she wouldn't take no for an answer. "Okay. When do you want to take my pictures?"

"In a bit," Diana said, watching the filming once more. "This scene is almost finished."

Leo nodded, hoping he could hide somewhere before the scene ended. But everywhere he stood to watch, he felt her eyes on him. She wasn't going to let him weasel out of this.

When he recalled his idea to give Asher one of his headshots, suddenly her photography session didn't sound so bad.

When the hospital scene ended, it was already evening. Diana approached him and he went with her willingly. He didn't tell J.C. and made sure Asher didn't see him. Embarrassment still flooded him at the idea, but he also wanted to surprise Asher.

But the surprise would be on Leo.

CHAPTER TWENTY-ONE

ALMOST DONE

THE MAKEUP "ROOM," A MAKESHIFT affair set up behind upright wooden flats to give Diana and the actors some privacy, was located at the farthest corner of the soundstage. Upon arriving, Leo understood why Diana liked staying near the action with her makeup kit. It was a long walk to the station. Isolated too.

As he stepped in between the two flats, he saw a longish makeup table that had a large upright mirror adorned with round lights, currently turned on. The area was large enough for three people to do makeup at one time. Brushes for hair and face, not to mention small makeup kits, sat on the table, and three chairs rested in front.

At one end of the space was a plain blue backdrop attached to the flat and a single chair beneath it. To either side were lights on stands.

Diana had a small desk of her own onto which she set her portable makeup kit. Beside it was a fancy-looking camera. Leo didn't know much about photography except for taking pictures with his phone.

Diana turned to him with a smile. "Your clothes are fine for the first shots, then I'll have you change shirts. Sit at the table and let me touch up your hair a bit."

Leo glanced into the mirror and realized he'd worn a striped tank top to the set. He noticed his veiny arms, especially the vein that ran down his biceps into the forearm. His biceps looked bigger than he remembered, but then he seldom looked at mirrors. He couldn't stand the thought of accidentally seeing his own death.

As he sat, Diana picked up a heavy-looking hairbrush and went to work on his shaggy auburn hair. Longish in the back, it covered his ears and sometimes his eyes if not controlled. He kept his eyes off his face and on his arms. He recalled how Diego, Asher, and especially Jaden had reacted to him when he arrived, complimenting him on his choice of shirt. The only other time he'd worn a tank top had been on location, so it didn't occur to him why they were staring. Even Donovan, Cassie, and Kristen had commented that he looked good.

He'd never thought of himself as particularly attractive, despite his mom's constant refrain that he was beautiful. Perhaps that's why Diana was doing this for him.

"There," she said, "perfect. What do you think?"

She pulled back the brush and Leo glanced at the lower half of his face, unable to really see the hair. "It looks great. Thanks."

She studied his face, so he had to keep his eyes averted from hers. "I think you look perfect as is. Not even any five o'clock shadow. Do you shave often?"

"Hardly ever, which I kind of like. Chet shaves every day, and he hates it."

She nodded. "I bet. Now, I want you to stand over here."

She led him to the blue background and pulled away the chair. Once he was positioned, she turned on the two lights and aimed them accordingly. One illuminated him from behind, the other from in front, both at angles.

She stepped back and studied him with intensity, making him squirm. "Perfect." She retreated to her desk and picked up the heavy-looking camera. She examined the settings, changed a few, and then stepped closer to Leo once more.

He'd never modeled before, so he didn't understand why she told him to look this way or that, to put his hands here or there, to tilt his chin up or down. She snapped away while giving him directions, and then stopped.

She rummaged through some clothes hanging on a rack behind the desk, pulling out a long-sleeved shirt in dark burgundy. She handed it to him. "Put this on, please."

Leo took the shirt, feeling awkward changing in front of her.

She laughed at his reticence. "Never fear, I've seen plenty of shirtless models over the years."

Leo hung the shirt on the back of a nearby chair, then quickly pulled off his tank top. He shivered slightly in the cool soundstage air. She eyed him as he reached for the shirt and said, "Hold up. Let me get a few this way."

Leo felt on display and almost said no, but she was being so nice he decided to just cooperate and get this modeling session over with.

No wonder Asher dropped out, he thought, as he posed this way and that, some in similar positions to before, others clearly designed to show off his physique.

After several more minutes and numerous clicks of the camera shutter, she told him to put on the shirt but not button it. Once more, Leo followed her directions. The shirt felt like silk, cool and soft against his bare skin. He left it unbuttoned, as instructed, and she snapped off what seemed like another hundred photos.

Finally, just when Leo was about to say he needed to get back to his friends, she said, "Almost done." She grabbed what looked like a green compression shirt off the rack and handed it over. "Last one, I promise. I think you'll look fantastic in this."

"Okay," Leo muttered, "but then I better get back. I carpooled over here."

"Five minutes, tops," Diana said with an infectious grin.

Leo understood what made her such a good photographer. She could coax great stuff out of even reluctant subjects like him. As he slipped off the long-sleeved shirt, she snapped a few more pictures and then turned to her desk, bending beneath it, probably to get some more equipment.

Leo hung the dress shirt carefully on the back of the chair and grabbed the compression shirt off the seat where she'd tossed it. He was about to slip it over his head when she turned around, still smiling.

Instead of the camera, however, in her hands was a lethal-looking crossbow, armed with a sharp metal-tipped arrow.

And it was aimed at his chest.

Startled, he dropped the shirt onto the floor and stared in horror at the arrow pointing at him. "Uh, Diana, is that, like, a prop you want me to hold?"

"No, dear boy. This is the prop I'm going to use to kill you."

His body turned to stone, and she laughed. When she did, she moved the crossbow slightly and light flickered off the metal arrow. Flashing through his mind was another image, one he'd seen multiple times: a shadowy figure and a flicker of light.

Of course! In looking for the others' deaths, he'd seen his own reflection, but the details were never clear enough for him to know that.

Today was the day he would die!

"Why?" He fought to keep his voice steady. "What have I ever done to you?"

Her sweet face darkened, like she was turning into medusa. "You killed the person most important to me."

Leo's heart pounded wildly, and he felt weak in the knees. She was too far away to use his aikido, so what could he do?

"I never…k-killed…anyone," he stammered.

"Not directly, no," she replied, keeping the crossbow leveled at his chest. "You're still responsible."

"How? When?" Leo needed to keep her talking.

She smirked. "I know your plan. Keep me distracted and maybe you can think of a way out. It won't happen, dear Leo. I've been plotting this moment since March."

Leo's brain exploded with understanding. "You mean you were friends with…"

"Partners really. There's nothing like serial killing to get the adrenaline going. I was behind the entire plan for Grant and Charles—the guy in the mask—as well. We used to gather for drinks after work, and we happened to share our sorrows one night, so I concocted a plan of revenge. Grant went along, with Charles as the instrument of death. For *his* victims, that is. I ordered that you be left for me."

Leo suddenly recalled what the killer and Grant had said about him, that he was off-limits. "You're crazy."

"No, just calculating." She paused, turning thoughtful. "But somehow, you ruined all our plans because you knew what would happen. Before I kill you, tell me how you knew."

"Go to Hell!" Leo trembled with rage.

She chuckled. "I expect that's where I'll end up, but not for some time. Goodbye, Leo."

Just then came a knock on the wood of the flat, and Asher stuck his head in. "Diana, could I—" His eyes darted to the crossbow and Leo standing in front of the background, and stepped between them. "That's a really cool prop. Can I hold it?"

"No, Asher, she'll kill you!" shouted Leo, rushing forward.

Just then, Robert leaped over the back side of the wooden frame and landed on Diana's desk. She spun in surprise, and he kicked the crossbow out of her hands just as Leo grabbed Asher and pushed him to one side.

Then, to Leo's further astonishment, into the small space flooded Kristen, Cassie, Donovan, Diego, Jaden, J.C., Laura, and Chet. Kristen and Diego rushed forward to grab Diana's arms, restraining her.

"Let me go!" Diana cried indignantly. "Why are you even here?"

Asher boldly stepped right up to her. "We came to save Leo."

Diana scoffed. "From a photo shoot?"

"No," Jaden said, shocking Leo by holding out his phone. He tapped it and Leo heard himself say, "Uh, Diana, is that, like, a prop you want me to hold?" and then her response, "No, dear boy. This is the prop I'm going to use to kill you."

Jaden tapped the phone and the recording stopped playing. "There's more, if you wanna hear it," he said coldly. "A lot more."

Diana's face fell and she said nothing more.

Cassie lifted the small walkie talkie she carried and clicked it on. "This is Cassie Stewart, AD. I need two security guards to come back to the makeup station. And bring restraints. We just stopped a murder attempt. Over."

A male voice crackled forth from the walkie. "Did you say murder attempt? Over."

"Yes," Cassie replied. "Please get security here asap. Over."

She reattached the walkie to her belt and gazed at Leo, who could only stare in amazement at his friends who'd saved him. "You okay, Leo?"

"How did you know this was going to happen?"

Cassie indicated Asher. "You can thank him."

Leo faced his friend, eyebrows raised.

"I worked with tons of photographers and makeup people my whole life," Asher explained. "Diana was always creepy nice to you, Leo. I saw her talking to you during the hospital scene, and when you were both gone after we finished, I got worried."

Leo nodded, his mind racing to understand the whole situation. "But all of you came," he said to the group at large.

Kristen smiled. "That's what friends are for."

"Whether you know it or not, Leo," Donovan said, "you're our friend for life."

Leo felt a surge of warmth pour through him that all these people considered him such a worthwhile friend.

Just then, he heard running footsteps, and two uniformed security guards stepped into the crowded room. The dark-haired man asked, "Where's the suspect?"

Cassie pointed to Diana, still being held firmly by Diego and Kristen.

"Her?" exclaimed the female guard. "I've known her for years."

"Not as well as you thought," Cassie said dryly. "Did you bring restraints?"

"Yes," said the man. "We also called the police."

"Good." Cassie stepped aside so Diego and Kristen could push Diana forward. The female security guard slipped some old-looking handcuffs around her wrists, snapping them shut.

"We'll take her now," said the man, waving the woman past him with the still silent Diana. "You all better wait near the front for the police. And don't touch anything here."

"We know," Cassie replied. "My dad's a cop."

Just as Diana was almost out of the cubicle, she turned and offered Leo a nasty smile. "You haven't seen the last of me."

Then she was gone, along with the two security guards.

"This is insane. She wanted to kill you because of something that happened when J.C. was stalked?" Cassie asked curiously.

Leo nodded. "She was crazy. You heard her, she helped Grant go after you."

"She always seemed so nice," Diego commented. "Just goes to show you, huh?"

Out of the blue, J.C. gaped at Leo. "Leo, why aren't you wearing a shirt?"

Everyone reacted with surprise, staring at Leo.

"Well, she took some pics," Leo said, clearly flummoxed, "and then she wanted me to change shirts, but then she wanted some with no shirt and… What does it matter, J.C.? The woman just tried to kill me."

"That doesn't give you the right to show off." J.C. looked petulant, then laughed. Everyone else joined in.

Leo relaxed, realizing the joke was on him. He reached for his tank top and had just slipped it on when Diego said, "Wait, Leo, you're saying she took, like, sexy pictures of you with no shirt on?"

Leo froze, feeling like that bug under the microscope. "Well, I don't know about sexy, but…"

Diego turned to Cassie. "Cass, is all this stuff considered evidence?"

Cassie shrugged. "I guess."

"The camera too? What about the film?"

A tiny smile crossed Cassie's freckled face. "I see what you mean. Unless there's something incriminating in the photos, they aren't evidence."

Diego grinned and nudged Jaden beside him. "Please ask your dad if I can have a set of those photos."

Leo winced. "What?"

Jaden gave Diego a small shove. "Hey, why do you get a set? I want one too."

Kristen grinned. "With a body that hot, I'll take a set, Cass."

Cassie shrugged. "I'll ask my dad. Anyone else want a set? Donovan?"

Donovan nodded eagerly. "Sure. I bet he's photogenic as hell. How about you, Asher?"

Asher's face reddened and he glanced shyly at Leo. "Yeah, I gotta have those."

Laura piped up with, "I'll take a set too. Chet?"

Chet smiled. "For sure. J.C.?"

J.C. eyed Leo a long moment, then sighed. "Probably just make me feel insecure, but why not."

They all sauntered out of the makeup area ahead of him, so Leo pushed his way to the front and stopped before them.

"Hey, what're you talking about with those photos? They're embarrassing."

Diego shook his head. "With a body like you got, Leo, no way they're gonna be embarrassing."

"Absolutely not," Jaden echoed.

Leo faced Jaden. "You're shy like me, Jaden, you know what I mean."

"Yeah, but I still want a set of those pics. Can't help myself." He shrugged.

Leo faced Asher in desperation. "Asher?"

Asher shrugged, looking down at the floor.

Leo stared at the group open-mouthed. Then they all busted up simultaneously, and Leo finally got it. He practically sagged with relief.

"You got me good," he said, offering a grin.

"I thought you would faint," Diego said, chuckling. "I was getting ready to catch you."

"Seriously, Leo, the look on your face." J.C. doubled over with laughter.

"Okay, let's leave him alone," Cassie said, losing her smile. "He just escaped death. For the third time this year."

Leo grinned and followed the group back toward the front entrance to the soundstage. Asher walked alongside him, while J.C. flanked Diego, who leaned into Cassie and said, "Seriously, Cass, talk to your dad about those photos. We really do want a set."

She cracked up and Leo rushed forward to shove Diego good-naturedly.

So, this is what it means to have friends, Leo thought, tossing a shy smile toward Asher. *I like it.*

It was Marisol and Edward who arrived with uniformed officers to take Diana into custody. Leo spotted his mom entering with the police. She gave him another crushing hug and then marched up to Diana as though to stab her. Leo was glad she wasn't carrying a weapon.

"I trusted you for the last ten years and this is how you repay me? By trying to kill my son?"

Diana laughed, the sound heartless and cold. "Like you care about your son?"

Cassandra's face dissolved into fury, and she slapped Diana hard across the face.

"That's enough, Cassandra," Edward said, grabbing her and holding her back.

Marisol motioned to two officers. "Mirandize her and take her downtown."

"Yes, Detective," replied a female officer. Then she and a short, stocky cop took Diana by the arms and led her out of sight to the exit.

Edward released his mom and she returned to Leo. "Are you sure she didn't hurt you?"

Leo shook his head. "My friends saved me." He waved an arm around at his stalwart group of friends, who grinned and nodded.

Cassandra smiled. "I'm glad you have such friends."

Edward turned to Marisol. "Do you want me to take their statements?"

"Yes, I'll examine the crime scene."

Jaden stepped forward. "I recorded everything on my phone. She bragged about everything she did."

Edward grinned and clapped Jaden on the back. "Good man."

Jaden beamed with pride.

Cassie approached her father. "Uh, Dad, can I ask you something before you take our statements?"

"Sure."

She pulled him to one side out of Leo's earshot, but he paid close attention to their facial expressions. Edward's eyebrows shot up at one point, but then he smiled and nodded.

She better not... Leo thought, as they both returned.

Cassie smiled innocently, but Leo didn't feel relieved.

CHAPTER TWENTY-TWO

THAT'S A WRAP

THE FOLLOWING WEEK WRAPPED UP shooting with the basement scenes. Since Leo and his high school friends couldn't show up until afternoon, they missed much of what they didn't want to watch anyway.

What weighed on Leo's mind as the film neared completion was the harsh reality that he wouldn't see much of his new friends, especially Asher. Leo would be in school, and they'd be working on other film projects.

Filming was due to wrap on Friday, with the wrap party held on Saturday for all the cast and crew. Leo needed to talk with Asher alone before everyone dispersed, but it was hard because Asher was in every scene being filmed that week.

Friday finally arrived and the last scene was completed. Leo's mom was present, of course, but it was Mr. Ketchum, as director, who called the moment.

"And that's a wrap, folks."

He grinned and everyone applauded. Leo joined in, but half-heartedly. His spirits lifted when Asher pushed through the back-slapping crowd to his side.

"Leo, I finally found you."

He sounded out of breath, even though the final shot was him seeming to die. He wore no shirt and fake sticky blood covered his abdomen and pants.

Leo stared a moment at Asher's defined upper body.

Asher looked down at his bloody torso and shrugged. "Better not let J.C. see me or he'll think I'm showing off."

Leo laughed. "You look great, you know, for an almost dead guy."

Asher laughed too. "Look, I gotta get cleaned up, obviously. You'll be at the wrap party, right?"

"Uh, yeah."

"Good, 'cause I really want to talk to you without everyone watching."

Leo's heart began pounding in his chest. Did Asher want to say they wouldn't be able to hang out like they'd talked about?

"That sounds cool. I wanna talk to you too."

They stared at one another awkwardly.

"Well, um, I better get cleaned up. See you tomorrow, Leo."

Leo nodded. "Tomorrow."

Asher grinned and moved off into the crowd.

Leo congratulated Mr. K and his crew for making such an awesome film, and then mostly hung out with Laura and Chet. J.C. went off to find Diego.

Laura pulled Leo to one side while Robert moved in to talk with Chet.

"So," Laura began, "tomorrow's party should be fun. Asher'll be there, right?"

"Course. He's the star."

"Just remember what I told you in that cemetery. No one expects you to be anyone but yourself, whoever you decide that is. We all love you no matter what."

Leo's eyes bulged in surprise.

She laughed. "Don't be afraid anymore." She squeezed his upper arm and then wandered off to chat with Cassie.

He stood where he was, basking in the glow of love that only friends could provide.

Leo struggled with what to wear for the party. Dress was casual, but he wanted to make a good impression on…everyone. He'd finally selected a lightweight long-sleeve blue shirt and cargo pants. The party would be held on the backlot to accommodate all the cast, crew, and their families.

Leo's mom offered to drive him, which was good because he was too nervous. But she was taking too long getting ready. He glanced at his watch again, nervously shuffling his feet in the foyer, waiting for her to come down.

Spotting a wall mirror, he hurried over to check his hair and overall appearance. The shirt seemed a bit snug in the chest and shoulders. Would J.C. accuse him of showing off again? Knowing J.C., probably.

Finally, his mother descended the stairs, and he stared in amazement. She'd styled her hair up, with dangly parts trailing past her ears. The dress she wore was deep red and form-fitting, showing off her impressive figure. She grinned and twirled around.

"How do I look?"

"Pretty amazing, actually."

"You look very sharp yourself, Leonardo." Then she frowned. "The hair though… Wait here."

She hurried back up the stairs while Leo checked his watch yet again. He glanced into the mirror. His hair covered much of his forehead and didn't look bad to him. She returned within moments holding a large hair-brush.

Standing beside him at the mirror, she began working his hair with the brush.

"Seriously, Mom, my hair looks fine."

"You want to look your best for…well, for your friends."

She'd been about to say something else, and he had a feeling he knew what. Within moments, she had his thick wavy hair mostly off his forehead and brushing the collar of his shirt.

"There, now we're ready."

He scowled but had to admit it looked better.

They carried on a genuine conversation on the drive to the studio, his mom sharing funny stories from other films she'd produced and expressing her opinion that this current one would be a hit.

Leo agreed with that assessment, especially with the lead actors.

When they arrived and his mom pulled into her reserved spot, Leo stepped out of the car and walked around to open her door, like he'd seen done in the movies. She reacted with pleasant surprise, then did something he never expected. She linked her arm in his and they walked side by side to the check-in station. Leo honestly felt like he was entering the Academy Awards.

He grinned when he saw Edward and Marisol, dressed in regular clothes, standing by the check-in table. Naturally, he and his mother didn't need to check in, so they passed by and stopped in front of the two police officers.

"Thank you for providing protection tonight," Cassandra said, "but please enjoy the party too."

"We will," Marisol said with a smile, her eyes fixed on the newcomers entering the area.

"Good to see you again, Leo," Edward said. "You look quite stylish. Even changed your hair."

"That was Mom's idea," he grumbled, then laughed at her pained expression.

"Well, all your friends are around somewhere, so have at it."

"Can I go find them, Mom?"

She offered a cryptic smile. "Of course, Leonardo. Have fun."

He unlinked his arm and hurried through the crowded backlot, spotting crew members he'd befriended drinking from paper cups and laughing it up together. He nearly collided with Tank, which could've proved fatal.

"Sorry, Tank."

"You can't say you didn't see *me*."

They both laughed.

"Have you seen Cassie or any of the actors?"

He shook his head. "Pierre's over there. I understand you guys know each other. Ask him."

Leo looked where Tank pointed and spotted Pierre wearing a flashy shirt and chatting with another guy Leo didn't know.

"Thanks, Tank."

Leo threaded his way through the crowd and stopped near Pierre and his friend. Pierre's face lit up.

"Whoa, it's Mr. All-Access Pass." He laughed, and so did his friend.

"Hi, Pierre. Having fun?"

"How can I not? I'm off-duty." He laughed again. "You're looking good tonight."

"Thanks. I don't know if you know them, but I'm looking for the director or assistant director?"

Pierre scanned the crowd. "Director's right there, chatting with your mom."

How'd she get this far so fast? Leo wondered.

"Thanks, Pierre."

He thought Pierre was about to say something more, but he'd already left to join Mr. Ketchum and his mom.

"Long time, no see, Leonardo," his mother chortled, sipping a drink from a plastic wine glass.

"Hi, Mom. Mr. K, have you seen Cassie or Donovan, or any of the actors?"

The two adults exchanged a cryptic look, then Mr. K pointed to an open soundstage door, the same soundstage where the movie had been filmed.

"I think I saw some of them go in there."

Leo eyed the open door beyond the milling crowd. "Thanks. I'll go check."

"Have a good time," his mother said as he moved on.

A few crew members greeted him as he passed and then he was at the open door, gazing inside. Lights were on, but he saw no one at first. Suddenly, Donovan appeared, as though he'd been waiting in the shadows.

"Hey, Leo, glad you're finally here. C'mon."

He smiled and led Leo farther into the soundstage. As they rounded a corner into the Moreton Bay Tree set, Leo spotted everyone standing in front of a table. Donovan hurried ahead to flank Cassie, and Leo, feeling uncertain, approached.

Asher was at one end, gazing at him with an unreadable expression. Even Laura, J.C., and Chet were present. So were William and Baxter, both looking healthy and happy. Jaden stood to one side, smiling.

Cassie stepped forward. "You look very nice, Leo. See? We both brushed our hair." She put a hand to her hair, which was smoothed out and brushed back, showing more freckles but looking styled for a change.

"I get credit for that," Kristen said, holding Robert's hand. She wore a lavender blouse and hip-hugging jeans, while Robert wore a loud Hawaiian shirt and shorts. "I like your hair, Leo. Mom help with that?"

Leo nodded.

"So, Leo, tell them the good news," J.C. said, indicating the others.

Leo furrowed his brow. "What news?"

"That you can look 'em in the eyes now."

Leo hitched in surprise. He'd forgotten all about that! He explained to the mystified group that once he changed someone's timeline, he couldn't see their death anymore. Which meant, he was safe to make eye contact.

"If my shyness lets me, that is," he added.

Jaden clapped. "You and me're gonna practice, Leo. We'll beat this thing."

Leo grinned. "Sounds like a plan. So, why are you all in here? Party's out there."

Kristen let go of Robert's hand and walked around the table past William and Baxter, then stopped. The others stepped aside, and Leo spotted many 8x10 photos spread out on the table.

Kristen looked seriously at him. "You may not want to hear this, Leo, but you're our hero. There's no telling how many of us might not be here if it weren't for you."

Leo opened his mouth to protest, but Asher put a hand lightly on his arm. "Let her finish."

"Like we told you," Kristen went on, "you're our friend for life and we want to hang out whenever possible. But work and school and other commitments might keep us apart for who knows how long. That's why each of us wants a memento of what you did for us. You may be embarrassed by the photos Diana took, but you look hot in every single one and we all want your autograph."

Leo thought he'd heard wrong. "My autograph?"

"Yes," Cassie said, joining Kristen. "Diana may have been a murderer, but she was an amazing photographer."

"And she had an amazing model," Diego added. Jaden nodded and grinned.

Kristen held up a sharpie. "Well, Leo, who do you want to start with?"

Leo could barely move, he was so overcome with emotion. He slowly walked around the table where Kristen indicated a chair for him to sit. The photos were scattered around the tabletop, he guessed so that everyone could pick one for him to sign.

Him, signing autographs? It was surreal.

He reached out a trembling hand to pick up a few of the color photos while everyone waited in silence. As he rifled through them, he felt like he was looking at someone else. Who was this handsome boy gazing out at him?

The headshots displayed his soft features with wavy auburn hair, small nose, full lips, and vibrant brown eyes. He almost gasped aloud at how much he resembled his mother when she was younger. He cringed when he got to the shirtless photos, but even then, Diana had framed him so that he looked like a fitness model. His breathing almost stopped at the sight of the person he'd lived with his whole life but had never truly "seen."

His favorites were the headshots, and the ones in which he wore the open button-down shirt, which displayed some of his chest and abs but covered up the scar he'd received from being stabbed the previous March.

"Well," Kristen said, sounding impatient, "who will you start with?"

Leo pulled his gaze from the pictures and focused on her beside him. "You're sure you want me to do this? I feel silly."

"That's because you still suffer from low self-esteem," she replied, but in a soft, gentle tone. "We want to change that."

Leo nodded, too emotional to respond, and sat in the chair. "I, uh, I'll start with you, Kristen."

"Naturally, you'd start with the best." She laughed and picked up one of the photos on the table, passing it to Leo. "This one is my favorite." It was the one Leo liked best, the open shirt, looking sideways at the camera.

Leo took the photo and set it down, grabbing the sharpie and considering what to write. Kristen had scared him at first. She was abrupt and self-absorbed. But she'd changed during the course of the filming, and she'd implied that he was largely responsible. He bent over the photo and wrote in his neatest writing, *Kristen, thank you for being my friend and not my enemy. You're much better at the former than you think. Love, Leo.*

He handed her the photo nervously, not sure how she'd react. She read his message, then leaned down to kiss him on the cheek. "It's perfect." Leo breathed a sigh of relief. Kristen straightened up and looked over the others. "Who's next?"

They all fished through the photos, selecting the ones they wanted.

Diego chose one of the shirtless ones and gleefully handed it to Leo. "What can I say, Leo, you're hotter than hot."

Rather than feel embarrassed, Leo laughed and wrote, *Diego, you're an amazing guy and I hope to always be your friend. Take good care of J.C. for me. Leo.*

When Diego read the message, he grinned. "Will do."

Cassie and Donovan approached next. Leo glanced around for Asher but found him at the back, already holding a photo, awaiting his turn. He noted that Cassie had one of the open shirt photos, while Donovan chose one in the tank top, where his veins were prominently on display.

To Cassie, Leo wrote, *Cassie, thanks for all your support. It means the world. Love, Leo.* And to Donovan he wrote, *Donovan, I hope we always stay friends because you're one of the best guys I know. Leo.*

He signed William's and Baxter's next. They chose different headshots. To William he wrote, *William, you're one of the bravest guys I've ever met. Thanks for being my friend. Leo*, and to Baxter he wrote, *Baxter, you're a fun guy to be around. Thanks for all the chips. Leo.* Both of his friends looked pleased.

Jaden inched closer and handed Leo one of the shirtless photos. "You kind of saved me from my shyness, so I'd like your autograph, too."

Leo smiled and took the photo. On it he wrote, *Jaden, from one Shy Boy to another, stay awesome. Leo.*

Jaden grinned as he took back the picture. "You, too."

Then Robert stepped forward. "I owe you my life three times over, Leo," Robert gushed. "Thank you." He handed over one of the headshots. Leo wrote, *Robert, thanks for letting me practice my lifesaving techniques on you. You're a great guy. Leo.*

When Robert read the message, he laughed out loud and started passing it around.

At that moment, they were interrupted by the appearance of his mother.

Everyone stopped talking as she approached, heels clicking on the hard floor. She eyed Kristen with a smile. "I see it's going well."

"Perfectly," Kristen said. "Thanks for helping set this up, Ms. Cantrell."

"My pleasure."

Leo stared incomprehensively. "Mom? You were in on this?"

"Naturally. Your friends came to me with the idea, and I loved it." She picked up one of the open shirt photos and gazed at it. "Now do you see that I was truthful when I called you beautiful?"

Leo blushed. "Mom, not in front of my friends."

The group laughed and J.C. gave Leo a playful shove.

Leo's mom walked over to him and set the photo down. "May I have your autograph, Leonardo?"

"Huh?"

"It occurred to me that I don't have a photo of my son on my desk here at the studio."

Leo stiffened with shock. "You...you want my picture on your desk?"

"Of course, dear. How else can I brag about you?"

Leo was glad he was sitting because he'd have fallen over otherwise. He searched his mother's face, careful to avoid the eyes, for any sign of mockery, but there was none. She was serious.

"Uh, what should I write?"

Her casual smile was enhanced by the red lipstick she wore. "Indulge yourself."

Leo stared a moment at the photo and then wrote: *To Mom, You're forever in my heart. Love, Leonardo.*

He handed it back, unsure how she might respond. She gazed a long moment at what he wrote, her smile widening. "Thank you, Leonardo. I'll display it proudly. Now, continue with your friends."

She turned and walked purposefully out of the soundstage.

"That was amazing," J.C. exclaimed excitedly. "I never thought I'd see the day. I wish *my* mom..." He met Leo's gaze and shrugged. Leo understood.

"I'm next," Laura said, interrupting the awkward moment. She slid her photo over. It was one of the tank top shots. Leo wrote, *Laura, I don't know what I'd do without you. Please stay my friend forever. Love, Leo.*

She grinned when he handed it over. "Right back at you," she said, then moved aside for Chet to step in. He chuckled. "I couldn't resist." He handed Leo one of the shirtless photos, and Leo raised his eyebrows. "I know you hate seeing that scar, Leo, but every time I look at it, I remember how you got it saving my life."

Leo almost choked up. "Yeah, well, it was a life worth saving."

"I'm not so sure."

Leo forced Chet to make eye contact. "I am."

He took the photo and wrote, *Chet, saving your life was one of the best things I ever did, and I value your friendship. Leo.*

Chet's face shifted with various emotions as he stared at the message. "Thanks, Leo. You're the best."

"I think we're all pretty awesome," Leo said, eyeing his friends gathered around him.

"Okay, enough about Chet," J.C. said, "I'm next. And you better write something super cool to me."

He laughed and Laura slapped him on the arm.

Leo took the photo J.C. handed him. It was another shirtless shot, but Leo was looking slightly more toward the camera. He glanced up at J.C., who shrugged.

"What can I say, Chet and I had the same idea. I hate that scar because I caused it, but I also love it because you got it for me. Weird, I know."

Leo smiled. "I don't think so." He considered what to write to his oldest friend, who'd stuck by him since second grade. He wrote, *J.C., you've always been there for me, and I can't imagine life without you. I love you, man. Leo.*

When J.C. read the message, his mouth twitched, and Leo saw he was trying to keep his emotions in check. "Same here, Leo. Every word."

Leo grinned and they fist-bumped. For a moment, Leo thought he was done, but then Asher stepped shyly forward, holding out his photo.

Leo took the photo, one with the open shirt, but tighter, more of a headshot that emphasized Leo's eyes looking at the camera. It was very similar to the headshot Asher had given him.

He smiled to himself and considered what to write. There was so much he wanted to say to Asher, and he hoped he'd get the chance, so he simply wrote, *Asher, I feel like I've known you my whole life and I hope you'll always be my friend. I need you. Leo.*

He handed back the photo, and Asher gazed at it without displaying any specific reaction. Leo frowned, worrying that he'd said the wrong thing.

Kristen clapped a few times. "Okay, people, there's a party happening out there. I, for one, intend to dance the night away." She batted her eyes at Robert. "Do I have a dance partner?"

"For sure," blurted Robert and everyone laughed.

"And we need to practice our new dance routines," Diego announced. "How about it, J.C.?"

"You got it," J.C. said with exuberance, accepting the high five from Diego.

Leo stood and each of his friends clapped him on the back before heading toward the exit.

Asher announced, "Uh, I need to talk to Leo about something, so I'll be out in a few."

J.C.'s face flashed a look of jealousy, but Laura took his arm, pushing him toward the waiting Diego. In moments, no one was left but Leo and Asher.

Leo faced him, worried about what his friend might say. "I, uh, I wanted to say something too."

"Sure, go for it," Asher said calmly.

Leo had practiced in his mind what he would say, and now that the moment arrived, it all flew from his head like leaves in a breeze.

"I…I've never met anyone like you who made me feel, I don't know, relaxed and calm inside. People always make me nervous, which is why until now I haven't had many friends. But when I'm with you, I feel… happy. Laura told me, and I think she's right, that because I kept myself bottled up my whole life, I don't know who I am or even who I might want to date. I never checked out girls, but I didn't check out guys either. I just kept to myself, or with J.C. But you make me feel…like I could kick it with you 24/7 and I'd be the happiest guy in the world. I…I really wanna keep hanging out with you, whenever we can, but if what I said creeps you out and you don't want to, I get that."

Asher's expression didn't change during Leo's rambling speech, and he held his breath, waiting for Asher to respond.

Asher's small lips spread into a wide smile, and Leo breathed again.

"Leo, you just said almost everything I was going to. It just goes to show how in sync we are. Our lives were different growing up, and I couldn't be as shy as you with a camera in my face every minute. But I always had to be someone other than me. That's what modeling's about, so I never really had friends either. Modeling's kind of a sleazy business. Older kids hit on me and sometimes adults, too, which creeped me out and made me wanna hide. But when I met you, I finally felt close to someone. I just knew I could tell you anything and you'd understand."

He blushed and glanced away a moment before making eye contact again.

"I never thought about, you know, dating guys before, even though they hit on me in the modeling world. I know this'll sound cringe, but if I ever even thought about dating another guy, it would be you. But that's not where I'm at right now. I just want to be your friend and hang out with you as much as possible. Is that okay?"

Leo was shocked that he had no trouble keeping eye contact with Asher, further proof of their connectedness. He couldn't help but grin when Asher finished.

"It's more than okay. It's perfect."

Asher grinned, practically bouncing on his heels. "Well, um, we better go back to the party. They might think we're doing something we're not."

Leo chuckled. "I don't care what they think."

"Me neither."

Laughing, they headed for the exit, and whatever awaited them beyond it.

THE END

ABOUT THE AUTHOR

Michael J. Bowler is the award-winning author of *A Matter of Time*, THE LANCE CHRONICLES (*Children of the Knight, Running Through A Dark Place, There Is No Fear, And The Children Shall Lead, Once Upon A Time In America),* THE HEALER CHRONICLES *(Spinner, Shifter, Spoiler)* The Film Milieu Thriller Series (*I Know When You're Going To Die, The Horror Film Killer, They Know When The Killer Will Strike*), and *Like A Hero (Book 1 of The Invictus Chronicles.)*

His screenplay, "THE GOD MACHINE," won First Place in the 2017 Scriptapalooza competition.

He grew up in San Rafael, California, and majored in English and Theatre at Santa Clara University. He went on to earn a master's in film production from Loyola Marymount University, a teaching credential in English from LMU, and another master's in Special Education from Cal State University Dominguez Hills. He worked producer, writer, and/or director on several ultra-low-budget horror films, including "Hell Spa," "Fatal Images," "Club Dead," and "Things II."

He taught high school in Hawthorne, California—both in general education and to students with learning disabilities—in subjects ranging from English and Strength Training to Algebra, Biology, and Yearbook.

He has been a volunteer Big Brother to eight different boys with the Catholic Big Brothers Big Sisters program, a decades-long volunteer within the juvenile justice system in Los Angeles, and is a single father to an adopted child.

He has been honored as Probation Volunteer of the Year, YMCA Volunteer of the Year, California Big Brother of the Year, and 2000 National Big Brother of the Year. The "National" honor allowed him and three of his Little Brothers to visit the White House and meet the president in the Oval Office.

His goal as an author is for teens and middle schoolers to experience empowerment and hope; to see themselves in his diverse characters; to read about kids who face real-life challenges; and to see how kids like them can remain decent people in an indecent world. As society, and as individuals, we're better off when we do what's right, not what's easy.

* * *

Website: michaeljbowler.com

FB: michaeljbowlerauthor

Twitter: @MichaelJBowler

tumblr: http://michaeljbowler.tumblr.com/

Pinterest: http://www.pinterest.com/michaelbowler/pins/

YouTube: https://www.youtube.com/channel/ UC2NXCPry4DDgJZOVDUxVtMw

Instagram: @michaeljbowler

If you enjoyed this book,
check out my multi-award-winning
HEALER CHRONICLES SERIES.

Here's Chapter One of my multi-award-wining first book in The Healer Chronicles, available at online retailers.

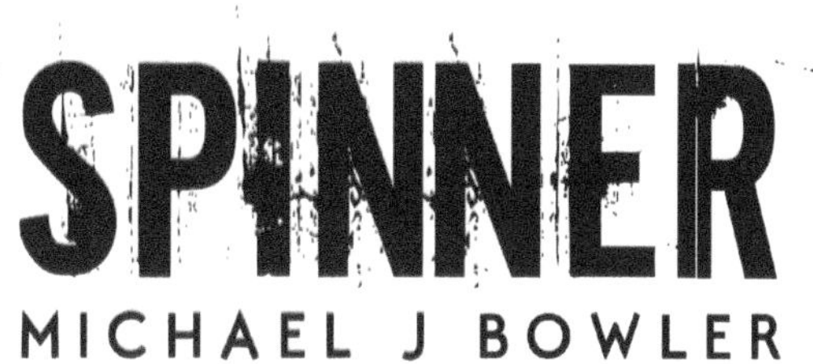

CHAPTER ONE

WHAT ARE YOU?

ALEX FIDGETED AS HE LAY in bed and listened to the wind outside. It had been an okay day at school – he'd only been called "Roller Boy" twice, which was almost a world record.

After school, he'd kicked it at Roy's house and they cranked *Hawthorne Heights* tunes and chilled. Even Jane hadn't bitched at him.

So why can't I sleep?

He didn't know the answer. His eyes returned to the dancing shadows that flitted across his floor from the window. His drapes were closed, but the wind whistled through the trees, and the shadows mesmerized him. The patterns of light and dark pulled on his eyelids, dragging him under. A dream loomed at the edges of his consciousness. One of *those* dreams. Sleep overcame him, and it began….

Ms. Ashley trudged down a flight of stairs from her second floor apartment, carrying several overflowing bags of trash. The traffic sounds were omnipresent, but otherwise the night was calm and clear.

A slight breeze ruffled her long brown hair as she slunk to the rear of the complex. Rounding the building, she passed alongside a sloping hill of ivy-covered ground toward the row of trashcans in the far corner.

Looking chilled and unsettled, Ms. Ashley lifted one lid and struggled to get all her bags in without spilling anything.

A rustling noise startled her and she whipped her head around.

The ivy-covered hill ascended upward into darkness, but there was no movement. Only a creepy silence.

She tossed her bags into the can and dropped the lid back in place with a hollow *clang*.

A large cat dropped onto the top of the can from somewhere above.

She uttered a startled cry and leaped back a few steps.

The cat meowed and she chuckled, extending one trembling hand.

The animal snuggled against it, wanting to be stroked. She ran her fingers through the fur around the cat's neck and under its chin.

More rustling leaves drew her attention to the ivy.

The darkness in this corner was deep and penetrating, with the vines and leaves snaking their way up the slope barely visible. Another cat materialized from beneath the thick cover of ivy.

Then another. And another.

In seconds, the hillside seethed with cats of all shapes and sizes. Their glowing eyes shone like eerie beacons in the night. The cat beneath Ms. Ashley's fingers hissed and swiped its claws at her, raking the top of her hand and drawing copious amounts of blood.

Startled, she cried out and yanked her hand back, gazing in shock at the dark liquid spilling onto the concrete at her feet.

Her body trembled with fear as she backed away.

The cats crouched on the hillside, poised and threatening.

The one she'd been petting wailed into the night, and then they were on her, leaping and clawing at her face and hair. Hundreds of cats streamed down the hillside and flung themselves at her while the big one sat and watched like a general commanding his troops.

Ms. Ashley screamed, but loud traffic sounds drowned out her cries. Flailing, she turned and stumbled along the side of the building toward the street, crying out for help.

Claws dug into her back and raked across her neck. Teeth sunk into her arm.

She shrieked in agony as they yanked out chunks of her hair and raked at her legs, shredding her sweat pants and digging into her

Her knees buckled, but Ms. Ashley managed to stay on her feet while stumbling headlong into the street at a frantic pace.

Suddenly aware that the truck was almost on her, she clutched at the nearest light post in desperation. One bloodied hand caught the post and slowed her momentum as the cats ceased their brutal attack. She gesticulated with her free hand, hoping to attract the attention of the driver. With her urgent gaze fixed on the truck, she didn't see the figure in black leap from behind the retaining wall right at her.

Strong hands pressed hard into her back and propelled her forward. The truck mowed her down in a splatter of blood and gore, flinging her broken body to the pavement and then crushing it beneath massive tires.

As the truck screeched to an ear-piercing halt near the corner, the figure in black melted into the darkness. Several cats sniffed the dead woman's remains before they, too, disappeared into the shadows. The first cat was the last to depart, watching as the horrified driver jumped from the truck cab and pelted toward Ms. Ashley's broken body.

The cat seemed to grin before vanishing into the night....

Alex screamed and bolted upright in bed, hair plastered to his sweat-sheened forehead. Heart thumping with urgent terror, he scanned his darkened room. The door leading outside was closed, but the ominous shadows still crept through the window. His desk was messy as usual, and the door to his bathroom stood ajar, but he'd left it that way. Everything looked like it had before he fell asleep.

Dropping onto his pillow, Alex fought to control his breathing and calm his pounding heart. God, he hated those dreams! Poor Ms. Ashley. He lay there, sweat making his t-shirt cling to his chest as his heart rate drew down. Could this dream be like the one about his parents? It seemed so real!

He lay in bed worrying about the morning, and what he'd find when he got to school.

Gradually, tree branches tapping against the house lulled him to sleep. The last image to assail him before he went under was that ugly- ass cat grinning at him before running off into the dark.

The following morning, Alex regarded himself in the bathroom mirror as he brushed his teeth. He'd showered and blow-dried his shoulder-length, choppy white-blond hair and it looked clean. People liked his blue eyes, when he didn't hide them behind his flowing bangs.

Alex finished pushing the brush up and down his teeth, and spat out the mint-flavored water, staring a moment at his soft, hairless cheeks and milky white skin. Sure, he seemed so innocent, a "sweet-faced boy," as his social workers had always described him to prospective foster parents. That's what made the whole thing worse. He *did* look like a nice kid. But no matter how hard he tried, he always screwed everything up. He always started spinning people. He couldn't help it. And once they figured out he was doing something weird, they got scared and wanted nothing more to do with him.

He'd already been through ten foster homes, and the only reason Jane kept him at this one was because she'd figured out what he could do.

"What are you?" he asked his reflection. As always, it didn't answer.

Jane Walters stood at the door with her ear pressed against it, while two boys sat at the kitchen table watching her.

Carlos, a burly high school junior, wolfed down his cereal, while freshman Juan glared with barely contained fury. Carlos grinned at the smaller boy. Juan flinched in fear and Carlos sniggered. Juan's cereal sat untouched in front of him as he reached with trembling fingers to touch his face, wincing at the pain. The left cheek and eye were black and blue and swelling rapidly.

A motorized sound came from behind the door, like a rising elevator.

Jane stepped away and jerked her thumb at Carlos. "You, out!"

Carlos's previous bravado with Juan dropped instantly. He swallowed his final mouthful and leapt from his chair. Snatching up a backpack from the floor, he bolted out the side door, never even glancing at Jane. She regarded the sullen Juan, folding her arms across her chest.

"You know what to do." Her tone left no room for argument. "What if he don't wanna this time? He said he wouldn't no more." "You know what'll happen to you if he won't," she snapped.

Juan nodded.

Jane observed her reflection in the large, ornately framed mirror, obviously looking pleased with what she saw.

She turned to him, practically pinning the petrified boy to his chair. "I'll be watching."

The motorized whirring s ground to a halt as Jane darted through the door into the hallway.

The door beside the rectangular dining table popped open and Alex rolled out in his wheelchair, wearing a *Hawthorne Heights* band t-shirt, black hoodie, skinny black jeans, his black and white high-top Converse shoes, and a backpack resting on his lap. He had Roy to thank for most of these clothes since Jane never spent a dime on him unless she had to.

He popped a small wheelie and shoved the door closed with a swipe of his hand, and then turned to Juan, whose head was bent toward his cereal bowl. Alex noted the behavior and frowned. It bothered him that he frightened Juan, but he didn't blame the kid. After all, he frightened almost everyone.

"Mornin', Juan," he offered in his most upbeat tone of voice as he dropped his backpack by the door. Was that upbeat? He so seldom felt that way he really didn't know what it sounded like.

"Hi, Alex."

Juan didn't look up. Alex noted the other bowl and half-filled glass of orange juice on the table, and frowned.

"Carlos must 'a heard me comin' and bailed, huh?" Juan said nothing.

Attempting to seem nonthreatening to the younger boy, Alex added, "Left his dishes this time. Jane'll be pissed."

Juan looked up, revealing his bruised face. "You mean 'Mom', right, Alex?"

Alex ignored the correction, gazing in shock at the other boy's battered face. Furious, he wheeled over to Juan. "Did she make Carlos—?"

Juan cut him off. "I fell, uh, hit the bed table. That's all."

He indicated the mirror on the wall with a slight head nod. Alex caught the movement and looked at Juan, blinking twice in response, his anger roiling.

Juan pleaded, "Alex, could you, you know…?"

His voice trailed off and he looked down at his cereal again. Alex scowled.

"I don't wanna go to school 'n look like this," Juan whispered, focusing his attention on the soggy corn flakes floating in his bowl like dead maggots.

Alex gazed long and hard at Juan. He was fourteen, but looked eleven or twelve, tiny and scrawny with brown skin, short hair, and big, fearful eyes. He wore baggy pants and baggy shirts, but they only highlighted how tiny he was. Had Alex ever seen the boy laugh or grin like a kid should? He didn't think so. But then, he didn't do those things either. How could they, living with a witch like Jane? He leaned in so Juan's head hid him from view of the mirror.

"You mean *she* don't want you to."

Juan's eyes looked round and filled with panic. "Please, Alex?" "Aren't you afraid, like the other times?"

He reached out to touch Juan's bruised cheek, but Juan recoiled even before Alex's fingers reached him.

Alex felt that punch to the gut sensation each time someone flinched from him, which was almost everyone, except for Roy and the kids in his class. "You *are* afraid. Guess I don' blame you."

Juan flushed red with embarrassment, turning his bruises a brighter shade of purple. "Alex, please?"

Alex sighed with resignation. His frown melted into a look of deep compassion as he brushed his bangs away from his eyes so Juan wouldn't be scared. At least, he didn't think he looked scary. The blue always seemed to calm people.

"Okay," Alex said, steeling himself for the pain to come. "Tell me."

Jane stood in a small closet directly behind the two-way mirror in the kitchen, smirking at the two men beside her. All the kids knew it was there, but they never knew when she might actually be on the other side. Another technique she'd developed to keep them in line. The men wore business suits, and one held a GoPro camera pointing through the glass at the two boys.

"Now watch real close," Jane admonished, though both men were already riveted to the drama playing out in the kitchen.

The younger of the two, Phil, watched intently, as though not surprised by what he was witnessing. As silver-haired Bob lifted the GoPro, his mouth dropped open in stunned disbelief.

Jane grinned as she turned from the boys to eye the two men. Shocked by what he saw, Bob lowered the camera and watched with his own eyes.

"You idiot, keep filming!" Jane snapped, her voice like a firecracker. Bob recovered from the initial surprise and whipped the camera up, continuing to record.

Phil's expression remained unreadable to Jane, but she didn't care.

These men were flunkies. The moneyman was all that mattered. "Wish we had audio," Phil muttered.

"You'll get it from the other camera," Jane said, directing his attention to the cupboard behind the boys. The door was ajar. From this angle, even through the two-way glass, she saw the blinking red light as it recorded.

Phil nodded while Jane watched, grinning at the stunned expressions of the two men beside her.

Through the mirror, she observed Alex spin his black magic, saw the pained expression on his face, and grinned when Juan, now uninjured, stared in wide-eyed fear at the freak beside him.

Yes, you're a freak, Alex, she thought, *but you're a freak who's going to make me rich.*

Alex's eyes remained closed, his features intent as his bruised face returned to normal. Several moments passed before his eyes fluttered open. "Man, Carlos—I mean that table—really hit you hard."

Juan had pulled away from Alex as far as his chair would allow. His eyes were wide and anxious, and his voice quavered. "Yeah. Well, I… uh, thanks."

He looked down at the table again, obviously afraid to meet Alex's gaze. Alex watched him sadly, and then glanced at the mirror. He scowled at his own reflection.

She was there, probably wearing that evil smile she had. Fighting down the temptation to flip his middle finger at her, Alex turned to Juan. "C'mon," he said with a heavy sigh. "We gonna be late for school."

He smiled as best he could manage, and Juan nodded. He rose from his chair and snatched his ratty backpack from the floor at his feet. Alex grabbed his own pack and rolled to the door, pulling it open. Juan skirted past him, making Alex feel like he had a horrible disease or something. He'd just helped the boy—for the seventh time already—and Juan was still afraid of him. But Juan's reaction was typical. Unless he spun them afterwards, everyone who saw what he could do pretty much freaked. He rolled outside and yanked the door shut behind him.

Inside the closet, Jane turned to Bob, who continued to run the GoPro even though the kitchen was empty.

"You can stop recording now," she said, folding her arms across her chest.

Bob suddenly realized there was nothing left to film and shut off the camera, staring at Jane with amazement. His face was ashen, as though he'd seen a ghost. Phil's eyes glittered with excitement, which Jane interpreted as astonishment at what he'd just seen.

"A million, remember," she insisted. "You tell him. Not a penny less."

Bob wiped his sweaty palms against his gray dress pants. "Oh, we'll definitely tell him, Ms. Walters. You can count on that."

Jane grinned.

Alex followed Juan along the side of the house. On their left rose a high, wood-slat fence separating Jane's property from her neighbor. He allowed his chair to roll itself down the sloping driveway past the five-foot hedge that took over for the fence and ended at the sidewalk.

Just as the boys reached the sidewalk, a little old lady stepped from behind the hedge and Alex nearly cried out with fright. The dream images of the night before had not fully retreated, and he realized he was more unnerved than he'd thought. Juan jumped like a frightened cat, but Alex knew why *he* was jittery. The stooped, white-haired old lady offered a toothy grin and held out a small brown bag to each boy.

Alex found himself grinning in return, and his racing heart settled into its normal rhythm. "Morning, Mrs. Rhodes."

She kept herself on her side of the hedge. "Mornin' Alex, Juan. I made you tuna today, plus my chocolate chip cookies."

Even though this was a daily ritual, Alex couldn't help but feel extreme gratitude every time. "Thanks, Mrs. Rhodes. I din' even get breakfast this morning." As though on cue, his stomach rumbled.

She glared a moment at Jane's house. "Doesn't surprise me." "*Gracias, señora*," Juan offered shyly.

Mrs. Rhodes smiled and turned away, observing Jane's house as she hobbled to her front porch. Alex noted that she was using a cane today, not something she normally did. Must be that arth-something or other that always bothered her, he realized. He'd spin her again as soon as he got a chance. She was always nice to him, and since she never figured out what he was doing, making her feel better was pretty easy.

While Bob and Jane discussed particulars of the pending deal, Phil wandered to the living room window and pulled aside the drapes. He observed the old lady hand lunch bags to the boys, and watched as Alex wheeled away down the street, the other kid following. Phil slipped out his phone and typed the following message: 'You were right.'

Alex didn't attempt to make conversation with Juan as they made their way toward school. Roy would be along any minute, but Juan would beg off and choose to walk. That's what happened every time Alex spun him.

Roy's F-150 truck rolled into view, and Alex couldn't help but feel good at the sight. Roy's dad had helped him buy the used pickup, and Roy worked all summer buying parts from junkyards and after-market places to soup up the engine and transmission. As far as Alex was concerned, Roy was a genius when it came to anything mechanical.

Roy dramatically honked the horn, as though the two boys couldn't see him right in front of them. It was their usual morning game and Alex chuckled like he always did. Roy pulled the pickup to the curb and hopped out. Alex barely had time to note Roy's skinny jeans, *30 Seconds to Mars* shirt, and shock of brown hair spilling across his face like an old mop before his friend bounded over and grabbed the back of the wheelchair.

Alex's chair was his one prized possession. A few years ago, when he'd had a cool social worker, he'd managed to get a super-sturdy chair built like the one a famous guy named Aaron used for his incredible stunts. Alex had only been seven when he'd seen on the news how fourteen- year-old Aaron mastered the world's first backflip in a wheelchair. It had amazed and empowered Alex to see someone who couldn't walk accomplishing something so spectacular.

His caseworker at the time, a lady named Sandy Quigley, had convinced the county to pay for his special chair on the grounds that it would be nearly indestructible and would not need to be replaced or repaired often. Alex had been so ecstatic he didn't even feel guilty for spinning Sandy into thinking he needed something like that.

Roy pushed Alex's chair around the front of the truck to the passenger side and yanked open the door. Alex tossed his backpack onto the floor as Roy extended his arms and grinned. The double piercings at each side of his lower lip glinted in the morning sun. Alex smiled and slid forward, allowing Roy to sweep him up and toss him onto the passenger seat, grunting as he did.

"Getting too buff, Alex," Roy said. "You should be tossing me into the car."

"Yer just mad cuz I'm younger and can beat yer ass at arm wrestling," Alex retorted as Roy grinned and slammed the door.

Roy grabbed the chair, popped out the cushion, folded it into itself and slipped both chair and cushion up and into the bed of his pickup. He noticed Juan walking away in the direction of Mark Twain and called out. "Hey, Juan, doncha wanna ride?"

Juan turned and shook his head. "Not today, Roy. Thanks." He hurried away, as though trying to put as much distance between himself and Alex as possible.

Alex watched through the rearview as his housemate scurried away like a frightened rabbit.

Roy climbed into the cab and slammed his door, flipping his ragged bangs off his face and jerking a thumb behind him. "'Sup with him today?"

Alex shrugged. "Jane had Carlos beat him up so I hadda spin 'im. You know how he trips."

Roy cast a disgusted look Alex's way. "I hate that bitch. You need to spin her but good."

Alex tried for a smile, but those horrific dream images returned in force.

"Don't tempt me."

When Roy didn't start the engine right away, Alex looked at him through his surfer-white bangs. "We're gonna be late."

Roy shrugged. He wore the black Levi's jacket Alex loved, the one with the rips in it that looked so cool. If Roy wasn't Special Ed like him, he'd be one of the sickest kids on campus.

Roy reached down to the floor beneath his seat and pulled out a small package wrapped in black paper. "Happy birthday, fool." He tossed Alex the box.

Oh, crap! Alex thought as he fumbled to catch the box that fell into his lap. He'd completely forgotten! What with his latest nightmare and having to spin Juan, his fifteenth birthday never even crossed his mind. Blushing and making his pale skin look like a tomato, Alex grinned.

"Thanks, man. I forgot."

Roy shoved his bangs aside again. "I didn't. Open it."

Almost giddy at receiving a real present, Alex tore off the paper with gusto, and gaped at what he found underneath. A Nexus phone, still in the box. Brand new!

His chest tightened, like the wind had been knocked from his lungs. Other than his wheelchair, he'd never been given anything this nice since he was four. He looked at the grinning Roy with open-mouthed astonishment. "Oh, man, Roy, I dunno what to say."

Roy laughed, a rarity for him. "How 'bout, thanks, Roy, for being my awesomest friend."

"Thanks, Roy, for being my *most* awesomest friend. But, this is too much, man. And I got no money for a plan. You know how Jane–"

"Screw her!" Roy spat. "You know I make money fixing engines and stuff and my dad let me put you on our plan. He hates that bitch as much as I do."

Alex felt funny, like he was taking advantage of Roy. "I never had a phone before…."

"It's time you did," Roy said, grabbing the box and ripping off the plastic covering. As he opened the box and slid out the smartphone, he added, "Now you can call me any time. I know7 we can't text a lot, but I'll put apps on it so we can see each other when we talk."

Alex grinned. Jane never let the boys use her house phone, and she didn't allow them to have cell phones, either. The others were on probation and she'd convinced their probation officers that "Cell phones are an invitation to trouble."

"I gotta hide this from Jane," Alex said, his face clouding over. "She'll take it away."

"Over my dead body."

Alex loved how protective Roy was of him.

"Thanks, Roy," he said shyly, gazing in awe at the bright, crystal clear home screen. *His own phone! Wow!*

"We better get to school," Roy said, turning the ignition. "You know how Ms. Ashley gets when we're late."

The mention of Ms. Ashley pushed aside all the joy he felt at receiving Roy's gift, and flooded his mind with bloodied images of her demise in his dream. He shivered, seeing once more the face of that huge, grinning cat.

"Yeah, let's get going."

Suddenly, he wanted to get to school. But he feared it, too, because deep down he knew his teacher wouldn't be there today, or any of the days to come.

Roy made a U-turn and pulled out into the quiet residential street toward Mark Twain High.

www.ingramcontent.com/pod-product-compliance
Lightning Source LLC
Chambersburg PA
CBHW030358310726
48979CB00001B/359

9798988611011